enjoys playing with her grandchildren and gardening. During rare spare moments you will find her snuggled up with a good book. Carol enjoys hearing from readers at carolarens@yahoo.com or on Facebook.

9112 0000 370242

Also by Carol Arens

Dreaming of a Western Christmas
Western Christmas Proposals
The Cowboy's Cinderella
Western Christmas Brides
The Rancher's Inconvenient Bride

The Walker Twins miniseries

Wed to the Montana Cowboy
Wed to the Texas Outlaw

Discover more at millsandboon.co.uk.

A RANCH
TO CALL HOME

Carol Arens

MILLS & BOON

All rights reserved including the right of reproduction
in whole or in part in any form. This edition is published
by arrangement with Harlequin Books S.A.

This is a work of fiction. Names, characters, places, locations
and incidents are purely fictional and bear no relationship to
any real life individuals, living or dead, or to any actual places,
business establishments, locations, events or incidents.
Any resemblance is entirely coincidental.

This book is sold subject to the condition that it shall not,
by way of trade or otherwise, be lent, resold, hired out
or otherwise circulated without the prior consent of the publisher
in any form of binding or cover other than that in which it is published
and without a similar condition including this condition
being imposed on the subsequent purchaser.

® and TM are trademarks owned and used by the trademark owner
and/or its licensee. Trademarks marked with ® are registered with the
United Kingdom Patent Office and/or the Office for Harmonisation
in the Internal Market and in other countries.

First Published in Great Britain 2018
by Mills & Boon, an imprint of HarperCollins*Publishers*
1 London Bridge Street, London, SE1 9GF

© 2018 Carol Arens

ISBN: 978-0-263-93292-8

MIX
Paper from
responsible sources
FSC® C007454

FSC
www.fsc.org

This book is produced from independently certified FSC™ paper
to ensure responsible forest management.
For more information visit www.harpercollins.co.uk/green.

Printed and bound in Spain
by CPI, Barcelona

To Caitlyn Iaccino

The world is a kinder place because of your sweet smile.

BRENT LIBRARIES	
EAL	
91120000370242	
Askews & Holts	25-May-2018
AF ROM	£5.99

Chapter One

〰〰〰〰

September 1883, Forget-Me-Not, Texas

A frizzle of unease teased Laura Lee's stomach. She rolled up the newest edition of the *Ladies' Home Journal and Practical Housekeeper* tight in her fist.

The elegant wedding gown that she had stitched with her own blistered fingers fell in lacy waves to the boardwalk, where she stood in front of Auntie June's boardinghouse waiting for her very own prince to arrive and carry her off to the preacher.

The pocket watch tucked within the secret pouch stitched into her petticoat marked time against her hip.

Tick, tock, tick… Seconds turned into minutes. Minutes crept up on half an hour.

As a distraction, she watched the breeze pluck

golden leaves from the trees and blow them over the rooftops of the main street of Forget-Me-Not. One leaf fell on the brim of a man's Stetson. He brushed it off, then went inside the bank.

At forty-five minutes, with Johnny nowhere in sight, she reminded herself she had nothing to fear. Her groom had no doubt been delayed by something that was far beyond his control.

Any moment now, dust would stir at the end of the street... Johnny urging his horse to a gallop through a veil of falling leaves. He would be wearing an expression of apology on his dashingly handsome face.

And truth be told, it wasn't uncommon for Johnny to be late. Once they were married, she would be able to help cure him of that habit.

Tick, tock, tick. Ten more minutes slid past. She gripped the *Ladies' Home Journal and Practical Housekeeper* tighter.

"Curse it! Where are you, Johnny Ruiz?" She loosened her hold on the precious magazine— her guide to all things domestic and wonderful.

As soon as the impatient words left her mouth, she regretted them. Ordinarily she was sweet tempered, the very soul of composure.

"Howdy, miss," came a deep male voice. Boot steps thumped on the boardwalk, bringing the speaker within feet of her. "May I be of assistance?"

She spun toward him and looked up…and up at a tall man wearing a black duster, a Stetson dipped over his brow. It was the man who had flicked the leaf from his hat and gone into the bank.

"Why, no." She had thought Johnny to be handsome but this man… *Well, my word.* It took all of a second to feel ashamed of the thought. Johnny was her true love and would forever be the most handsome man in her heart. "Thank you, but I'm fine as can be."

"Name's Jesse Creed, ma'am," he said, dipping his dark hat in greeting. "Couldn't help but notice you've been standing in this spot for a good long time now. I reckon that fellow you just mentioned might not show up."

He might assume so since she had blurted it out. Which did not mean it was any concern of his.

"Perhaps I simply enjoy taking in the morning sunshine." In a wedding gown.

It cut her heart that this stranger thought her to be abandoned, given that was the very fear that had plagued her for the past ten minutes…as ridiculous a fear as it was.

Johnny loved her. Nothing could keep him from being here unless something horrible had happened. What if he'd been injured…or worse?

"It's not my business but—"

"Just so. It is not." She unrolled the magazine and pressed it flat to her chest. "And just how do you know how long I've been standing here, sir?"

"I've been to the bank, the livery and the blacksmith. Passed in front of you three times."

She'd been so intent on watching for Johnny that she had only noticed him once.

"Well, you may go along your way knowing that I am perfectly fine."

"Good day, then." He tipped his hat and continued down the boardwalk.

One shop down, Jesse Creed stopped, turned. His olive green gaze settling upon her was more than a bit distracting…the sound of his voice far too appealing. In fact, it stirred her in a way she didn't understand. "If you find you do need something, Auntie June is the one to ask for help. Here in town she's everyone's honorary aunt."

Was that handsome fellow a married man? she wondered before she could stop. She chastised herself for wondering, given that she was an engaged woman.

A very lucky engaged woman. Johnny was dark-eyed and dashing…fun loving…passionate.

And striding out of the front door of the hotel across the street.

Jesse Creed would have laid a wager that the pretty woman's "Johnny" was not going to show up. That she was as abandoned as her expression said she was.

Looks like he'd have lost that money. Just as he mounted the steps to the general store, a cowpoke, spiffed up and looking swank, sauntered out of the hotel. The lady rushed across the street and into his arms.

What she did not seem to notice was that another woman drew aside the curtain of a second-story window. She peered down at the couple with resentment contorting her mouth, narrowing her eyes. A red robe drooped off her bare shoulders.

The bride-to-be, and clearly she was that, was not going to find life an easy path with that faithless fellow as her husband.

Sometimes Jesse wished that he didn't notice so much, but his former career as a bounty hunter made him take note of details that many folks would not.

Hell, the woman's future was none of his business. He didn't even know her. Still, he'd go on his way easier if he didn't guess what her future held in store.

In the end, he knew she would not welcome his observation if he told her. She probably wouldn't believe him. There was nothing to do but continue on his way to the general store. It was a shame, though, a pretty thing like her headed for such trouble.

Coming up the steps of the store, he nearly smacked into Auntie June on her way out. Carrying a sack of what he guessed to be sugar, she wasn't looking where she was going, but up the street instead.

Her short, pillow-like body listed left, but he caught her by the forearms and righted her.

"Jesse Creed! I do declare I ought to watch out where I'm going. But I can't rightly say I mind being rescued by such a dashing fellow."

"Always a pleasure, Auntie June." And it was. The woman was one of the kindest souls he had ever met. It had been Auntie June who had convinced Corum Peterson to sell his ranch to Jesse, when he had been a stranger in Forget-Me-Not.

"I'm just relieved to see that her young man showed up." She turned her attention again to the couple kissing in the middle of the street. "She sewed all night long on that wedding gown."

"Looks like it was worth the effort," he answered, meaning that she looked fetching in it, not that he thought the man deserved the trouble she had gone to.

"I hope so." She glanced back at him, brows arched over honey-brown eyes. "I'm not convinced."

"Seems like she is, though."

"Yes…and I do remember what it's like to be blinded by love." She stroked the bag of sugar with one finger, shaking her head. "The light of day was a harsh thing to face, I can tell you."

"Whoever the fellow was who broke your heart, he was a fool."

"What a pity you weren't born forty years sooner. I turned many a head back then." Reaching up, she patted his cheek. "I'd best get on my way if I want to get this pie baked in time for supper."

Jesse stood for a moment, watching the good-hearted lady walk away. In his opinion, she still could turn heads. After she turned aside into the dressmaker shop, he entered the general store.

"Mornin', Thomas," he said, walking past a display of frilly yard goods. The scent of coffee on the simmer hit him like a welcome home.

And home he was. After a lifetime of living here and there, often without a roof to keep out the night, he'd purchased a ranch and settled down in the sweet town of Forget-Me-Not.

"Say, Jesse! Bingham's nearly busting with excitement. I'm mighty grateful you hired him to come along with you to pick up your horses."

"No thanks needed. He'll be earning every bit of his pay."

"Grateful for that, too. The boy was headed for trouble, taking up with the Underwoods like he was. Good honest work will give him something to be proud of."

Jesse understood that. He'd earned a lot of money as a bounty hunter but the profession had darkened his soul. Ranching was something to feel honorable about…to let him lay his head on his pillow at night and sleep without regret.

"I'll take good care of your boy, don't you worry, Thomas."

"I won't. Or not overly. I'd rather see him bucked off a stallion than spend an hour with Hoodoo and his brothers. Those young men grow wilder by the day."

For the large part, Forget-Me-Not was a peaceful place to lay down roots, but every town had its problems. Most folks waited anxiously for the day that the Underwood boys left home and went looking for adventure that couldn't be found in this tranquil place.

In Jesse's opinion and with what hard experience had shown him, those five hoodlums' quest for adventure would land them in prison or dead.

Something, cans he guessed, clattered to the floor in the storeroom. A series of clanking sounds indicated that they were being set to rights. Heavy boot thumps crossed the floor. Something else rattled but didn't fall.

The curtain separating the rooms fanned out and Bingham Teal burst into the room, his saddle pack slung over his shoulder.

"I'm ready to go, Mr. Creed." A grin as wide

as sunrise split the kid's face. He rushed out the front door of the store, his hat nearly brushing the frame, hurrying away without a goodbye. His father raised his arm as if to call him back but then let it fall to his side.

All at once, Bingham charged back into the store, took his father's hand and pumped it up and down. "See you in two weeks, Pa!" He stepped toward the door again but spun about and wrapped his father in a great hug.

Once again, Bingham hurried out of the store.

"Mind your manners!" Thomas called after his great, lurching offspring. "If you catch a whiff of jasmine along the trail, Jesse, it'll be his mother watching over him. I reckon she's bursting her heavenly buttons over what a fine boy he grew into."

"I'll bring him home safe, two weeks…three at most."

Thomas lifted a blanket from behind the counter. "Never know when the night might turn bitter cold."

Jesse took the heavy wool cover, tipped his Stetson in farewell, then followed the boy outside.

While this was a great adventure for Bingham, it was more so for Jesse. He'd moved onto his ranch only a month ago. There had been enough time to make repairs to the barn and paddock, but being anxious to pick up his herd of horses, he'd neglected fixing up the house.

No matter. It was something he could do over time. He'd lived in worse conditions than a slightly run-down home.

Today he was bound for Cartersville to get his breeding stock. Bringing them home would fulfill the dream of a lifetime.

No, not fulfill, but begin.

It felt like the sun came out from behind a big black cloud, seeing Johnny walk out of the hotel. What a silly duck she had been to worry.

And truly, this was not the first time she'd been a little restive over his loyalty to her. But on those few occasions, he had handily put her anxiety at ease. From all the way across the street, she felt how much he loved her...saw how he was committed to her by the joyful turn of his smile.

Within an hour, she would be Mrs. Johnny Ruiz. She would be free to show him how much she loved him...in all the ways a woman could show her man.

She hugged him, squeezed her eyes shut tight.

"I thought the night would never pass," she whispered against his collar.

He must have dabbed on cologne. His neck smelled like a bouquet. What a sweet gesture for their wedding day. He didn't normally wear cologne.

"I didn't sleep all night, baby doll."

Opening her eyes, she spotted a couple of fellows coming out of the hotel. One of them shot her and Johnny an odd glance. Could he really be smirking at them?

No doubt he was jealous over the affection they felt for one another. Clearly the fellow had never been in love and didn't understand the way it was between nearly married folks.

Uncomfortable under the scrutiny, Laura Lee pushed away from her intended but did not let go of him.

"I love you so much, Johnny!"

He lifted a dark brow. The corner of his mouth ticked up. "I am a dashing fellow. All the ladies say so."

She gently swatted his arm with the *Ladies' Home Journal and Practical Housekeeper.* "And such a tease."

"I love you, too, Laura Lee." He kissed her on the mouth, right there in the middle of the street for all to see.

Well, in a few more minutes it would no longer be improper.

"Say—" he leaned in, his whisper tickling the hair near her ear "—let's go up to your room… We can get a head start on being married."

"We've already kept the minister waiting."

"Won't take long, I promise. Then we can come back here and have the whole day and night just the two of us, fine and married."

"We see the minister first, then we spend the whole day and night just the two of us."

"Ah, come on, Laura Lee, I'm really aching for you. It's been two weeks since I came for you in Tanners Ridge and we've hardly had a private hour."

That wasn't quite true. They had spent several nights under the stars when they traveled between towns. In town, she had naturally wanted her own hotel room.

But what an impetuous fellow he was. His impatience only showed how much he loved her. Ever since they had run off to get married, he'd wanted to take liberties.

Truth to tell, she wouldn't mind giving him what he wanted, but right was right and wrong was wrong. She would not begin their future on the wrong side of the bed.

"Don't you love me?" His dark brow lifted. He kissed her again.

"With all my heart. You know that."

Close by, a window slammed. She heard the young men who came out of the hotel laugh heartily.

"Come on, Hell Dog! Finish kissing your girl goodbye and let's get outta here."

Johnny dropped his arms from about her. "Shut your trap, Hoodoo. I'll be along when I'm ready."

Laura Lee turned to give the men on the porch a closer look. She could not imagine why Johnny would have even answered the fellow who had spoken.

"Who are they?" She stepped closer to Johnny because the men looked disreputable. Like they had been carousing all night, with their clothes rumpled and their hair in disarray.

They were nothing like her Johnny. He was always dashing and dapper, with his hair neatly groomed and his clothing in order. It was a lucky thing he was completely devoted to her because she could not count the times she'd noticed other women's gazes lingering upon him.

Three more men came out of the hotel and stood with the carousers.

"Who is Hell Dog?" she murmured. The name could describe anyone of the men on the porch. Still, it did not escape her that the only man doing any kissing was Johnny. "I don't care for the way those men are looking at us."

"Don't pay them any mind. Those are just the Underwood brothers."

"Why are they talking to you?"

A smile crept across Johnny's face. His back

straightened and his chest puffed out. "Because I'm Hell Dog."

"That's not a bit funny!" She slapped his arm with the magazine, not playfully this time. She didn't like feeling so riled at her intended, but they were late for their appointment with the minister. "Tell them goodbye and let's be on our way."

"You going to let that little hen peck at you?" the one named Hoodoo called.

If Hoodoo was an odd name, the man was more so. He was tall, rail thin, with posture as curved as a fishhook. His long nose and his sharp black beard both pointed toward the ground.

Even though the morning was cool, sweat dampened Laura Lee's neck. Something was very wrong. In a million years, she could not imagine Johnny taking up with the likes of those men.

"What have you been doing all night, Johnny?" While she had been sewing the lace ruffle on the hem of her gown, restless and dreaming of her one true love, what had kept him restless?

"Made me some friends."

"Of the wrong kind, if you ask me." All five of them looked like they were about to erupt into misdoing.

"Not that I did ask you." An expression crossed his face that she'd never seen before. She'd known him for a nearly a year...been in love with him for four and a half months, and she had never seen a hint of bully on that handsome face. He'd always been the soul of congeniality.

For the first time, she doubted her decision to go away with him. It cleaved her heart in half, wondering if she had made a mistake. That he might not be who she knew him to be.

"Don't look sad." He took her by the shoulders. "I'm sorry, really sorry. That sounded harsh. And just ignore those fools. They aren't such a bad sort when you get to know them."

"I don't intend on getting to know them. I intend on marrying you and settling down. Someday getting our own little house and raising lots of babies. You haven't changed your mind about that, have you?"

"Of course I haven't!" He squeezed her to him.

All of a sudden, life felt right again. He was her Johnny, not Hell Dog…whoever that might be. No doubt the name came from a misguided night with that bunch.

But in the end, one night did not hurt what she and Johnny were to each other.

"Let's go get married, Johnny." She looked up into his deep brown eyes, her excitement over their future restored. She tugged on his sleeve, half dancing her joy.

"Hold up a minute." He set his boots firmly in the dirt. "I've got a wedding present for you."

"We're losing time here, Hell Dog." The speaker

was short and round. His head was topped by an unruly bush of black hair, his long beard a wild match.

"You go on, Ivan," Johnny called while reaching into his pocket. "I'll be along."

"What do you mean, you'll be along?" she said.

"Just you wait and see!" He unfolded the paper he had taken from his pocket, looking as pleased as she'd ever seen him. "Here's your dream come true, Laura Lee." He smoothed open the crisp sheet of paper and held it in front of her face to read.

"A deed? To a house?" Carefully, as though the dream might crumble under the pressure of her fingertips, she took the document from him.

"Your house, baby doll. I was up all night getting it for you. It's why I was late."

"I never dreamed…" Words failed. She wanted a little home of her own more than she wanted anything on this earth. "Three hundred and twenty acres? How, Johnny?"

He looked so proud, preening like a peacock with his feathers splayed. How could she not adore him?

"I met an old man last night. We hit up a friendship and he told me how he was headed east to live out his days with his granddaughter. He sold his place to me but I told him to make the deed out to you. I know how you've got your heart set on a house of your own."

A house of *their* own, she knew he meant to say. "But how did you pay for it?"

They had planned to work and save and finally make that dream come true. Now here it was, not a flight of fancy, but a reality in her hands. She could scarce believe what she was looking at.

"Well, that's the thing, Laura Lee." He cast a glance over his shoulder at the men walking single file down the boardwalk, then turning at the ally running between the hotel and the stream that trickled through town. "I've still got to pay it off. There's a mortgage."

"We've got to pay it off, you mean. The both of us will work hard and get it done." She hugged him about the middle as tight as she could. Any man who would do this for her must love her more than…air or food or…or anything. She regretted thinking badly of him for knowing those men and for being called Hell Dog.

Johnny Ruiz was a man among men.

"The fortunate thing is—" he loosened himself from her grip of gratitude and shoved a slip of paper in her hand "—I know a way of getting it paid off quick. But I've got to go away with the Underwood boys to do it. But that there is directions to where the ranch is."

"I don't trust them." Here she was with her

dream in her hand, a deed of ownership in her name and so fresh that the ink smelled damp, and she was turning shrewish again.

"I told you, Laura Lee, they're not so bad as they seem. Trust me, what we're doing isn't illegal."

"Or dangerous? I couldn't go on if something happened to you."

"Don't you worry." He held her away from him, took two long steps backward. "You go on home and fix the place up. I'll be back before you know it."

"When? You must have some idea of when."

"Hard to say—not long, though. Before first snow, I reckon."

"We could get married now, before you head out."

"I'd like that, you know I would. But the fellows are waiting."

She held on to his arm. "Thank you. This is more than my dream come true."

Pounding hooves trembled the dirt. Five animals carrying Underwoods galloped up the road. One horse was being led without a rider.

Johnny peeled her fingers from his arm. He backed away.

"Bug-ock, bug-ock!" clucked one of the Underwoods. This one was short, slim and had blond hair that curled tightly to his scalp.

Johnny turned to glance at him. When he looked back at Laura Lee a smile blazed across his face.

"Goodbye, Johnny!" All of a sudden, she wasn't sure the house was worth the cost of having him go away. She ought to be a married woman by now. "I love you!"

"Wait for me!" he called, mounting his horse.

"I will! I promise I'll be waiting!"

Maybe he heard her promise. She couldn't be sure, though, because galloping off with his friends, he did not glance back.

Chapter Two

Two wagons were for sale in the livery. One was small and weathered. It would carry her home but would not work to transport all the goods she would need in order to set up housekeeping.

The other one was large and new. She smelled the freshly sawed wood the moment she walked into the livery. It would only take one trip to bring everything she needed. But it would require a pair of durable workhorses to pull it. Saffron, her sweet saddle mare, was not used to such hard work.

Laura Lee knew exactly how much money was in the pocket of her petticoat by the weight of it. It had gotten heavier, but only slightly, since she left the Lucky Clover Ranch.

Before Johnny came for her in Travers Ridge, she, along with Agatha Magee, had worked as cooks. First for a hotel that went bankrupt, then for a traveling circus.

Laura Lee had managed to collect her pay from the hotel owner, who was a good and decent woman. Sadly, the owner of the circus was neither good nor decent and still owed her a week's wages.

If she had her way, she would have gone after him and pestered him until he paid, but Johnny had come for her, and what really mattered other than that?

Loving man that Johnny was, he thought their time would be better spent in a hotel room. Naturally, she'd reminded him that an even better use of time would be spent with a preacher.

Given that they were traveling together, and in constant company, he'd tried to convince her it was like being married. He vowed that he was as devoted to her as he would be when they were officially wed and that waiting was hard for a man. Especially when he loved a woman so. In the end, he'd accepted the wait. He even promised to replace the money the circus owner had cheated her of.

He had more than kept the promise. He'd bought her a house...and land! Even though she was not yet Mrs. Johnny Ruiz, she soon would be. Johnny would return, just like he swore he would.

Yes, it was disquieting to remember the look on his face when he rode away, like it was the dream of a lifetime to be running free.

When that image threatened to subdue her joy, all she had to do was remember the deed packed away in her trunk.

That piece of paper proved his vision for their future was the same as hers...to settle down in their own little home and raise babies.

A huge gray-and-brown dog wandered into the barn, distracting Laura Lee from her woolgathering. Bartholomew Rawlings, the liveryman, shooed it outside with the bristle end of a broom. He shook his head, sighed, then set the broom against the gate on the larger wagon.

She dearly wanted that one. Did she dare risk spending so much of her money on it? Johnny had been vague about how long he would be gone. What if a mortgage payment became due before he returned?

She would need an income in order to cover it.

Mending and washing laundry...she knew those skills with the best of them. But one needed clients before she could begin earning money that way. The only person she was acquainted with in Forget-Me-Not was Auntie June.

Besides that, she did not particularly enjoy mending and washing.

"You can't beat this wagon, ma'am." Mr. Rawlings gripped the large front wheel of the wagon, shook it to demonstrate how solid it was. Then he pointed a finger to a stall on the far side of the barn. "Whittle and Bride are only two years old but are already working well together. You couldn't ask for a better bargain."

Given that a bargain was only a bargain as long as one could afford it, Laura Lee nipped her bottom lip, silently watching the horses eating hay. As large as they were, there would be some expense in feeding them.

Still, the ranch had three hundred and twenty acres that would need tending, not the acre or two that she had envisioned.

"I wonder, Mr. Rawlings…does the town have a market day?"

"Oh, yes, it's quite an event. Every other Friday, farmers come from all over to sell what they have. In the winter, the ladies gather in the library to sell their jarred goods."

Farmers worked hard, built up strong appetites. Pastries and coffee would be welcome while they sold goods on market day, she imagined.

She could set up her own little booth. In her mind's eye, she watched her business flourish. All over town, folks were eating her muffins and pies, happily sipping her freshly brewed coffee. In time, perhaps, people would seek her out to provide pastries for parties and festivals.

If she could satisfy the appetites of circus performers, surely she could do the same for the folks of Forget-Me-Not.

"This Friday or next?" The idea sent a shiver of excitement through her. She would earn a bit of money doing something she loved and the enterprise would keep her busy until Johnny returned.

"This. Only five days from now."

"I'll take the large wagon and the team, Mr. Rawlings. As long as you include their tack and load the wagon with a week's worth of feed."

She extended her hand to shake on the deal, hoping he would accept her conditions. If she had to buy the feed and the tack, she would not be able to purchase the other things she needed to begin life in her own sweet home. Especially now that she would need to invest a bit of her precious funds in her new business venture.

The liveryman stood with his hands in his pockets for a long moment, rocking back on the heels of his boots.

When she thought she might faint in anticipation of his answer, he reached out and accepted her hand.

The deal was made.

At this point, it would have broken her heart to be forced to purchase the smaller wagon. Once she'd made up her mind on a course, nothing else would do.

Just like when she'd realized she was in love with Johnny, she'd decided that they should be married and no other man would do.

With a skip in her step, she approached the horses. She stroked Bride's brown nose, then Whittle's black one. Because she had spent much of her life on the Lucky Clover Ranch, she felt comfortable around the large beasts.

Of course, the acres Johnny had given her were dwarfed by the vastness of the ranch she had grown to womanhood on. She carried deep attachments for those countless acres and for everyone who'd worked along with her to keep them running. For many people, living out their lives on the Lucky Clover where they had grown and raised their families was their dream.

That was not the case for Laura Lee. She needed a place to call her own. To know that come what may, it was her own spot on the earth to just…be.

When she was small, her father had a need to wander and was never happy to settle in one spot overlong. About the time Laura Lee would make a friend or feel secure in a new bed, she was dragged off on another "adventure."

All she'd ever wanted was a place to call home.

Her toes were nearly dancing inside her boots because very soon she would be sitting in four snug walls that were her own. She would rise with the sun and plant a garden…and a peach tree so she could sit under its shade on a hot afternoon.

As much as she would miss the Lucky Clover,

would even bring her children to visit one day, she now had a home of her own and her heart was bursting with the joy of it.

"You ready, Bride?" she asked, gazing into a large, gently blinking brown eye. "Time to go home."

With Saffron tied to the back of the wagon, Laura Lee sat tall on the wood bench, her gloved hands gripping the team's reins. As advertised, the horses got along well and were easy to handle.

Seeing a movement beside the wagon, she glanced down. The dog that Mr. Rawlings had chased from the barn trotted beside the wagon wheel. It glanced up, woofed quietly in greeting and wagged its long, fanlike tail.

She pulled the team up short.

"Go on back home." She pointed toward the livery with her finger.

The dog plopped its hairy rump on the dirt, stirring up dust with its tail.

"Mr. Rawlings!" she called over her shoulder. Luckily the man was standing in the livery yard. "Your dog is following."

He crossed the road, grinning. "I reckon I ought to have mentioned." He clapped his palm on the wagon wheel. "The dog comes with the horses."

"But I don't need a dog."

"Oh, he's useful enough. With his size, coyotes and wolves won't bother you much."

"I've never been over bothered by the beasts as it is."

"Haven't heard of the great wolf migration three years this past February then, I reckon?"

To her knowledge, wolves did not migrate. She shook her head. What she wanted was for the dog to migrate back to the livery.

"The story goes that a fellow named Biggers, a newspaperman, was riding out on the frontier one day when he spotted thousands of animals on the lope. He was a curious fellow, given his occupation, and he went to investigate. Turned out to be wolves. Now, no one knows quite why they did it, mass exodus like that, but Biggers wasn't the only one to report it. Supposedly it's the truth."

Supposedly might be a long stretch from the truth. He wanted to be rid of the dog was what she thought.

"Truth or not, I didn't agree to purchase your dog."

"The thing is, he's not my dog. When I bought the horses, he came along. Followed me just like he's following you." Bartholomew Rawlings petted the dog between his ears. "I doubt you'll be rid of him. But he's a good boy for all he's a hairy giant."

"Go home," she said to the dog since she was

having no success getting the livery owner to keep him. "I can't feed you."

"Don't trouble yourself over that, miss. He's a hunter. It's fair to say you won't see a rat in your barn or a rabbit in your garden once he moves in." Apparently Bartholomew considered the matter finished because he tipped his hat and walked away.

"What's his name? How old is he?" If the animal really was not going to leave the horses, she ought to know that little bit about him.

"I believe he's two, same as the team. Don't know the name he started with since I was a mile from the auction when I noticed he was coming along. He's been answering to 'Hey, dog!' for the last six months."

The very last thing she needed was to be responsible for a nameless dog.

After another tip of his faded brown hat, the liveryman crossed the road and went inside his stable.

With any luck, while she was busy purchasing her goods, the dog would attach himself to someone else's horses.

Glancing out the window of the general store, Laura Lee spotted the great beast. Not only had he not taken up with someone else, he looked quite content where he was…asleep on the four-foot-high pile of hay in the wagon.

Turning her attention to the task at hand, the last of many, she examined several bolts of lace with which to sew curtains.

An especially sweet one caught her eye, having hearts and flowers embroidered on a sheer fabric. It would be romantic for Johnny to see them hanging in the windows when he came riding home with the money to pay off the mortgage for the ranch. She only hoped she had time to sew them and hang them in the windows before he did.

The problem was, she didn't know how much fabric she would need since she had no idea how many windows the house had. The one and only thing she knew about it was that her name was on the deed…the home belonged to her.

It might be a palace or a cozy cottage. The knowledge that she was only hours from seeing it for the first time left her breathless. Tearful emotion cramped her throat when she set the fabric bolt on the counter and told the clerk she wanted only half of it.

There was no sense in spending more than she needed to. She would be back in town on Friday for market day and could purchase more if her house turned out to have an abundance of windows.

In her mind, there were dozens. She'd always

dreamed of a house with lots of windows for her to sit beside. There hadn't been a time when she didn't long for a cozy spot with a plump chair to watch the wind blow and the snow fall, to see heat roll off the ground in waves during the summer, peer through the glass when spring rains pelted the earth.

"This will be all, Mr. Teal."

She'd been in the store for more than an hour. Her stash of money was going to feel a lot lighter going out than it had coming in.

"Are you sure you want to head out now? It'll be dark in a few hours."

"I've been waiting all my life for this house. I can't wait a moment longer."

"A woman on her own…it just doesn't seem right or safe. Let me find a fellow to ride out with you. For the life of me, I can't picture where your ranch is."

"You and Auntie June are of a mind. And I thank you, but I'd rather do this on my own." If she decided to weep for joy or dance around the parlor like a mad woman, she would rather do it privately. "At any rate, it appears I'm not on my own after all. I've been adopted by that big dog on the hay pile."

She scooped up the fabric and walked toward the door because she really could not wait another moment.

Mr. Rawlings followed, carrying the crate of baking pans she had purchased. "You going to be warm enough in that coat? Nights turn cold this time of year."

If Laura Lee hadn't just met Mr. Rawlings, she would hug him. His concern for her seemed fatherly in a way she had never known.

Her own father might be alive and well somewhere in the vast world but she had no way of knowing since she hadn't heard from him since she was twelve years old. He'd left her at the Lucky Clover Ranch because she had begged him to. He'd waved her goodbye and ridden away with a great smile on his face.

Same as Johnny had. The thought left her feeling uneasy.

George Quinn did love her in his own way. Just not as much as he loved his adventuresome way of life. Every once in a while, he had looked at her as though he was surprised to see her.

Oh, Laura Lee, he would say, as if she had just returned from a distant place. But really, the only place she had been was out of the sphere of his attention.

"I have a warmer one, Mr. Rawlings. In case it's not enough, I'll snuggle up to my hairy new companion."

The storekeeper gave her a hand up into the wagon seat. Not that she needed the help. My word, she'd been climbing in and out of wagons on her own for as long as she could remember. Back on the Lucky Clover, she'd often driven wagons like this one for miles across open land, delivering food to the chuck wagons.

Even though it wasn't needed, the helpful gesture did make her feel at home in Forget-Me-Not.

"Thank you," she said, her smile down at him springing from a joyful heart. "I'll see you on market day."

Two hours later, Laura Lee was riding toward the sunset. On her right was a farmhouse with children playing in the yard. A woman stood on the porch of her white two-story home. When she saw Laura Lee, she waved her arm. A breeze snatched hundreds of fall leaves off the trees behind the house and blew them into the yard. The fading sunlight caught them, giving the appearance of golden rain drifting to the yard.

From what she understood, her own ranch was no more than an hour past this pretty place. Laura Lee waved back, certain that she would become fast friends with her neighbor.

With the sun setting and the land darkened, the earth seemed hushed, except for an occasional breeze that stirred the grass. It whispered through the trees growing in small groves on hillsides rolling away from both sides of the trail.

It was a clear night, so the stars shone as bright

as a million candles. She breathed in a deep lung-ful of cold air, grateful that the moon also shone down to light her way home.

As fast as the temperature had fallen, she might have been shivering had Hey... Dog not come to sit beside her on the bench.

She hadn't intended to have a dog. Would have refused him if she could have.

But now? She could not deny that he gave off a great deal of warmth, that his solid, hulking presence made her feel safer.

She leaned into him. The chill in her cheek melted when she snuggled against the fur on his shoulder. It was interesting that for such a huge fellow he did not have the unpleasant odor that some dogs had. She had to glance up to look into his face as he sat so tall beside her. He woofed softly and set his chin on top of her head. It was a relief to discover that his breath smelled as fresh as his fur.

Since sundown, she'd noticed coyotes stand-ing on distant hilltops. They lifted their noses, sniffed the air, then vanished back among the trees. She could only guess that they scented a dog and hoped to find an easy dinner. One glance at Hey... Dog must have made them think again about who was going to be a meal.

As long as she did not cross paths with thou-sands of migrating wolves, she ought to pass the boundary of her land before much longer. There was no way of knowing where the house was. There were a lot of acres; it could be on any one of them. She might spot it in half an hour or two hours.

Forty minutes rolled past before she came upon a split rail fence that looked in good repair. She pulled the team to a halt.

"Here we are," she said to the dog. "Home! I don't know about you, but I've never had one of my very own."

She stood up, stretched, then stepped up on the wagon bench to get a better view of the land. Acres stretched before her, sloping slightly down-hill, which gave her an excellent view of large meadows surrounded by trees that, with sunrise, would be flushed with fall color.

Moonlight glinted off what she thought must be water, possibly a large stream gouging the shape of a question mark across her property.

This piece of paradise could not possibly be hers. And yet, thanks to a man who was devoted to her, it was. He'd borne the pain of separation to make sure the mortgage would be paid, so that no one could ever take her home from her.

For probably the fourth time today, her throat tightened with emotion. Joyful tears pricked at her eyes. Hey... Dog looked at her and whined, nudged her hip with his nose.

In the darkness, she still could not spot a house and she knew that the horses must need a rest.

"Come on, boy." She ruffled the dusky colored fur growing between the pointed brown ears. It was odd that such a fierce-looking creature would have fur that felt like down feathers. "Let's go for a stroll about."

Now that the horses' hooves were not plodding the dirt and the new wood of the wagon not creaking, she heard the sound of running water. So it had been a stream she spotted running through her land.

Climbing on the load at the back of the wagon, she rummaged through her spanking new goods until she found a water bucket.

"You thirsty, big fella? I reckon the horses could use a drink, too."

Climbing down the spokes of the rear wheel, she realized she could use a drink as well. She followed the gurgling noise of the stream. Come summer, she would hear the soothing song of crickets and frogs, but now there was only the rush of water running icy cold.

"Here it is."

She stooped and drew her coat tighter against the night. The air wasn't freezing, but it might be before morning.

Glancing about at bushes that cast shifting shadows in the night breeze, she remembered how Mr. Rawlings thought it was dangerous for her to be out alone.

All at once, she was not sure he was wrong. Any kind of predator might have come to drink at the stream. As if to confirm that fear, a large shrub to her left rustled, and not with the wind.

The dog lifted his face from the water. Icy drops dripped from the fur on his chin. His growl was a low rumble in his deep chest.

The shrubbery went still. Suddenly a large shape burst from it, flying over the water in one graceful leap.

Hey... Dog bent his head and lapped once again, not bothering to watch the big cat race over the ridge of the hill.

She would be well and truly grateful to be within the safety of her own walls.

Some creatures owned the night. She was not of one of them.

Chapter Three

Jesse lay on the lumpy hotel bed, arms cradling his head on a pillow while he stared at the wood ceiling. Moonlight streamed inside the window, giving enough light to expose a network of spiderwebs in the rafters. Given a choice, he would have slept under the stars, but even the extra blanket from Bingham's father would not have kept the boy warm enough.

It was only the first night away from his ranch and already Jesse felt a yearning to be home. Even though he'd only owned the place for a month, was still a stranger to some of the folks in town, he felt a strong sense of belonging.

He'd only ever known that sense of kinship to a place once before. On the rainy afternoon that a welfare agency dragged him from the whorehouse where he had been born and raised, he'd truly felt like the six-year-old orphan he was.

Living on a ranch for the next ten years, along

with four other orphans, hadn't been horrible. Hadn't been home either. His adopted parents raised workers, not sons.

Bedsprings creaked near the opposite wall. Footsteps padded lightly across the rug. The door handle turned.

"Where are you going, Bingham?"

"To get a breath of fresh air, is all."

"I'll go with you." Jesse sat up. He'd bet his new herd that fresh air wasn't all the kid wanted.

"You don't need to, Mr. Creed. I've been breathing on my own since I was born."

"You walk around in this town with that smart mouth and someone will shoot you as soon as answer."

"The Underwood brothers come to Black Creek all the time. No one's shot them yet."

"Not yet. Put on your coat." Jesse could lecture the boy all night and not teach him as much as a walk through the streets of this sordid town would.

Once outside, Jesse regretted the need to teach the kid this way. The air was bitter cold. A breeze twirled puffs of dust down the road. He shrugged closer into his coat, hugged the lapels across his throat.

If Bingham was cold, he didn't show it. All he seemed to notice were two women waving to him from the upper balcony of the saloon.

Jesse resisted the urge to wave back. These were not the women who raised him. Those ladies had doted upon him, loved him freely. He'd come to find out later in life that most soiled doves were not like the ones who had brought him up. With most of those adrift souls, nothing was given for free.

"How about we go inside, have a drink?" Bingham stepped toward the open front door where bawdy sounds spilled into the night.

No doubt it all sounded like a fine time to the boy. Jesse had thought the same at his age. Cold crept through the soles of his boots. It wouldn't be long before his toes went numb.

Jesse grabbed Bingham's collar and yanked him back.

"I'm of an age." The kid gazed longingly at the saloon door.

"When you're old enough to know better, you'll be of an age."

"You sound like my pa."

The scent of jasmine wafted past Jesse's nose. Odd to smell that this time of year. He glanced about and didn't see the plant growing nearby.

"I hope I do." Once they walked past the saloon, the night grew quieter. It wouldn't stay that way because there was another saloon on the next block. "Your father is a fine man."

"I know, and I love him. But the thing is, he's

happy just being at work or home. And that's all right for him because he's old. I'm ready to experience everything out there!"

"It's fine to want that."

How did he tell the boy what he'd learned without sounding like a Sunday morning preacher? Not that Jesse had anything against Sunday morning preachers; it's just that he figured the boy didn't pay much attention to them.

He sure hadn't. He'd learned about life the hard way. Made some grave mistakes that other folks paid the price for. If he could keep Bingham from doing the same, it would be worth more than the herd of horses he was going to fetch. And they meant the world to him.

"You too cold to keep walking, boy?"

"I ain't a bit cold, sir." His red nose said otherwise but he didn't appear to be shivering.

"I'm glad. I've got some things to say to you."

"I did come along to learn everything you know."

"Everything you think I know."

Bingham slapped his hands on his forearms as though he could ward off the frigid air. "I reckon you've had more adventures than even than Hoodoo Underwood."

Many more. Although calling them *adventures* was giving his experiences glamour when they didn't deserve it.

The one and only thing he wanted now was to settle on his property, breed horses and raise children. Wake up every morning with their mother in his bed.

Out of the blue—or the dark—a vision flashed in his mind of the woman he had met earlier today. The one who was going to end up brokenhearted because she chose the wrong sort of man.

Hmm... She lay in his bed, hair the color of shimmering cream splayed about the pillow. A playful smile on her face. In his mind, he allowed himself to brush a feathered kiss across her lips because what was the harm? A pair of blue eyes gazed up at him in love, even though she knew his every secret.

Odd how something he only imagined left his heart half shaken. Slightly bereft.

"I've lived life, and I think maybe you envy that. The thing is, Bingham, I'd have traded every last adventure to have parents like yours."

"What was it you did, when you were living life before you settled in Forget-Hoping-Anything-Interesting-Will-Happen?"

"I was a bounty hunter." A robber of freedom. A maker of widows and orphans. He'd taken a life...and worse.

Bingham halted midstride. His mouth hung open, making him look like a fledgling bird expecting a worm to be stuffed into its beak.

"That's enough talk for now. It's cold. Let's go back."

"But I want to see—"

"Adventure? Look around, boy!" Jesse nodded toward a man who had just stumbled out of the saloon.

Even in the dark, he recognized the fellow who held the heart of the lady on the boardwalk back in Forget-Me-Not. The very lady he had just been fantasizing about. Although, the strange thing was, the vision seemed more solid than fantasy. The oddest part being, he was not a man who indulged in fantasy.

"What do you see?" he asked Bingham.

"A fellow having a high old time. Could be he just won money at cards."

"The truth is more like he's so drunk he's going to vomit at the hitching post. He lost money because his mind couldn't think a straight thought. He'll wake up in the morning feeling sick to death, then he'll do the same damn thing tomorrow night. And he'll keep on until he's out of money. I've seen it over and over, son. Haggard and hungry isn't adventurous."

"But you were a bounty hunter!"

What he wouldn't give to forget that. To live on his sweet little ranch and wake up next to a blue-eyed, blond-haired woman who forgave and forgot.

Yes, one who made him forget.

* * *

Within moments of passing the split-rail fence, Laura Lee drove the team over the rise of a hill. And there it was…

Home.

Moonlight touched the single-story structure with shimmering, magical light.

As least, that's how her heart saw it. If the reality of the house was different by the light of day, so be it. Setting the place to rights would be an act of love. The porch looked like it circled the house. She longed to spend time there. Someone had even left behind a rocking chair.

While Laura Lee's shivers were of pure delight, she doubted the same was true for the horses. No doubt the beasts wanted nothing more than warmth and rest.

Not too far in the distance, to the left of the house, she spotted a tall red barn. A wide bridge lay across the stream cutting between the structures.

"Let's get you settled in." With a glance back at the house, she led the team toward the bridge. The enchantment of her four walls would not vanish because she settled the animals first.

The barn proved to be in excellent condition. It was as though the previous owners departed only yesterday. They had even left behind a huge supply of hay, which meant she would not have to unload the wagon tonight.

An hour later, the animals fed and put in stalls, she took one last, loving glance at her barn.

"Good night, everyone." She patted the dog's head, then closed the barn door.

She hadn't walked more than ten steps before she heard scratching and whining. Evidently Hey... Dog preferred to spend his nights outdoors. Hurrying back, she opened the barn door. The dog pranced out, his great tail wagging.

"Even though you have plenty of fur," she said to him while he trotted beside her toward the house, "it's awfully cold out."

Moments later, she stood in the spot she had dreamed of standing since...since as long as she could remember. It was fitting to pause at the foot of the stairs and simply gaze in awe of her lovely whitewashed house.

In truth, the paint was a bit chipped and faded but that didn't dim its appeal one whit in Laura Lee's eyes. It only meant that her house needed her as much as she needed it.

"Tomorrow night, I'll find you a blanket," she said to the dog. She didn't need to reach down to pet him. He fit nicely under her hand. There was no denying that she found his presence a comfort. If she managed to sleep tonight, she would do it more soundly knowing that he was keeping watch on the porch.

"Good night, then."

She mounted the steps, walking backward and looking one last time at her property. If the rolling hills, meadows and groves of trees looked this pretty by moonlight, how would they look in the morning with sunshine bringing everything to life?

She stared at the door. What if it was locked? Johnny had given her a deed and directions but not a key. With the stress of separation looming between them, he must have forgotten.

"I suppose I could break a window." As horrible as it would be if the first thing she did to her house was to break something, she did have to get inside.

To her great relief, when she turned the knob, the door swung open with barely a squeal.

Stepping inside, her emotions burst from her in a flood. She sobbed out loud because she had never really believed she would have a place that was her own. Even all those times she and Johnny spoke about it, dreamed about it, it had been only that. A dream.

Now there were wood floors under her feet. She couldn't see much in the darkness, but there seemed to be a stone fireplace that spanned the length of a wall. And if she was not mistaken, bedrooms, one to her left and one to right, flanked each end of the big parlor.

Paws scratched at her front door.

Wiping her cheeks with the backs of her hands, she sniffled one more time, then opened the front door.

"You ought to have stayed in the—"

Apparently Hey… Dog had no intention of sleeping on the porch because he trotted happily past her, his tail thumping her skirt in passing.

She closed the door against the frigid air rushing inside. If he meant to stay inside, there was really nothing she could do about it. It's possible that he weighed more than she did.

"Well, what do you think?" Glancing about in the dark, she only imagined what the place was like or what might be in it.

To her relief, she did spot a chair. It was so big and comfortable-looking that a king might feel at home sitting upon it.

How thoughtful it was of the former owner to leave it behind. She would like to express her gratitude for the hay and the chair, but of course, she had no idea how to go about it.

For all that she thought she would not be able to sleep tonight, the chair seemed to open its arms and call her name. Perhaps she had become more worn down than she thought, running about getting ready for the move. Or perhaps it was simply a sense of security wrapping her up. Her own four walls saying, *Welcome home…come and rest your soul.*

She plopped down in the chair with a great sigh, loosened her hair and fluffed it out behind her.

The dog pressed his face close, licked a lingering teardrop from her cheek. With a soft woof, he sat on the floor. The weight of his head settled on her thigh. For as much as he resembled an extra-large wolf, he seemed to have a sweet and loyal spirit.

"You need a name of your own," she said while twining her fingers in the thicket of gray-brown hair on his neck. "From now on, your name is Chisel because you chiseled your way into my house…and into my heart, you great hairy beast."

He sighed, as though he was happy to finally be worthy of a name of his own. Actually, he might have sighed for many reasons, but she hoped it was that one. Shifting his weight, he lay down upon her feet. The warmth was welcome since it was shivering cold, even inside.

With everything the previous owners had left behind, they'd no doubt left firewood as well. Still, in the moment, she was too weary to go exploring.

Shrugging deeply into her coat, she felt her eyes grow heavy. As she did every night, she carried a vision of Johnny's handsome face off to sleep with her.

Drifting on a sleepy daze, she imagined the

sigh of his breath upon her cheek, the brush of his lips lightly grazing hers. He whispered her name and his voice sounded different. More tender and less demanding. The pitch was different, too, deeper. Compelling. She had to admit she liked the difference. Ordinarily, Johnny was bold, taking—or trying to take—what he wanted. In this dream, he wanted to give.

In her slumbering vision, she lifted her hand, trailed her fingers through the short whorls of his dark blond hair. Which was odd since Johnny had long dark hair. He smiled, and she felt a yearning for him to her very soul. His olive green eyes gazed at her with more love than she'd ever felt before.

Olive green eyes! Laura Lee sat upright with a start. Johnny had deep brown eyes.

Could she have been…? No, she absolutely could not have been dreaming of the stranger from town whom she had met for one brief moment. Why would she?

What a faithless creature she was! Johnny had bought her a house! He was out…somewhere… working hard to pay off the mortgage.

She owed Johnny everything. And yet…the yearning for a stranger lingered in her heart.

How wicked she was. She deserved to shiver the night away wide awake. Ah, but the dog's warmth crept up her ankles to her calves, then her knees.

She drifted back to sleep barely aware of wind hitting the window and making it rattle in its frame.

Could it truly be morning? It was hard to re-member when she had slept so soundly, even at the Lucky Clover, where she'd felt safe for the first time in her life.

The ranch had been her first home really. She'd been given a small room of her own in the main house, the same as the rest of the unmarried girls. For many years, it had been her sanctuary.

Even though she had been happy, it had never been her dream to live at the Lucky Clover for-ever. Here, within her own walls, was where her heart always longed to be.

Like a veil being drawn from her eyes, the fog of sleep cleared from her brain. She bounded up from the chair she had slept in.

Everything she had not been able to see in the dark was now visible.

The chair was deep blue and the only piece of furniture in the room. As she'd suspected, there was a bedroom flanking each end of the main room. Behind the fireplace, she thought there might be a kitchen. If she was very lucky, and it appeared that so far she was, there would be a stove so that she could cook her pastries for Friday.

Skipping because there was no one to witness her acting like a loon, she passed through the main room to the area behind the fireplace.

To the right was a table with one chair and to the right of the table was a stairway that led to... She lifted up onto her toes trying to see. There was no way of knowing without climbing the steep stairs, but she thought the space might be a loft.

When she and Johnny had children, the boys could sleep up there. She could nearly see them peeking over the edge, their eyes green and—no, no, no! Brown eyes, warm and happy like their father, peering over the edge.

She shook herself. Perhaps she was still more sleepy than she realized. When she was wide awake, she would no longer recall the dream or how the man had made her feel so cherished.

Spinning left, she was grateful to see a kitchen with a wood-burning stove. As though in a deliriously happy fog, she moved toward the black-iron beauty that had six burners and an oven.

"Hurry home, Johnny! I need to give you a kiss." And after they'd been to the preacher... Well, she blushed right there in her own sweet kitchen just imagining the kisses they would share.

Chisel, whining at the front door, snapped her to the here and now, which was a wonderful place to be.

"It looks like rain," she announced, opening the front door. He bunched his legs, then leaped from the porch without touching the stairs. He raced across the yard, over the bridge and through an autumn-brown meadow.

He must be claiming the land as his, the same as she was claiming the house.

And what better way to do it than to explore the loft, then to clean the grime off the windows? After that, with a fire crackling in the fireplace, she would sit in her chair and sew her curtains.

If life could be any better, she could not imagine how.

If life could be any better, Jesse Creed could not imagine how. Sitting beside the campfire, he could smell his horses, hear them snorting and shuffling their hooves in the dirt.

After a week and a half on the homeward-bound trail, they would soon be grazing in their home pastures. It would take until after dark to get there. They might even encounter some rain. Where he was, it was clear overhead, but far off to the west, clouds were massing.

Rain or not, he didn't care. All he wanted was to be home.

During the time he'd been gone, he'd seen more of the outside world than he wanted to. There had been no way to ignore tainted reality since he'd been constantly dragging Bingham away from this or that "adventure," lecturing him on how a horse was better company than the Underwood brothers.

But he was a kid and curious. There was only so much Jesse could do to set the boy's feet on the right path.

"You anxious to get home?" Jesse asked.

Bingham, lounging against his saddle beside the campfire, didn't answer at first. An owl hooted in a branch overhead and a distant coyote yipped while the boy seemed to consider what to say.

"I'll be right glad to see my pa. The thing is, I'm worried I'll dry up with boredom. Next time you buy horses, I'd like to go along. You don't even have to pay me."

"You deserve to be paid. You're a hard worker."

There was a matter Jesse had been considering, going over it in his mind all during the journey home. Bingham was at a point in his life where his future might go one of two ways. He could work hard and become a man, or he could take up with the Underwoods and remain a boy for the rest of his life.

Jesse owed society recompense for the wrong

he'd done. If he could keep this good-hearted boy from going astray…prevent Thomas Teal from having a broken heart, he would do it.

"With all these horses, I've got more work than one man can do alone," Jesse began. "I'll pay fair wage if you'd work for me when your father doesn't need you at the store. You've shown what a good hand you've got with the herd, that you're willing to work hard."

Bingham leaped to his feet and crossed to Jesse's side of the campfire with his hand extended. The kid stood tall with the star-studded sky behind him. It looked for all the world that he wore a sparkling crown.

But there were also flames reflecting on his face.

Yep, the kid could go right or wrong at this point. If Jesse had any say in the matter, Bingham would grow to be a responsible citizen.

"I'll take that job, sir!"

"You'll need a horse of your own, son. Pick one out of the herd tomorrow."

"You're giving me a horse?" Bingham's long jaw dropped open.

"No, not giving. You've worked hard and earned yourself a pony."

The boy slapped his thigh. "I reckon I won't sleep a wink wondering which one to take."

Half an hour later, Jesse heard snoring from the

other side of the campfire. He heard it because he was the one who could not sleep.

Images of home played in his mind. He could nearly hear the sound of the stream that cut between the house and the big red barn. He imagined the solid thud his boots would make on the wooden bridge when he crossed it.

He pictured the horses in the paddock, saw them racing across the meadows, resting in groves of cottonwood and aspen that were scattered over the property.

He'd been so busy getting ready for the herd that he'd neglected the house. It had suited his needs for a while, with the one chair on the porch and the other before the fireplace. It was hard to remember what he'd stuffed into the loft built over the kitchen, but he was anxious to get it out and put his house in order.

Gazing up at the stars, he knew he was a blessed man. He didn't deserve any of what he had.

In the end, he did fall asleep halfway into a prayer of thanksgiving.

Chapter Four

It was late in the evening when Laura Lee hung a curtain on the last bare window. Listening to rain tap on the porch, she adjusted gathers over the rod, smoothing them with her fingers until they were evenly spread.

Then, hands on hips, she stood back to gaze at her handiwork. It looked like bouquets of snow-white flowers bloomed in the windows. Even though she was accustomed to sewing, her fingers ached…along with her back, her legs and her arms. Still, she could not remember a time when she'd felt better.

Glancing down, she saw the hem of her skirt winking in the high shine of the floor she had spent hours polishing.

The attic had been a treasure trove. She was surprised that the previous owners had left such useful items behind.

When Johnny returned, he was going to be

pleased to see the place looking like home. There was a red rug on the floor, which she had managed to beat most of the dust out of before the rain started.

He would also appreciate the fact that he had sturdy dinnerware on which to eat the delicious meals she planned to make for him. She had been beyond pleased to find a cast-iron skillet and a pot in the loft. Basic tools but along with what she had purchased, she was well equipped to prepare food with the same skill as her mentor, Mrs. Morgan from the Lucky Clover.

There was still only the one chair, but one of the rooms had a big, comfortable bed with room and more to stretch. She'd found an extra blanket in the loft, and a good thing, too. The weather was turning colder by the day. It couldn't be long before frost covered the ground.

Walking over to the chair, she glanced about, satisfied at how two weeks of hard work had turned her house into a home. With a tweak and a fluff, she plumped a pillow and set it back in the chair to make it look welcoming.

She smiled at her well-read copy of the *Ladies' Home Journal and Practical Housekeeper* where it lay open on the end table beside the chair. Over the past few months, she'd all but worn out the pages of the magazine. Just this week, she'd spent many an evening in her chair, studying this and dreaming of that.

Hmm… One chair… A pair of newlyweds.

Sighing, she wondered where her fiancé was. It had been too long since she'd seen him and, oh, but she did miss the sound of his voice and the hint of mischief that always lurked in his brown eyes. She could not help but wonder where she would be when Johnny returned, what she would be doing or wearing.

However it happened, their reunion would be utterly romantic.

But where was he? She thought he would have returned by now. Worry over him was beginning to shadow the joy of being in her own home. It couldn't take this long to conduct a business deal. Surely he was as anxious to get home as she was to have him here?

More and more she had to banish the fear that something might have happened to him. If only he hadn't gone off with those men. They did not look like the decent sort, in her eyes.

It took some effort to forget Johnny's smile, how he looked so gloriously happy to be off on an adventure when he rode away from her. It couldn't mean anything, but still, she'd have rather seen a frown of regret.

In her opinion, it would have been a fine thing for them to work side by side to pay off the mortgage. Still, paid was paid and she should be grateful for it.

She tried not to think it, but would she be able to keep her property if something prevented Johnny from returning?

Yes, she thought so. Her booth at last week's market had been a great success. It had been wonderful meeting so many friendly people, even if some of them did seem baffled about where her ranch was. She'd explained it, but in the end, they'd simply shrugged and welcomed her. There had been a few new ranchers to the area so the confusion was understandable.

Ten gongs chimed from the clock she'd found in the loft and placed on the mantel.

Time for bed and every muscle in her body was glad for it. Without a doubt, she was going to sleep like a stone. And a good thing, too. She would need to rise early in the morning to begin baking for market on Friday.

"Bedtime," she announced to Chisel, who was already asleep in front of the hearth.

The dog twitched one ear. Clearly he was in no mood to move to another place to continue his doze. Leaning over him as far as she could, she banked the fire.

"Sweet dreams, my hairy friend."

The soft woof he gave in answer must mean the same, she figured, except for the hairy part.

Moments later, she fell into bed and was sleeping before she got three blessings counted.

Jesse drew the pocket watch from his vest. He wiped a smear of rain from the glass to find it was already one fifteen in the morning.

Hell, it was good to finally be home, no matter the hour.

A steady sheet of rain blurred the figure of Bingham racing across the bridge for home. Jesse had tried to get the boy to spend the night but he'd wanted to wake up in his own bed and was all but bursting to show his pa the horse he'd earned. The moment they'd sheltered the horses under the large lean-to in the corral, the kid had lit out for home.

Given Bingham's youth, the extra hour of riding wouldn't hurt. While Jesse was far from doddering, it had been a long, exhausting trip and he was weary to his bones. Walking over the bridge, he knew that if it weren't that he was soaked to the skin, he would fall face-first onto his bed and not wake until the afternoon.

Through wavering sheets of rain, he spotted his house. In his mind, it had arms, wide open and ready to give him a welcome-home embrace.

Funny how something that wasn't even alive could make him feel like that. It must be because a place of his own, that sense of belonging, had eluded him all his life.

It had taken a tragedy to get him here but—

What was in the windows? A white film? Fog, maybe?

He picked up his pace, his boots sucking in the mud with the effort to run. At the porch steps, he came up short, skidding and nearly going down with the shock of what he saw.

Not fog, not a white film, but curtains…lacy ones with dainty embroidered flowers.

Must be one of his neighbors played a joke on him while he was gone. Although he couldn't imagine who it would be. He didn't really know anyone well enough for that kind of humor.

He only hoped it wasn't Martha Timbly, a widow more than ten years his senior. As new as he was to town, she had set her cap for him. She might have had the forwardness to decorate his place in order to show him what a fine wife she would be.

It didn't seem likely that she had, but in the end, he could not imagine why there were curtains in his windows. He did know that in the morning they were coming down.

Given that his boots were more mud than leather, he shucked them off outside. His clothes weren't much better so he shed them, too. Hopefully they would be dry enough come morning to put them back on so he could tend to his stock. Regretfully, all the clothes he owned were in the saddle packs he'd left behind under the lean-to. He would have remembered to bring them up to the house had he not put so much effort into trying to convince Bingham to stay the night.

He opened the front door, grateful that whoever had played the trick or done the courting hadn't locked the door when they'd sneaked out. He doubted that many of his neighbors even had locks on their doors. Forget-Me-Not wasn't a locking-doors kind of town.

He probably ought to check the barn to be sure no animals were in there to indicate that the prankster was still here. In his old life, he never left his door unlocked. The person he had been would have checked the barn and the trees surrounding it as a matter of habit.

But this was now. Goose bumps rippled over his bare flesh. Water dripped from his hair in an icy jag between his shoulder blades. He couldn't get to his bed soon enough.

He paused for a moment to listen for any sound that shouldn't be.

Nothing. Only the relentless pelting of rain on the roof.

Already half asleep, he plodded toward the bedroom, wondering if the jokester or the widow had done anything but hang curtains. He was just too tired to look right now.

Reaching for the blanket on the bed, his eyes already closed, his fingers curled about something that was not wool. Whatever it was shifted between his fingers like threads of silk…or hair?

His eyes jerked open.

There was a woman sleeping in his bed!

And not just any woman! It was her! The one he had met in town two weeks ago, the one he had daydreamed about so vividly.

Now, with his eyes wide and blinking, he could see that she had left a lamp burning low. It cast the room in a soft amber glow.

Just as in his imagination, the lady lay with shimmering cream-colored hair fanned out across his pillow. The same playful smile he'd conjured now lurked at the corners of her mouth. She must be engaged in some sweet dream.

Awake as he now felt, the room and the lady still bore a dream quality. Something about the shape of her mouth, the way her brown lashes deepened to black at the tips, felt more like a memory than the here and now. Could be he was in the grips of some magic spell. As if he believed in magic spells.

But…just maybe she would open her eyes and gaze upon him with love like she had in the daydream.

Or maybe he really was asleep again, dreaming that he was awake. Maybe the woman and the situation he knew her to be in had touched him more deeply than he realized so she was appearing in his dreams…day and night.

The only thing to do was wait and see what would happen next, if he would wake up or she would.

It was while he watched, eager and hoping to see again that devotion in her eyes, that he heard a growl.

Something lunged and knocked him sideways. The hit left him dazed. He closed his eyes, struggling to make sense of things. Footsteps pattered quickly out of the room and then returned. He cracked his eyes open. The world went black.

"I think he's coming around," said a voice so sweet it could only belong to an angel.

Jesse was halfway afraid to open his eyes and find that eternity had landed him someplace other than heaven. Still there was the voice and a gentle brush of fingers across his forehead.

He wasn't mistaking the scent of lilac and citrus either. Someone, although he could not recall who or how they would know, had claimed that heaven smelled like that.

No rush to find out where he was. For now, he was happy to feel the angel rustle her fingers in his hair, to feel the soft, moist puff of her breath on his face.

Except…he felt like he was suffocating, being bound in robes that were far too tight. And whatever cloud he was reclining upon was rock hard.

"Get back, Chisel. Let the man breathe." The fingers in his hair gently traced his scalp, running from ear to—

Pain, red-hot stabbing misery, shot through his head. He tried to sit up but firm yet feminine hands held him down.

"Lie still, Mr. Creed. You'll only make it hurt worse."

As if it could. Soothing unconsciousness claimed him before he could decide which side of the mortal coil he was on.

Laura Lee hadn't meant to hit the man quite so hard, but a skillet was a skillet and the situation had been dire.

She'd been sleeping when he crept into her room, deeply sleeping in fact and betraying Johnny by dreaming of the man who lay unconscious on the floor beside her bed.

One moment, his compelling green eyes had been looking at her with dreamy longing. In the next instant, he was real, bending over her naked and dripping water on her nose.

Before she knew for sure she was awake, Chisel

had knocked the man to the floor. She'd rushed for the frying pan and walloped him, in her fuzzy state not certain he was who she thought.

Not that it would have made a difference one way or another. Knowing who he was was not the same thing as knowing him.

And a wet, naked man leaning over one's bed was a shocking thing to wake up to.

Naturally, she'd wanted to toss him back into the storm where he came from but he'd been much too heavy for her to drag. Which was why he remained beside the bed where he had fallen.

Upon their first meeting, she hadn't judged him to be a lewd-minded man. To the contrary. He had been concerned for her predicament, even though she had not been in one.

She could not guess why he had invaded her house in the wee hours.

The storm was much worse than when she had gone to bed. Perhaps that was the reason. Maybe he was seeking shelter. Or he could be lost and had mistaken her home for his. From what she'd seen, the ranch homes in this area were not so different from one another. It might be hard to tell the difference through the deluge pounding the earth.

And if he had been very tired? Given the hour, he might have been confused.

Carefully, she slid a pillow under his head. He

winced but didn't awaken. There was no reason she should feel responsible for his pain. He was the one who'd trespassed. Any woman would have reacted the same way to a bare, damp-skinned intruder in her bedroom.

A gloriously built intruder. One she had gazed upon far longer than was appropriate under the circumstances. Under any circumstances, she had reminded herself before she dressed him in the only garment at hand.

He wouldn't like it. What man would? But his clothes were a dripping heap on the hearth. He could wear what she put on him or continue to shiver on the floor. Besides, he would have no idea how absurd he looked until he came to.

When he did regain consciousness, and she dearly hoped it was soon since she would hate to have to fetch a doctor in this weather, she would discover his reason for being here. Depending upon what it was, she would make up her mind on whether or not to have Chisel escort him back into the rain, or sleet, as it was becoming.

For the moment, though, she would have to tend to him since she was the one who'd laid him low.

"I'm sorry I hit you." She ought to touch the lump to assure herself that it was going down, to wash the blood out of his hair and cleanse the gash, but every time she tried, he moaned.

"Nearly sorry anyway. You can't just sneak into a body's home. And in case you hoped to shock me, I've seen a man without his clothes on before."

One time when she and Johnny had been camped by a stream, he went to bathe, then came back without wearing a stitch. That had been the first time he'd tried to convince her to take premarital liberties. He'd pivoted this way and that, making sure she got a good look at what she would be missing by turning him down. In spite of the fact that he seemed as confident in his allure as a rooster strutting about the hen coop, some things were meant to be waited for.

In the moment, she had been fascinated by the way he looked, so trim and dapper. There had been the slightest softness to his belly, which she didn't mind since she chose to take it as a compliment to her cooking.

Johnny was pleasant, but seeing him like that had not made her blush in the least.

The same was not true of Jesse Creed. She'd had to look away several times while getting him decently covered. She'd felt her cheeks flaming each time her fingers touched him while she yanked and tugged fabric about him.

Where Johnny was spare and reedy, Mr. Creed was muscled. Every inch of the man looked ripe with power.

It was a good thing it was Johnny she was marrying. She would hate to spend her life feeling the odd edginess that sidelong glances at Mr. Creed gave her. She took a deep breath, expelled it in a rush to purge her mind of comparing naked men.

Since she could do nothing for Mr. Creed at the moment but watch him sleep, and it was getting close to dawn, she decided to go to the barn and tend her horses.

Walking into the front room, she drew aside her pretty curtain. She'd been right about the sleet. It was coming down heavily.

Responsibilities came with having all this land. Back on the Lucky Clover, animals got fed no matter the weather. Her obligation had been to feed the hands who fed the stock. Today, it was up to her to feed the animals.

"Stay here, Chisel. Watch over our prisoner. Or our guest. We'll figure it out later." Yanking the blanket from the bed, she spread it over Mr. Creed.

For safety's sake, she snuffed out the bedroom lamp. She shrugged into her heavy coat, then went outside and dashed for the barn.

By the time she reached the big red doors, mud caked her legs well past her knees. Her dress and petticoats would never be the same. She didn't even want to think about her shoes.

A whinny of greeting met her while she still

had her hand on the door latch. Then another and another…then three more.

She didn't have that many horses! And hers were in the barn, not the paddock behind the barn.

Jesse tried to stretch. His arms would not straighten. He needed to take a deep breath but his chest was banded by something that kept his lungs from expanding.

Confusion set heavy upon him. The only thing he knew with certainty was that he was lying on the floor and it was cold.

Easing onto his elbows, he felt something soft yet inflexible cage the roll of his shoulders.

The fabric smelled pretty, though, like citrus and lilac. He'd noticed that fragrance recently, but when? His head pounded. His eyeballs ached. With great force of will, he opened his eyes.

A rose-patterned ruffle fluttered across his chest to the tempo of his breathing.

Sitting up suddenly, he cursed the pain shooting from the back of his brain to the front. He heard a seam rip. Looking down, he saw his legs sticking out of the bottom of a woman's flannel nightgown. A wide band of lace tickled the hair on his legs inches below his knees.

What the blazes! He'd been in and out of a dream state was all he could recall.

But this was his room, as solid and real as he'd last seen it.

He sat on the floor beside the bed, his naked butt numb with cold. Glancing down, he saw a pillow. Someone must have put it under his head.

A woman—but no, not simply a woman—the woman. She must be the one who dressed him in this…this flannel nightmare.

Also the one who, no doubt, hit him in the head with the skillet that lay on the mattress. It was the only thing that made sense.

She'd hit him because—

Of his horses!

Her beau was the cowboy who was involved with those hell-raising Underwoods. They would have known he'd gone to purchase his herd.

"Damn!" he shouted, then regretted it because it hurt like blazes and because in a shadowed corner of the room, something growled.

Slowly, Jesse came to his feet. So did the animal. In the dim, predawn light, he saw it bare its great, long teeth.

"Good dog." Or wolf or bear. "Good, good fellow."

There was no time to deal with the beast. At this very moment, the Underwoods and their fetching accomplice could be riding away with his stock.

As he thought about it, it made sense. Just because Bingham believed the gang of brothers went to Black Creek on a regular basis did not mean that this time they weren't following Jesse. It had been no secret in Forget-Me-Not that he would be away purchasing his horses. If the brothers were set on thievery, they knew where to find a victim.

The woman had proved to be a skilled conspirator, luring him over the bed and then knocking him senseless. Could be the reason she looked familiar was from seeing that pretty face on a wanted poster. Although, he didn't think that was something he would forget.

How long had he been unconscious? Plenty long enough for them to ride off with nineteen prime breeding animals.

The dog's tail thumped the wall. It emerged from the corner.

"Hey… Dog! Is that you?" he muttered in relief. "What the glory blazes are you doing in my house?"

When Jesse ran out the door, he heard the dog padding behind him.

It was a good thing his closest neighbor was a fair distance away. He'd look like a fool, running barefoot in the freezing rain wearing a woman's nightie. And a double fool for having no weapon at hand.

In the future, no matter how blamed tired he

was, he was not leaving his rifle on his saddle under the lean-to.

But if sheer anger could count as a weapon, he was well armed.

For all that his toes felt frozen, numb in the sucking mud, it didn't cool his anger at himself and the folly of being duped by a pretty slip of a woman. He was ashamed to admit that he'd succumbed to such beguiling bait…even dreamed of her while wide awake.

Slipping and sliding, he rounded the corner of the barn where the paddock was located.

As he'd feared, it was empty.

No mind, he was a tracker by former profession.

Looked like Hey… Dog was a tracker, too, although not so skilled as a dog ought to be. He trotted to the large barn doors, scratched and whined.

A seam of light glowed dimly through the door crack.

Either someone remained in the barn or the thieves had committed the sin of leaving a lamp burning when they hightailed it.

"Hush up, pup," he whispered, not wanting his presence known before he snatched his rifle from the saddle where it lay across a sawhorse ten feet away. "You ready to catch us a thief?" he asked, retrieving the weapon. The dog thumped his muddy tail on the nightgown.

Slowly, so as to make the least noise possible, he drew open one of the doors and eased inside, his rifle at the ready.

He spotted his horses first thing.

Then he saw the woman. She stood on a wagon bed, her skirt rucked up about her waist and her shapely bare legs caked with mud. Gripping a pitchfork, she shoveled hay onto the barn floor. Because she had her back turned, he had a moment to watch her golden hair shimmy with the sway of her hips. She hummed an off-key tune while she worked.

The relief he felt finding that she was not a thief seemed excessive. He'd only met her the one time, for pity's sake. It couldn't rightly be said that she was even an acquaintance. There was just something about her…a sensation of knowing…

Wasn't that as logical as a frog flapping butterfly wings?

But here she was, making herself at home in his house and in his barn.

"Howdy, ma'am," he said because his sense of knowing did not include the knowledge of her name.

Chapter Five

❧❧❧

"Oh!" Startled by the voice, Laura Lee's fingers clamped hard around the handle of the pitchfork. Turning quickly, she sucked in a breath and held it. Not because she believed the man intended to shoot her; the weapon was nose to the dirt and his finger nowhere near the trigger. She couldn't breathe because of the effort it took not to laugh out loud.

Her guest—she supposed that was what she must consider him to be—looked absurd. Seeing him standing in the doorway of the barn, his legs spread in a no-nonsense stance, holding his weapon while rain dripped off his eyebrows… *oh, my.*

Still, it wasn't that which nearly brought her to her knees in hilarity. It was the sight of this large man, so bold looking in every way, dressed in pink flannel with delicate flowers and leaves stretched across his chest, with wiry brown hair poking from the stretched-out neckline, that made her need to cover her mouth with one hand.

She might have managed to keep control had it not been for the sodden lace clinging to his shins, seeing those muscular calves captured by embroidered rosebuds.

Pressing her fingers to her mouth did no good. A giggle burst from her lips.

"I do beg your pardon," she said with a slight, high-pitched hiccup.

She stabbed the prongs of the pitchfork into the hay, then climbed down from the wagon. She yanked her skirt from the waistband, smoothing it down so that it covered her legs in a proper manner. He'd already seen more of her than he should have...but not nearly as much as she'd seen of him.

Why did that have to pop into her mind? Now she was blushing and he would guess why.

"Your own clothes are wet and this is all I could spare that didn't require a corset." No! She could not have possibly blurted that out. "I meant...well, you were wet and shivering. Most of the time, flannel is wonderfully warm. I hope you—"

"Thank you for bringing my horses in," he said, saving her from continued babbling.

Which she did not normally do. It's just that the events of the last hours had been...unusual, and vastly perplexing. At least she understood now what he was doing on her property. He and his horses needed shelter. He had been naked because—she didn't know why for sure, but there could be many reasons that did not involve an assault on her person.

No doubt being soaked, he had removed his clothes out of for respect for the many hours she had spent polishing the floor. A more suspicious part of her brain argued that he would have no idea how much care she had given the floors and that it had been too dark to see the shine.

"You are welcome. Come, Chisel." She would rather have the dog standing beside her than Mr. Creed. One could only trust one's judgment to a certain degree.

Except where Johnny was concerned. Naturally, she trusted her fiancé completely. But where was he? Two weeks would be enough time for him to do what he needed to. If he really… But no, she trusted him with all her heart.

Obediently, Chisel trotted forward and licked her hand. Seconds later, he joined Whittle and Bride in their stall. Saffron and the other horses mingled in the large open area between the stalls, munching hay.

"I'm sorry I hit you, Mr. Creed." She might as well clear her conscience about that now. Judging by the increasingly bad weather, they might be stranded together for a few hours. "But you did give me a start."

"I didn't expect anyone to be in the house."

It was a relief to know she was right about the reason he was here. Any reasonable person would have sought the nearest shelter in this storm. She knew nothing about Mr. Creed other than his name and that he had a scar on his left hip. She also knew that he looked… well, never mind that.

It was blamed difficult to never mind it, though. Her eyes had seen what they'd seen and there was no changing that. If soaking flannel was not clinging to him, it would be easier. But it was clinging to him, an intimate reminder.

"Your herd is beautiful," she said as a distraction.

"Plenty hungry, too. Again, many thanks for bringing them inside and feeding them."

Setting his rifle against the wall beside the door, he crossed the barn and leaped up on the wagon. He picked up the pitchfork and began shoveling out the hay. The smooth pull and draw of his muscles, which she could see because of what he was wearing, made the job look easier than it felt when she did it.

"It was the neighborly thing to do," she answered while refocusing her attention on the long black mane of a pretty brown mare.

"And I reckon we're neighbors?" His brows knit together, as though something was puzzling him.

"I suppose we are but I've only been in Forget-Me-Not for a short time."

"It's a good place to settle." In one leap, he hopped off the wagon.

She watched him while he walked to the wall where the tools were hanging, taking note of the long rip down the back of her nightgown. She would have to repair it before bed.

It was interesting to note that he knew the exact spot to put the tool even though he had never been in her barn. A barn was a barn, she guessed, pretty much the same anywhere. Tools went where they went with no great mystery involved.

"Must be getting close to dawn," Mr. Creed remarked while leading the two stallions in his herd, each to a separate stall.

It made sense that he would put the stallions away. But it struck her as forward that he had not asked for her permission. It was her barn, for all that he seemed so at home in it.

"I'll fix us something to eat." Since he had unloaded the hay wagon for her, she owed him a meal before she sent him and his livestock on their way.

"Appreciate it. I'm not much of a hand in the

kitchen. I'll build us up a fire in the parlor. Reckon it's nearly as cold inside as it is out here."

Jesse ran toward the house, his saddlebag slung over his shoulder, his rifle in his fist.

The sooner he peeled out of this blamed sleepwear the better. He'd toss it in the fire he was about to build if he didn't guess the woman would need to take it with her when she left.

He had hoped it would happen after breakfast, but during the dash from the barn to the house, the weather took an intense turn for the worse. This was the kind of storm that living things ought not to venture out in.

The lady dashed a few feet ahead of him, through the mess of rain and sleet. She sure was a shapely little thing. Rude as it was, he couldn't help staring at how gracefully she bounded up the stairs, how her hips swayed—

He forced his gaze down, watching his knees bump the lace border of the nightgown. He purely hoped she hadn't married her unfaithful beau. She seemed far too fine for the likes of someone who'd picked the nickname of Hell Dog.

Standing on the porch, he opened the front door for her to enter before him. He was as soaked and muddy as when he last came in the house, but this time he thought better of shedding his clothes.

The dog rushed in first, heedless of the debris sticking to his fur.

"Hey… Dog, get out of the house!" he called.

"He belongs to me now and I've named him Chisel," the lady announced, brushing by him. "I do allow him inside."

The hell she did! He opened his mouth to say so, then noticed the high gleam reflecting off the floor. Words dried in his mouth like a stream in a three-year drought.

Curtains in the windows, a shine on the floor… How long had she been squatting in his house? And what was he going to do about it?

He'd think about it while he set a fire in the hearth. Surely he'd come to some sort of decision while he changed clothes.

Walking into his bedroom, he yanked the nightgown off over his head. The room smelled different, like citrus and lavender, same as it did when he'd lain helpless on the floor.

Nothing about this situation made any sense. Being caught in a storm and seeking shelter, he could understand her need for refuge. But the weather had only turned bad yesterday. How could she have made his place shiny and frilly in that short of a time?

Apparently the woman was unusually industrious.

A thought occurred to him and it made him

drop his pants with only one leg inserted. What if that worthless fiancé of hers had abandoned her?

If that were the case, she would have needed a place to stay. Auntie June knew Jesse was out of town. Hadn't he been the one to advise the woman to turn to Auntie June for help?

That's it! Auntie June had advised her to stay here. That combination of *if*s was the only thing that made any sense.

A houseguest, then. He hadn't planned on having one, but if the aromas coming from the kitchen were anything to go by, her presence would be a welcome treat.

Welcome or not, the plain fact was she couldn't leave. So welcome was better than not. They would just have to make the best of it for a time. Thought about in a neighborly fashion, this was a fine way to get acquainted.

But not only that. There was a part of him that would always be a bounty hunter. That part wondered if that no-good Hell Dog was a wanted man, up to something that would jeopardize the peace of Forget-Me-Not. Keeping company with the Underwoods made it seem likely.

If the lady was, or had been, intimate with the fellow, she would be privy to what he was up to. In the event there was something to discover, it wouldn't take long for Jesse to root it out.

In the meantime, he'd dine as fine as a king.

Fastening the button of his shirt collar, he followed his nose.

Rounding the corner where the parlor joined the kitchen, he saw her standing beside the stove holding out a thick slab of ham for the dog to eat. There were times in his life when he hadn't eaten half as well.

The thought must have shown on his face.

"Usually, he hunts his own food." She looked at Jesse with wide blue eyes that reflected a forthright spirit. But at the same time he sensed her grit to be tempered with naïveté. While she charmed him, made his heart grin, she also caused his watchful nature to wake up and sniff about. "I won't send him out to do it, not right now."

The thought of the weather not being fit for man or beast had crossed his mind. Sure as shootin', no matter how skilled a hunter the dog was, he wouldn't find game this morning.

"I wonder if I might have the pleasure of knowing your name?"

It was a fair request given that she knew his name...and a whole lot more about him than that. All he knew about her was what he tried to piece together. Which meant he knew nothing. Except that if she had or was going to marry that faithless man, her life would be a sorry one.

"Laura Lee Quinn." She wiped ham-smudged fingers on her frilly apron, then extended her hand in greeting. "Please make yourself comfortable, Mr. Creed."

She indicated a chair at the table with a sweep of her hand. Seems like he's the one who ought to welcome her, but since she was the one cooking the meal, he didn't remark on it.

He sat down where she pointed. "Sure does smell fine, Miss Quinn."

He breathed in the scent of ham, warm butter and frying eggs while he waited to see if she would correct the *Miss*.

She didn't. He was relieved, for her sake…but also—he shook his head. For his sake was what his mind suggested before he thought better of it.

Without knowing more than Laura Lee Quinn's name, he felt an odd draw toward her. He'd noticed it the first time he saw her standing on the boardwalk wearing a wedding gown and looking bereft.

At the time, he'd assumed the attraction to be the watchful feeling that any man would have for a woman in an unfortunate circumstance.

If that were the case, he would have put her out of his mind after advising her to seek the help of Auntie June. But she hadn't gone out of his mind. She'd haunted his daydreams the whole time he'd been away from Forget-Me-Not.

Why was that?

And then to come home and find her in his bed? It was almost…fate?

He shook his head again. Fate had nothing to do with her presence in his house. It was logical circumstance. Auntie June, knowing his house to be vacant, had sent her here.

Auntie June could have rented Miss Quinn a room, but no doubt Hell Dog had left her destitute. As caring a woman as Auntie June was, she was still running a business.

Logically, there was only one reason Miss Quinn haunted his dreams. She was a woman in need. It had been soiled doves, women treated cruelly and without respect, who had raised him until he was six years old. From a young age, he'd learned to watch out for them, to run for help when one of them was in danger.

From what he guessed, Miss Quinn was a woman in need, if not in immediate danger. That was why she had been on his mind, invaded his daydreams. It was why his feelings toward her were inexplicably tender.

He'd feel the same for any lady who had fallen under his temporary care.

It sure as hell was not a fairy-tale notion that made him approach her on the street a couple of weeks ago. Life was action and result, not foggy fantasy.

Then again, the plate of food she just set on the

table in front of him seemed something out of a dream. He cut a piece of ham, put it in his mouth, then closed his eyes in appreciation of the rich, sweet-salty flavor.

Swallowing, he opened his eyes to see her smiling at him.

This was bound to be a cordial visit. He found that he was glad for the company.

"Welcome to my home," he stated.

In the very same instant, she said, "Welcome to my home."

Wind howled under the eaves while a long, stunned silence pervaded every corner of the house.

"I must demand that you leave," Laura Lee stuttered when she at last remembered how to speak.

The man might have slapped her in the face, so bald-faced was the lie that burst from his attractive mouth. Weather be blamed, she could not have this invader in her house.

"And I must demand the same of you, Miss Quinn."

"This is my home! You may not demand anything." Red-hot emotion bubbled in her chest, erupted from her tongue. "Why, you lowdown, vile trespasser!"

She slid her chair backward, then slowly stood.

Like a mirror image, he did the same. How she wished the man was not so tall. Locked in eye combat across the table, he held the advantage of being able to glare down at her.

"A court of law will say differently," he said. She felt the scorch of his breath puff on her face. "Just because Auntie June sent you here for temporary shelter does not make my property yours."

"Auntie June?" She squinted her eyes, narrowed them to arrows of authority, daggers of indignation. "What has she to do with this?"

"You know better than I do, Miss Quinn, but if you require an explanation—Auntie June knew I was away purchasing my herd. When your fiancé jilted you and left you penniless, she sent you here."

"Jilted me!" This had gone too far. Propelled by righteous fury, she rounded the table. She jabbed him in the ribs with her finger. What a horrid, desperate man he was to suggest such a thing. "Left me destitute! What he left me with is a deed to this property!"

He caught her finger, swallowing her hand in his big fist. She yanked, certain that he meant to do her harm. But for as much as they stared murder at each other, for as strong as his grip was, the pressure he exerted was gentle.

"It's a fake." The insufferable man sounded so sure of his falsehood. "You've been tricked."

"I will not allow you to steal my ranch."

"It isn't yours for me to steal."

"Oh, no? Look around. What here belongs to you?"

"The walls, the floors, the windows." Rain pummeled overhead. The hiss of two people breathing heavily wound Laura Lee's nerves tight. Any second now she was going to snap like the string on an over taut violin. "The roof."

"No one lived here when I moved in. And all of a sudden, you claim it's yours?"

Glancing down, he looked surprised to see that he was touching her. He let go, straightening his fingers slowly, one by one.

"Whose chair did you put that ruffled pillow on? Whose hay was in the hayloft?" He dipped his head, his nose within inches of hers while those green, dark-lashed eyes stared at her unblinking. "Whose bed were you sleeping in?"

Not his, certainly! If that were the case, it would mean that Johnny had betrayed her. And Johnny would never! How foolish and disloyal would she be to believe the word of this stranger over the word of her one true love?

"Everything I found here was left behind by the previous owner."

"Whose name was?"

"Corum Peterson."

That made him back up a step. Judging by his startled gaze, his arrogance took a tumble.

"Show me your deed, Miss Quinn."

"Show me yours. Assuming it exists."

The storm had nothing on Mr. Jesse Creed as he pounded up the staircase to the attic. If she didn't know better, she'd think it was thunder pounding the treads.

There hadn't been time to go through everything up there yet, but she'd bet her happy future with Johnny on the fact that there was not a legitimate deed stashed in a dark corner.

Listening to boot steps thumping the floor overhead, she went to her bedroom, easily located her deed, then came back into the parlor, where she sat down on the only chair.

Let him prove his point standing up while she confidently reclined. No doubt he would stand before her shifting from foot to foot in shame, given that she had a deed and he did not.

Sitting back, she smiled. Partly because she wanted to cover how nervous she was with this situation, but also because Mr. Jesse Creed was going to leave her home like a dog with his tail tucked between his legs.

Imagine having the gall to besmirch Johnny's character with such a whopping lie!

"When he comes downstairs with nothing in his hand, you may eat him for dessert," she said to Chisel, who slept in front of the hearth. He twitched one ear in acknowledgment, lifted an eyelid, then went back to sleep. No doubt the dog didn't care one way or another who owned the property, as long as he got to enjoy the warmth of the fire.

Johnny didn't care for dogs. She had no doubt that he would come to care for Chisel, though. He had to. She had become fond of her canine companion and it would break her heart to send him away. Even if it could be done. It was hard to imagine who would have the boldness to try to separate Chisel from Whittle and Bride.

Besides, Johnny would never break her heart. In spite of what Mr. Creed believed, she knew he would not.

Footsteps clomped down the steps. As soon as the man rounded the corner into the parlor, she fanned her deed in front of her face. And yes, she did it a bit smugly because—

No! It could not be!

He had something gripped in his fist. Something that looked the same size and color of what she gripped in her fist.

Stomping around in the attic gave vent to a bit of Jesse's temper. By the time he'd located his deed and come down stairs again, that emotion changed direction.

Now that his ire was cooling, he couldn't forget how stunned Miss Quinn looked when he told her the truth about what she supposed to be her property. It was obvious that she had been betrayed by that no-good man of hers, but it was going to take a while before she knew it.

By the time he was on the sixth step down, he almost wished he did not have to deliver such heartbreaking news. All she was guilty of was having a trusting heart. He'd bet his last acre she had no idea that her intended was carousing with loose women.

While Miss Quinn was about to face a severe disappointment, her intended was probably taking up with any lady of questionable morals who glanced his way.

For all that Hell Dog had a black heart, he did have a face that made women take a second look. Jesse would give the reprobate that much. Didn't much care to give him anything, though.

Rounding the corner of the parlor, he watched Laura Lee's fair-skinned face go bone-white. She would not have expected him to have a deed.

"Come to the kitchen." By rights he could gloat, well aware that his deed was legitimate, that his property was paid for in full. But knowing that she was about to discover the man she adored had betrayed her…he didn't have the stomach for it. "Lay your deed next to mine on the table. We'll see what we've got."

It was a relief to see the color flood back into her cheeks even though he had no doubt that she would gladly kill him at the moment. Given what she believed to be true, how could he blame her?

Whatever anger still sickened his gut was now directed at one faithless fraud named Hell Dog. Johnny might be his given name, but the one he'd been appointed by the Underwoods, or even chosen himself, suited him better.

"What we have is proof of your trickery, Mr. Creed."

He remained silent because he had no wish to plunge a dagger in her heart sooner than he had to. Walking lead-footed into the kitchen, he smelled something burning.

"My pie!" Laura Lee lurched toward the stove, where smoke curled out of the crack in the door.

She reached for the handle without using a mitt. Rushing up behind her, he snatched her hand away an instant before her fingers curled around the searing iron.

She looked back at him, her blue eyes wide with dismay. "I've never done that before...with everything—"

She glanced down at his fingers, clutching hers, wrapping around hers. He ought to let go but didn't want to. She eased her hand from his grip and put it behind her back. "It was pumpkin. There's a patch growing behind the back of the house."

"I'm familiar with it, though I could never figure out what to do with them but feed them to the horses."

"I forbid you to touch my garden!" Now she was pale again. He'd never seen someone's emotions show that way before. Was she distressed because she'd nearly burned herself or because of the peril to the pumpkins?

"If you make me another pie, I'll leave them alone."

"You act like you will be here long enough for me to do that."

During the rush for the stove, she'd had the foresight to slap her false deed down on the table. He set his genuine one beside hers.

"I can't see that either one of us is going anywhere with the weather the way it is," he announced.

She didn't have anything to say about that but her cheeks did brighten from pale to splotchy.

He had to admit, Hell Dog and his friends had done a good job of forging the deed.

That shouldn't be surprising. The elder Underwood worked for the county recorder. When the office burned down last year, Jesse had been told that he worked from an office behind the saloon. Given that the boys spent a lot of time there, they could easily have access to county records.

What he couldn't figure out was why Hell Dog would give his fiancée a fake deed. To impress her, make himself a hero in her eyes?

Maybe he wanted out of the engagement and was too cowardly to say so? Handing her a false future left him free to ride away.

Either or both of those things seemed likely.

"They are identical." Her voice sounded like it was trapped halfway up her throat. "Mine has got to be the real one because why would Johnny give me one that was not?"

Because he was Hell Dog more than he was Johnny. Love was blind. Auntie June had said so. Blame it, here was the proof blinking her wide, innocent eyes at him.

He could argue with her all night long but he doubted she would recognize the truth. Glancing about at the curtains in the windows, the high shine on the floor, he knew she would not.

"I reckon this place is your dream as much as it is mine."

"Your dream, Mr. Creed. My reality."

Her color evened out while she spoke so he figured her high emotions must be settling.

"How well do you really know—" he began.

She folded her arms across her chest, arched her brows. He could tell her the truth about her

Johnny, but she would not hear it, as blind and besotted as she was.

"I reckon this is a matter for Judge Benson to decide," he said instead.

Eventually Jesse would know Hell Dog's reasons for betraying this fine woman. For now, all he could hope for was a truce. A bit of peace while they rode out the storm.

Be it the one outside or the one between them.

It had been a difficult day. Laura Lee suspected Mr. Creed was trying to make peace between them, even going out into the storm to bring in another pumpkin.

Which did not make up for the fact that he was trying to steal her ranch. No matter how accommodating he tried to be, how much he acted the gentleman, he wanted what belonged to her.

The blasted weather had only worsened over the hours, so here they sat after dinner, to a stranger's eye enjoying a cozy evening in front of the fireplace. She sat in the chair mending her laundered nightgown while Mr. Creed lounged upon a dusty quilt he'd brought down from the loft. He reclined against Chisel, his head cradled on the dog's furry flank.

Anyone peering in the window would see a picture domestic bliss.

As much as she wanted Johnny to walk in out

of the storm, she didn't want him to do it at this moment. She could only imagine what he would think. That she had tossed him over for someone else was what! That the man with compelling green eyes and a body ripe with well-formed muscles had discomfited her. Turned her head.

Which he had not! Much.

Shamed, she determined to keep her wonderful fiancé foremost in her mind. She would be relieved when Jesse Creed finally left her in peace. He looked far too at ease with his long legs stretched out on the floor, his head nuzzling Chisel's fur.

It was disturbing to see the confidence in his serene pose. It gave the impression that this was his house and she was the one stranded in foul weather.

Something wind-driven smacked the wall outside. She glanced up from her work to see Mr. Creed gazing at her face. How long had he been doing that?

His mouth lifted slightly while at the same time a line furrowed the flesh between his eyebrows. He studied her with neither a smile nor a frown.

Whatever the expression was, it made her uncomfortable.

"I was just thinking," she said in order to redirect that speculative gaze. It felt far too warm, too familiar for her peace of mind. "You owe me money for keeping your herd in my barn."

There could only be one reason she reacted to Jesse's every little look and that was because she missed Johnny so much. It was simply that she was longing for the attention of her one true love.

"You short on cash?" His eyebrows shot up. Apparently in trying to dull his curiosity, she had only sharpened it.

Her circumstances were none of his business.

"I am not!" She plopped her mending on her lap so forcefully that she nearly nicked her thumb on the needle. The man was a hazard to her. First the near burn, now the near stabbing. "The state of my finances has no bearing on your horses taking up room in my barn."

He sat up, hooked his elbows around his bent knees. "I see it a bit differently, Miss Quinn. It's your animals in my barn. And my house." The man slid his gaze at Chisel but she didn't miss his affectionate smile.

"I can't help but wonder," he went on. "You say Johnny gave you the ranch as a gift. How did he come by it? I reckon he's a wealthy fellow to be able to surprise you that way."

She ought to tell him to mind his own business, but with identical deeds, he might innocently believe the ranch was his. The sooner she convinced him otherwise the better. Telling the truth at this point hurt no one.

"He isn't wealthy." She picked up her nightgown and resumed sewing. Neat, even stitches were a far sight more soothing than those probing green eyes were. How on earth could a simple look make her feel so flustered, even when she wasn't returning it? "Not in money, at least. But he does love me. That is worth more than any fortune."

She felt him look away more than saw him, since she was intent on her work and not on him.

"I wonder why he isn't here with you?"

"Like I said, he isn't a wealthy man. But he's found a way to pay off the mortgage. He wants me to feel secure. To that end, he has gone away to earn the money to pay off the debt all at once. I assure you, he would rather be here with me. It shows his good character that he is making such a sacrifice for us."

"Anything can happen. It's a wild country out there away from Forget-Me-Not. What if he's delayed in getting back?"

Wild country was something she knew a bit about. Until she was twelve, gunshots and slamming doors were her lullaby. Instead of her mother's arms about her in the dark, there had been fleas in her scratchy blanket.

"I may be a woman, but I am capable of keeping a roof over my head."

"Seems like you've done a competent job of settling in."

Why, the gall of him glancing about at all she'd done and frowning about it.

"A far better job than you have done," she shot back. "Assuming you did not show up here last night for the first time."

"Can't deny the house is in a bit of disrepair."

"As vacant homes tend to be."

"I wonder, Miss Quinn, who will you make a mortgage payment to when one comes due?"

For all the wondering she'd done about it, she did not know. Her intention had been to inquire at Wells, Fargo & Co. in the unlikely event that Johnny did not return within another week or so. Of course, she had no way of knowing if the financial institution had anything to do with her loan.

There was no denying she had lost a bit of sleep over the matter.

"The bank," she said, pretending a certainty she was far from feeling. "Just like I assume you do." She arched a brow, then leaned forward in the chair while she watched for him to react to the fact that she had just neatly pointed out that his deed was a fake since they were not both making payments to the bank.

"The ranch is paid off, Miss Quinn. No one will be coming after you for a payment. Unless I decide to charge you for keeping your animals in my barn."

It took all her power of will not to poke him with the needle for smiling with such a cocky turn of lip.

"I can't imagine why I should trust the word of a man who would bend over a lady's bed in all his naked—" not glory…no, not that "—nakedness."

"And I can't figure out why you would trust the word of a fellow who—" Jesse Creed snapped his mouth closed on something he clearly wanted to say. He shifted his gaze from her eyes to the leaping flames.

"Would give me a dream come true? The very thing I've longed for all my life?"

His gaze still riveted on the fire, he shook his head. Amber lights shimmered in his hair. She wanted to touch it, feel the soft strands glimmer under her fingertips.

She was shamed to her core, ill at heart over her treachery toward Johnny.

Once again, a long silence ached between them.

When he finally spoke, he began with a deep sigh, his broad shoulders slumped. "We have that in common then. Love of home."

That was a horrible thing to find out. If, for

reasons unknown to her, he truly did love her land, he might do anything to wrest it from her.

"As I see it, we've got identical deeds," he said. "The thing is, I know mine is genuine, but as long as you believe the same of yours—" now she really was going to impale him with her fire-sparkled needle "—we've got a problem that can't be solved between the two of us."

"We are in a predicament." There was no harm in admitting the obvious.

Turning his face away from the fire, he gazed at her with an expression so agreeable that she felt suddenly friendly toward him.

That wouldn't do! The last thing she wanted was to feel amenable toward a thief, whether he was intentionally one or not.

Apparently, what she wanted was not what was in her heart.

So when he said, "I propose that as soon as the weather clears, we take the matter up with Judge Benson in town. But until then, we've got to share this space. I'd like to do it peacefully, Miss Quinn," she thought it the most sensible thing to do.

"Yes. It seems the only thing to do." She rose from her mending and set it behind her in the chair. "I believe I'll make us a pie from the pumpkin you brought in."

The thought of making a pie for Mr. Creed was not as horrible as she might expect.

Once again she was being completely disloyal to Johnny by baking for this intruder, but she'd offered him pie and there was no taking it back now.

What a long, miserable night it was going to be, trying to figure out why she didn't mind spending time in Jesse Creed's company.

Because truly, it was very last thing she should want.

Chapter Six

According to Jesse's pocket watch, it was four in the morning. The rich scent of chocolate drifted on the air. He yawned and stretched out across the thin layer of blankets on the floor of his spare bedroom.

He couldn't say it was the scent of baking that woke him. As tired as he'd been when he'd gone to—not to bed really, Miss Quinn slept in the only bed—but when he'd lain down on the blankets on the gleaming floor of the spare room, sleep had been elusive.

Still, he wouldn't have minded an extra half hour of a light doze before the animals needed to be fed. With any luck, the storm had moved out and he could go to the barn without getting wet. Winter was coming, no way about it, but a few dry days would be welcome. More than that, if the weather cleared, he and Miss Quinn could go to town and pay a visit to the judge.

Judge Benson would set things right. Tell Miss Quinn that Jesse was the legal owner of the ranch.

Jesse would gladly pay Laura Lee Quinn's board at Auntie June's until her no-good fiancé came to claim her. If he did.

He'd pay a good amount to have his life back the way it was. Simple, quiet, the welfare of his herd his only concern. With no lacy curtains in his windows and no shiny floor to worry about messing up.

It had been a while since he'd felt the familiar lumps of his own mattress, since he'd given up the stress of a day by relaxing into the cushions of his chair. Sure seemed like an age since he'd felt the tranquility of home settle about his shoulders.

Peace and privacy were what he craved.

His lovely and betrayed squatter disturbed his peace of mind in a way he could not have imagined. He'd lost count of the number of times his heart softened toward her, the same way it had in the dream.

That fanciful emotion hadn't been real. If he had risen from his nest on the floor, crossed the parlor to the other bedroom, then stood over the bed to watch her sleep, she would not have opened her eyes, gazed at him with love and forgiveness for his ugly past.

No. She'd have hit him with a skillet and he'd have deserved it.

A dream, whether one was awake or asleep when it happened, was only that. A vision to cherish until it faded from memory.

Sitting up a bit stiffly from a night on the floor, he pulled on his socks, then stepped into his boots while listening for the beat of rain on the roof. Coming to his feet, he scraped his hand across the beard stubble on his face. No rain, he thought, but plenty of wind.

And something else. He tipped his head to one side, trying to hear.

A song drifted out of the kitchen, slightly off-key but as pleasant a sound as he reckoned had ever filled this house.

Assuming she would stop if she knew he was listening, he tiptoed out of the bedroom, then leaned against the kitchen doorjamb. This time tomorrow, his house would be still. It might not be a bad thing to take a moment to smell what was baking and listen to the melody drifting through the rooms.

Watching the lady from behind, swaying happily while she worked, he thought Hell Dog was making the mistake of a lifetime. What man would not be blessed to have Laura Lee Quinn in his home?

Well, not Jesse. Not under these circumstances, but someone else would be a lucky fellow.

It was just too bad she thought the world of her

fiancé when all the while he was betraying her in the worst way.

If there was a chance of her believing him, Jesse would say something.

Later on today, he'd have a word with Auntie June. Maybe if Auntie June told her the truth about Ruiz, Laura Lee would listen. She would move on her way—whatever way that was—and at least be free of the burden that being married to that man would bring.

"Looks like you aim to feed the whole town," he said because he couldn't stand in the doorway forever. Not with livestock to be tended and legal matters to be seen to.

"I hope to." She spoke to him with her back turned, her attention on something that looked so fluffy it might float to the ceiling with just a huff of breath to lift it. "Today is market day and even though I am not penniless as you suggested, every bit of income is helpful."

"It looks like the weather cleared enough for us to go to town. We'll face some mud and wind, but we'll get there."

"Where do you plan to go after we meet with the judge?" She softened the hard edge of her question by turning and placing a pastry that smelled like cinnamon and butter heaven in his hand.

"Home." He bit into the treat, nearly groaned

out loud in pleasure. Hell Dog was a fool in a million. "How about you?"

She gazed at him with wide blue eyes, confident and unblinking. "Home. Right back here to my kitchen."

Guiding Laura Lee's wagon into town, Jesse was grateful to see that the market was being held inside today. Even with the sky turning bright and cloudless, it was biting cold. Wind seeped through his duster. His fingers grew numb and stiff around the reins. Miss Quinn's skin looked as white and brittle as porcelain, except for her nose. It was red.

A curl of smoke rose from the chimney of the library.

"Ought to be warm inside," he commented, pulling the wagon to a stop in front of the steps. "For a chocolate cookie and a cup of coffee, I'll take your wagon and team to the livery."

"Two cups of coffee," she said while he gave her a hand down from the wagon. "Be sure and let Mr. Rawlings know that they won't be there for more than a few hours."

"As soon as we get you set up inside, I'll hunt up Judge Benson."

"Honestly, Mr. Creed, I can set up my own booth."

No doubt she could, but what kind of man

would he be to let her? He knew the boxes to be heavy because he'd loaded them into the wagon earlier this morning.

"It'll be quicker if I help. You wouldn't want to miss a sale."

Without giving her a chance to argue, he lifted a crate containing mugs and the coffeepot. He carried it inside, listening to the rustle of her skirt while she hurried behind him with the bag of coffee beans clutched to her chest.

"That's my table." She pointed at the one to the right of the fireplace.

Crossing the room with the load, he noticed people smiling at Miss Quinn. Being the bearer of warm drink no doubt made her everyone's favorite citizen.

He wondered if she would stay in Forget-Me-Not once Judge Benson gave her the bad news. Sure did seem like she would fit in well here.

Auntie June bustled out from behind her table of preserved peaches smiling at Miss Quinn, her arms open wide and her skirt swaying with her gait. It was a relief to think that Miss Quinn would be watched over after the truth was revealed. Knowing it, his step felt lighter going back outside.

When he returned toting two large boxes of baked goods, Laura Lee was being rocked in a hug and cooed over. Auntie June had not given birth to children of her own but that didn't keep her from mothering anyone who crossed her path.

As soon as he set the goods on the table, Auntie June let go of Miss Quinn and turned the hug on him.

"Welcome home, Jesse! Did you collect your herd?" Finished squeezing, she stepped back. "I see you've met our Laura Lee."

Not knowing quite what to say, how to explain matters with so many folks looking on, he said, "Yes, I have."

His gaze slid to Miss Quinn. Would she reveal the situation? She slid a gaze back at him.

He was quickly learning that it was a mistake to look into her eyes because he so easily got lost in them. He barely knew the woman and yet peering into her sky-colored gaze made everyone else in the room grow fuzzy.

It was as if there was a connection between them that could not be explained. He was caught, like a deer staring down the barrel of a gun. All he could think of was, did she feel the same draw? Had anyone noticed his preoccupation with staring at her?

He blinked, corralling his thoughts and his racing heart.

Laura Lee blinked, too. She sucked in a breath, then turned abruptly toward the table, unloading her goods with brisk efficiency.

Blame it! Someone had noticed. It was Auntie June, whom he suspected could read a person's very thoughts.

"Auntie June," he whispered. "May I speak to you privately?"

"Yes, I think you should, young man." She snagged his elbow and arched a fine salt-and-pepper brow.

"It's not what you think," he explained because she chuckled while she led him past row after row of shelved books.

"Is it not?" Reaching the privacy of a dim corner, she let go of his arm.

"No," he whispered because even though they were so far in the back of the room that the book spine he stared at had an author named Ziesloff, he did not want anyone to be privy to what was about to befall Miss Quinn. "It's worse."

"My word, Jesse. There is the complication of her engagement to be dealt with, but if you ask me, her fiancé is not a decent sort."

"He's going to break Miss Quinn's heart."

"That's been my belief all along. Anyone with eyes can see it."

The scent of coffee brewing drifted from the front of the library, sounds of laughter and folks visiting intermingling with it.

"She's got blinders on when it comes to him," Auntie June went on. How, Jesse had to wonder, could Auntie June say so much with a simple flick of her brows? "I believe it's your duty to explore whatever it is between the two of you."

"The only thing between us is my ranch."

"Oh, her ranch borders yours? There's been some confusion about where it is."

"Her ranch is my ranch." The words might have been acid on his tongue. It stung just to speak them.

"I don't understand."

"It's an ugly thing, but her fiancé gave her a deed to my ranch. Claimed to be giving her a wedding gift."

Auntie June gasped and pressed one hand to her throat. "What a cad he is and such a peacock. Oh, he can turn the girls' heads all right, strutting about like he does, flashing his devilish smile. If you ask me, it's to cover how weak he really is."

"I saw him when I was in Black Creek, drunk and—" he shook his head, feeling repulsed by what he had to tell "—keeping company with loose women. I doubt he's coming back for Miss Quinn."

"That sweet lamb deserves better." The look Auntie June shot him made him feel like she thought he was the "better."

"I sure do hope you aren't matchmaking, Auntie June, because I—"

Light, feminine-sounding footsteps tapped on

the floor, weaving a way through the maze of shelving.

Laura Lee rounded the last corner, a friendly smile on her face. "There you are, Mr. Creed. I've brought your coffee." She placed the mug in his hand. She sure did have a pretty blush. He was certain the pink hue came naturally to her.

"I've just been explaining our predicament to Auntie June."

"Quite a pickle it seems," Auntie June said.

"Only until Judge Benson takes a look at our deeds and informs Mr. Creed that mine is the valid one. I hope you have a room for him at the boardinghouse."

"Oh, dear," Auntie June fussed. "Judge Benson is out of town. Gone to visit his ailing cousin, I'm afraid. Who knows how long he'll be gone"

"That doesn't change the fact that my deed is the genuine one." Laura Lee Quinn straightened her shoulders, stiffened her spine and looked like she grew an inch taller. Pricklier, too.

"Auntie June." He hated to do this to Miss Quinn; he did think she was a fine woman. His feelings toward her were becoming tender. But he was not going to give his home to her because of it. "You were there when Corum Peterson signed the deed and gave me his property. You witnessed my purchase. We don't really need the judge."

His ally, his witness, reached for the mug in

his hand. She took a long swallow of coffee while glancing back and forth between him and Miss Quinn. She handed it back to him, her expression unreadable.

"Was I?" she said with a slight shrug of her shoulders. "Perhaps, but I don't recall it."

Jesse Creed looked like he had been run through by a pitchfork.

Rightly so. Laura Lee had been within half a second of committing violence against him, the way he looked so certain that Auntie June was going to support his lie.

Now, she could peacefully keep her hands and most of her temper to herself. The man looked as vanquished as anyone could.

"How can you not remember?" Steaming coffee sloshed over his fingers. He placed the mug on a shelf, then blew on his fingers.

"At my age, one's memory isn't as sharp as one would like." Auntie June smiled back and forth between them.

Mr. Creed resembled a match tip in the instant it sizzles to full-blown flame. While she ought to feel reassured that Auntie June did not recall the incident, Jesse did not look like a man caught up in a lie. He appeared outraged...genuinely rattled.

Not only that, during her brief acquaintance

with Auntie June, Laura Lee had never gotten the impression that the woman was forgetful.

After a deep breath or two, Mr. Creed's color evened out. His hands unclenched.

"It seems that until the judge returns, we are at an impasse." She heard tension in his voice, but it was lessening. Although he did turn a severe look on Auntie June, who did not appear at all distressed over it. "Do you have a room for let?"

What a relief that he was going to be reasonable and go to live at the boardinghouse. Perhaps she would bake him a pie or two and bring them to town. Really, there was no reason they could not be friendly. It was not his fault someone had cheated him out of his money.

Why, she nearly pitied him. It might not be out of line to bring the poor man a dozen cookies to go with the pie.

"I will gladly pay for Miss Quinn's stay until Judge Benson returns."

"My stay! Not on your life!"

Without thinking, she flung her arms wide, incredulous at his high-handed maneuvering. Her fingers hit the mug and knocked it over. Coffee dripped over book spines in a rich brown waterfall, pooling on the floor with a steady plop, plop, plop.

Drat! The only cloth at hand was her skirt. She grabbed the green-flowered hem and wiped the spill off *Sketches of Africa*. On the next shelf down, she cleaned off *A Common Man's Guide to Ranching*. Kneeling, she swiped at the pool of coffee on the floor. How could she have been so careless?

Really, this was all Jesse Creed's fault! He'd shocked her into reacting in haste.

All of a sudden, he was on the floor across from her, vest in hand, wiping coffee off the lower shelves.

"I will not leave my home." Yes, that was a hiss spewing out of her mouth. "It's mine and you will not force me off my land."

He sat back on his haunches. For a second, she forgot to breathe. Of all the moments to be struck by how manly…how utterly handsome he was, why did it have to be now?

Why did her heart pick this very moment to recognize the width of his shoulders, how his long bold fingers flexed around his crumpled vest. Why must a lock of hair dip across his forehead toward his left eye, as if to say, *See how my gaze makes your belly feel all aflutter?*

"You—" she rubbed hard at the floor even though the spill was gone "—cannot force me."

"No?" He wadded his damp vest in a tight ball. "I'm not leaving either. If you value your reputation, you will stay with Auntie June."

"If I— Why, if you were a gentleman, you would take the room and save my honor!"

"In any case, I do not have a room to let." Auntie June's voice drifted softly down upon them.

Glancing up, Laura Lee saw her smiling. A great wide cat-that-ate-the-canary grin.

Why would she be grinning when down here on the floor futures were at stake? It was almost like she was up to something. For the life of her, Laura Lee could not imagine what.

"Oh, I doubt we need to be overly concerned about reputations, my dears."

Auntie June crouched down, eye to eye with them. She picked the mug up from the floor along with the chip that had broken off when it hit the wood. With the agility she displayed, Laura Lee wondered whether the woman was of an age to be all that forgetful.

"Given matters," Auntie June whispered, "no one will think badly of either of you for standing your ground. It's not as though you are lovers flouting your sin. You, Laura Lee, are an engaged woman. And, Jesse, everyone knows how honorable you are. Haven't I heard that Bingham Teal is coming to work for you? He can act as chaperone."

"That'll make three hours of the day acceptable," Jesse grumbled.

"I do agree that you must both occupy the property, but do so without a hint of impropriety."

"Can't see how that's possible." Jesse Creed was no happier with events than Laura Lee was and it showed in his curt tone.

"I would suggest that you, Jesse, rent a room to Laura Lee."

Preposterous! It would be the same as admitting the property was his. She would not accept that.

It wasn't until a pin dropped out of her hair and pinged on the floor that she realized how forcefully she was shaking her head.

"And you, Laura Lee, will rent a room to Jesse. With money changing hands, you have a business arrangement and no scandal to it."

"That's not what Johnny will think!" How would she ever explain it?

"He'll think you've done your best under trying circumstances." Auntie June picked up the hairpin, caught an escaped curl bouncing about Laura Lee's nose, then secured it back into her hard-won coif. "And that perhaps he should not have been gone so long. If he thinks otherwise, he is not the man for you, my dear."

Oddly, she thought she heard Jesse Creed grunt. Perhaps his knees were becoming sore from kneeling on the wood floor.

"I won't be responsible for folks thinking badly of Miss Quinn," he stated.

"Let me ask you this, both of you. Do you feel that I'm living a scarlet life when it's only me and my renter, Mr. Hobbs, in residence?"

"I've never given it a second thought." Mr. Creed crossed his arms over his chest and stared hard at the coffee-soaked vest setting on the floor near his knees. "But he's—"

"Don't you dare say 'an older gentleman,' Jesse Creed. I promise age makes no difference in affairs of the heart."

"I reckon I would see matters in a different light if he weren't paying rent."

"All that is needed is for you to keep your relationship friendly...businesslike, and all will be well." Auntie June shifted her happy, crinkled gaze from Mr. Creed to her. "Don't you agree, Laura Lee?"

"If I must, then yes." If only that little voice in her head wasn't shouting a warning to be careful of Jesse Creed. There was something about him, an allure that—

Never mind, she was completely devoted to her fiancé. "Five dollars, then," she said. "You may live in my house for five dollars until Judge Benson returns."

"Agreed. I offer you the same."

He extended his hand to shake on the deal. It

looked damp with the coffee he had spilled on it. She pressed her hand against his hot, work-calloused hand. When the handshake ended, the dose of sugar she had added to the drink made her skin stick to his.

Her nerves tingled as his flesh drew away from hers in a slow sensuous pull. The voice in her head screamed so loudly for her to beware, she half thought someone would hear it.

With the deal agreed upon and disaster diverted...for a time...all three of them stood up.

"You are witness to our arrangement, Auntie June," Jesse said, apparently trying to quash the woman's bright smile with a slash of his brows. It only made her eyes twinkle. "You won't forget?"

Auntie June gave his cheek a playful pinch. "Of course not. I have an excellent memory."

She did? Hadn't she claimed only a moment ago that age had challenged her memory?

A frizzle of dread crept up Laura Lee's neck. Perhaps the woman was pretending not to recall witnessing the signing of Jesse's deed.

But why would she?

There was no reason. Laura Lee would not let her mind go there, because if she did and found Jesse's claim to be true, her whole life would fall apart.

Everything she dreamed of would be lies under her feet.

Chapter Seven

It was dark by the time Jesse went to the barn to check on the horses. A few were already sleeping. Awake or asleep, he sure did enjoy looking at them. After spending so many years dreaming, all he wanted to do was watch them swish their tails, listen to them whicker softly to each other…picture which ones would give birth to the prettiest foals.

"Sorry to be so late." He knelt down, stroked the muzzle of a mare who had bedded down on a pile of straw. Most of the animals dozed off while standing, but some were lying down for a deeper rest. "Didn't get back from town until half an hour ago. I've got a renter now so I needed to shop for an extra bed and chair. A few more blankets and such."

The mare sure was a pretty animal. Reflected in lamplight, her glossy coat was a near blue-black.

"I reckon if I've got to have a houseguest, I'm glad it's her. The woman cooks like a saint. If saints do that kind of thing. I never tasted better food. She's in there now, fixing a late supper. When the time comes for her to move on, I'll miss her cooking and I don't mind saying so out loud."

There was more he would miss, but he didn't feel he should say those things out loud. Speaking made them real. Made it so you couldn't go back from whatever you'd stated.

"What I can tell you is that there is something going on in here." He tapped his heart with his thumb. "Damned if I know what the hell it is, though."

He'd grown up with a soft spot when it came to women. That's the only way he could explain what he was feeling.

"What the hell *what* is?" Laura Lee's voice came from only yards behind him. How much had she heard?

"What you're cooking for supper," he answered quickly so it sounded like the truth.

Pivoting his head, he glanced over his shoulder. He was no longer living alone and would need to take care with what he confided to his horses.

"Fried chicken and mashed potatoes. I came to tell you supper is ready."

"I appreciate you cooking for me, Miss Quinn. I know you don't have to."

"And you don't have to feed my animals. I appreciate that." She knelt beside him and stroked the mare's glossy mane. "What a good mother you are going to be…and your babies so beautiful."

"Which stallion shall I breed her with?"

He purely hoped this was the start of a truce between them. Circumstances had put them at odds with each other, not natural animosity.

Still, it had been a long ride from town with not a word spoken by either of them. Mile after mile of fertile pastureland rolled by and not a comment made on its beauty. In his opinion, that was a crime against the Creator.

"They are both beautiful. Does one of them have a better temperament? Of the two of them, which is the more trustworthy and less likely to—" she glanced up at him, her cheeks flushing pink "—to wander?"

All of a sudden, she stood up, brushing a bit of straw from her skirt.

"I'm sure I don't know which of the horses would suit. I've only come out to invite you to share the meal with me, Mr. Creed." Rather than looking at him while she spoke, she stared at the tools he'd placed on the wall the first day he moved in. "No point in eating alone, I reckon."

"I'm obliged, ma'am."

She walked beside him toward the barn door. He plucked his coat and hat from a rusty nail on the wall. Only Corum Peterson would know how long the makeshift hook had been there.

Going outside, he was struck as always by the stars winking brightly overhead.

"I imagine it's the same all over the world," he commented. "Looking at them in China is much the same as looking at them in Texas."

She was quiet for so long he wondered if she would not engage in conversation. But when she spoke, he wished she hadn't.

"I imagine Johnny and I are both seeing the same ones." Her face was turned upward, so beautiful in profile he wanted to reach out and trace the slope of her nose, the curve of her lips and chin. "I believe he's aching for me as much as I am him."

And Jesse imagined all too well that he was not. He shrugged deeper into his coat against the deepening chill.

What, he wondered, would Miss Laura Lee have done had Auntie June "remembered" how she had been there when he signed his deed, how she'd been so happy for him that she'd opened a bottle of wine. She'd handed him a glass, Judge Benson, too, and the three of them had toasted to the success of his horse ranch.

Auntie June had even promised to purchase his first foal.

Wind whipped up his pant legs, twirled the hem of Miss Quinn's skirt.

"How did you meet?" Sneaking out of another woman's bedroom? Cheating at cards or stealing a horse?

Her face lit up. All of a sudden, he wished he hadn't asked. Didn't want to know what wickedness the fool had been up to.

"He saved my life."

"Oh?" he uttered blankly.

"No need to look so surprised, Mr. Creed." Her laughter sounded like a small, happy bird flying toward the moon. "I promise he is not the cad you believe he is."

"If you don't mind talking about it, I'd like to know about…his heroics."

"All right." Wind snapped her skirt, whirled it around her knees. "After I've told you, I hope to quit seeing that skeptical look in your eye whenever I m-mention Johnny's n-n-name."

The bone-chilling cold must be making her stutter.

"Tell me over dinner. I'll race you to the house."

What he wanted to do was wrap his arm around her and share his warmth, but a race would do as well. Better, since he had no business touching her for any reason.

As much as Laura Lee wished to have her house to herself, she was not sorry that Mr. Creed was here to revive the fire in the hearth.

Dashing inside the house, her fingers clumsy and half-frozen, there was every chance she would have burned the hearth rug in the attempt to do it herself. If mid-October was this cold, what would winter be like?

Clapping her hands together, rubbing her fingers briskly against each other, she regained enough feeling to put supper on plates and carry them into the parlor.

"Dinner by the fire?" she asked.

He glanced up from his task, smiling. The warm friendliness in his gaze held her. In the future, she would have to remember how easily his sea-colored eyes could draw her in, make her want to stare trancelike into them.

And turn her into a disloyal Jezebel.

When he stood and took a plate, his fingers brushed hers. Transferred warmth flooded her hand, chased the chill from her bones as quickly as her sudden inhalation of surprise.

Johnny's touch was cooler. She didn't know that there was such a difference in the feel of a man's hands. It wasn't something she'd ever wondered about before she'd crossed paths with Jesse Creed.

Evidently she had been staring at Mr. Creed's fingers for too long. Her mind had wandered completely astray from dinner and onto a slippery path. Luckily it was a private path that no one else could travel. And it was absolutely none of her business what his hands were like when they touched a woman in tenderness.

But still…were they slow, patient and coaxing? Would that kind of touch feel better than Johnny's quick, insistent one?

"Looks mighty fine." Judging by the grin on his face while he looked at the plate, Mr. Creed's praise was genuine. "I thank you."

He sat down on the plush new chair he had purchased from town, then balanced his plate on his knees. He waited for her to sit down before he picked up his fork.

She couldn't recall a man ever doing that before. Her father would rarely notice when she set a plate of food in front of him. The ranch hands she cooked for would dig into their food before it was fully on the table.

Johnny, being a hand on the Lucky Clover, never knew any better, but he did grunt his appreciation while he ate.

Once she was seated, Mr. Creed scooped up a spoonful of mashed potatoes with gravy dripping down the side. He held it up as though it was a glass of wine he was toasting with.

A toast was a toast, she supposed, no matter if it was with wine or potatoes. She held up a spoon of potatoes in response, heard a glob of gravy drip back onto her plate.

"To friendship, Miss Quinn. Circumstance might have set us at odds, but since we are each other's renters for the next few weeks, I reckon cordial relations would be easiest. And the truth is, I like you. I wouldn't mind calling you a friend."

She would like that as well. There was nothing to say that a friendship with Jesse would keep her from loving Johnny. No, naturally not.

"To friendship, then." She touched the tip of her spoon to the tip of his. "To mutual understanding."

To the near future, when she would become lost in a brown-eyed gaze and not a green one. But Mr. Creed was right in that cordial relations would be easier.

"I'd be pleased if you'd call me Jesse, ma'am."

"I'm not usually known by 'ma'am' or 'Miss Quinn.' Just Laura Lee. And I think that I would like to call you a friend, too."

She had a fiancé; that role was filled. But one could never be hurt by having another friend.

"Laura Lee is a right pretty name."

"Oh, it's common as apple pie, but my parents weren't poetic people."

"I didn't know mine," he said but didn't look distressed over it. No, indeed, he took a bite of fried chicken and slowly blinked his eyes in apparent bliss.

"You were an orphan?" Once in a while, she wondered if she would have been better off as one. To have been adopted into a family who noticed she existed might have been better.

"Can't say that exactly, since I had half a dozen mothers."

"Were you raised in a convent then?" Oh, to have been so lucky!

He laughed, wiped those long calloused fingers on a napkin. "No, they were soiled doves. My mother was one. She died when I was a baby so the others tucked me under their scarlet wings and clucked about like mother hens until I was six. I hope you don't think poorly of me for it. I couldn't tell you who my father was."

Thinking poorly of Jesse Creed was becoming more difficult by the day.

"I think you were lucky to have someone to cluck over you. Growing up, I only had my father. Most of the time, he didn't know I was there. I was twelve when I got a job in the kitchen of the Lucky Clover Ranch. I imagine it took a good month for him to notice I wasn't trailing behind him when he left, even after I told him I was staying."

"The Lucky Clover outside Cheyenne?"

"I knew the ranch was well-known in Wyoming, but we're a ways from there."

"I grew up near the Lucky Clover. The folks

who adopted me after the Children's Aid Society took me away from the ladies, they hired me out to work there one summer. Me and a couple of other boys they adopted."

"I wonder if our paths crossed."

"I was fifteen, the summer of '72."

"I was thirteen. I'd been at the ranch a year already so it was possible," she allowed. His expression said he was digging deep, trying to remember her. "School would have been out for the summer when you were there, so I would have spent most of the day in the kitchen. Besides, even if we did meet, we couldn't expect to recognize each other now. I know I've changed a great deal over when I was thirteen. I reckon you have, too."

A crease formed between his brows while he seemed to be searching lost memory for her. At last he shrugged, smiled. "I was a spindly-looking kid."

Watching him now while he sat, one long leg cocked to the left, seeing firelight glint in the shadow of his beard stubble… Yes, he had changed quite a bit. "So was I."

"How about your Johnny? Did he grow up on the ranch? You said he saved your life."

Her Johnny? Why was it when Jesse said it, it sounded as though he were not? Just because her fiancé had been gone for a while did not mean he was not still hers. Surely it did not.

"No. He hired on as a cowboy only a month before he rescued me from a mad coyote."

His shoulders shivered dramatically. "I've seen rabid animals a time or two. Hope I never do again."

It hadn't happened so long ago that the details weren't fresh in her mind. "I was walking from the main house to the married cowboys' homes, taking dinner to a woman who had just given birth. It was only about a fifteen-minute walk."

It had been a lovely evening with the sun close to setting, not a single cloud to blur the intense orange and pink. A breeze had rustled the grass and cooled the sweat on the back of her neck. The scent of warm, freshly baked bread had wafted out of the box she carried.

"I was halfway there, alone on the path because it was suppertime. The cowboys who weren't on the range were at the bunkhouse or their cabins. It was so peaceful with the sun going down, I didn't mind it. Not until I heard growling behind me. I turned and saw that poor sick beast. I was scared to my bones. The thing looked more zombie than alive."

The evening had been soft and lovely, and she hadn't been paying the attention she should have to potential danger. Not that paying attention would have changed the situation.

"I was out in the open with no place to go. I

couldn't hide from it. Couldn't run fast enough to get anyplace safe, so I prayed. That's all I could do. Then I heard hoofbeats pounding fast. There was a blur that turned out to be Johnny leaping off his horse and placing himself between me and the coyote. He shot his gun three times while it was leaping. The last shot brought the animal to a halt smack at Johnny's feet."

And that was the moment she'd fallen in love with him. He'd been so handsome and brave... and quite the hero on the ranch. No matter how the other girls had sighed over him, it was Laura Lee who'd won his heart.

"I reckon he's been your white knight ever since?"

After what she had just told him, how Johnny had risked his life to save hers, she expected that he would see her fiancé differently. Yet there was something in his tone that gave her the impression that he did not.

"He's never given me reason to doubt him. And now that he's given me a ranch for a wedding gift...yes, he will always be my white knight."

Jesse had been thinking of naming the stallion he was leading about the paddock White Knight, even though the animal was gray. Now that the name was tainted, he would have to call the horse something else.

"Let's let Laura Lee give you a name."

Last he noticed, she was in the garden, taking advantage of a sudden warm spell and trying to salvage what the storm hadn't ruined.

He opened the paddock gate, then closed it securely behind him. Although the stallion would never be broken to saddle, he didn't want the critter to be wild either. The same was true of all the horses he'd purchased for breeding.

To that end, he'd be spending a lot of time walking them about and getting them comfortable on a lead. Making them feel easy around him. In about a year, he hoped to welcome his first foals. He didn't want the mares skittish when he handled their babies.

Pulling a well-worn book from his vest pocket, he began to read. It would get the stallion used to the sound of his voice.

"""Tom." No answer. "What's gone with that boy, I wonder? You Tom!" No answer.'" He could read *The Adventures of Tom Sawyer* by Mark Twain a hundred times and never tire of it. It didn't matter that he wasn't a kid. A great story was a great story.

He took his time getting to the garden, reading and leading the horse, getting him familiar with his surroundings. At first, the horse shied away from walking over the bridge that crossed the stream, but after some sweet talk and coaxing, he did it.

Taking the long way to the garden, Jesse walked past the front of the house. Funny how he didn't mind the curtains in the windows so much anymore.

"Come on, boy, let's get you a name."

The garden was only a couple hundred feet behind the house. Laura Lee, sunshine glimmering in her hair, knelt over a limp tomato vine. She cupped a shriveled red fruit in her hand.

She must have heard the horse's hooves clopping the damp earth because she looked up suddenly and swiped the hem of her apron across her eyes.

"Say, Laura Lee! This fellow needs a name. I was hoping that you—"

Standing only a foot from her, he saw that it had not been mud that she wiped off her face but tears. He knelt beside her, tipped her chin up so that she looked into his eyes and not at the ruined fruit.

"Hey, darlin'? Don't be sad," he coaxed. She blinked, away the tears still streaming from her sky blue eyes. "There's still a few pumpkins and look…over there, a corn stalk with an ear or two still on it."

And then it hit him. A punch to the gut could not have been more startling.

"I remember you," he said. "From the Lucky Clover."

Firmly, she gripped his fist, slid it out from under her chin. She stood up, fluffing and straightening her apron with exaggerated care. "I don't see how you possibly can." With wilted tomato in hand, she spun on her heel and walked away.

But he did remember. Vividly. It made no difference that she had been short and skinny; her eyes were the same. She'd been crying that evening, same as she was this morning.

He'd heard that a person never forgets. Memories were just buried deep in the brain. It must be true because what he thought was forgotten seemed as fresh as if it happened yesterday.

It had been mid-July, that moment when the sun was half above and half below the horizon. Shadows were long and deep blue. After a hard day of shoveling hay, he was hungry but supper was running late that night so he'd gone to the garden to find a bite to tide him over.

What he'd found was a girl weeping, half hidden by a trellis of twining green beans.

Back at Dollies, where he'd spent his first six years, he'd often seen grown women cry. He would cling to their bosoms, tell them he loved them and after a while, they would pat him on the head and dry their eyes.

He was old enough now to know that he could not cling to this girl's bosom…or what would one day be her bosom. He could hardly say he loved her since they had never met.

So he sat down beside her, his arms wrapped around his bony, jutting knees.

"Howdy," he said. She blinked quickly, probably ashamed to be caught out crying by a stranger. He decided to pretend he didn't notice. "Crickets sound right pretty."

"Yes." She dabbed her eyes with the apron she wore.

"I came here to listen to them." He didn't want to admit to coming to raid the garden.

"Me, too." She drew her knees to her chest, wrapped her arms about them, then rested her chin on top. "They sure do sound nice."

Silent, they listened for a moment.

"I don't remember seeing you around," she said at last. He was grateful to hear that her voice no longer quivered.

"I'm working here for the summer, me and my adopted brothers."

"Well, you're lucky…to have brothers."

Not as lucky as she might think but, "Most of the time," he answered because he knew she was right when it came to the deep-down heart of the matter. "But I'll be going out on my own as soon as I can. I mean to have my own ranch someday."

"So do I. Not a ranch, I don't mean, but a sweet little house to call my own. If I work hard enough…and…and I—" It sounded like she was about to cry again.

"Look up there!" He pointed to the sky. "It's the first star. What do you say we make wishes?"

He snagged her hand off her knee, twined her slender fingers through his gangly ones and lifted their joined fists skyward.

"To a house for you and a ranch for me!" he announced, sending the wish heavenward.

"Yes," she said, her voice once again steady. "To home."

"Say." He sniffed about. "I smell smoke." He thought the odor came from her dress.

Stabbing him with a tearful stare, she yanked her hand free, then stood and ran off without a word. He heard her sobs through rows of corn and nodding sunflowers. Later, he'd found out that dinner was late because one of the kitchen girls burned both the meat and the potatoes. It explained the reason for Laura Lee's tears.

Now he knew that sense of knowing and the tenderness he'd been feeling for her was not so mystical after all. His feelings had a logical explanation as a long-buried memory.

The same could not be said for the fact that the ranch and the house they had wished for under the stars turned out to be one and the same place.

Mysterious workings did not ordinarily cause him undue thought, but this inexplicable crossing of fate would keep him restless all night long.

Laura Lee ran for the kitchen, the place that always settled her nerves, made her feel in control of life.

She concentrated on breathing slowly, evenly, while she snatched up flour, eggs and…she was barely aware of what her hands were grabbing for. But whatever, she was going to bake it.

Stirring up batter under her wood spoon would help her put life in perspective again. How could a morning that began with sunshine and birdsong turn sour so quickly?

Nothing had happened to make it that way. It was only her imagination that had gotten the better of her.

Sitting in the garden, gazing out across the land, she'd pictured Johnny galloping toward her, as eager as she was for a reunion. But there, walking past her line of vision, was Jesse, leading one of his stallions and reading a book. He was solid, Johnny was dreamlike.

How else could he be since she had no idea where he was? It was as easy to imagine him playing poker in some tawdry saloon as it was herding cattle. She hadn't heard from him, so how was she to know what he was doing…who he was with?

Those horrid Underwood brothers might lead him into all sorts of trouble.

With no effort at all she saw him being dragged along to rob a bank or a train…or a helpless old lady in a general store.

But what if—and this was the thought that brought on the tears while she knelt in the garden cupping a shriveled tomato in her palm—what if they hadn't dragged him?

As hard as she tried, she could not forget his smile as he rode away from her on what ought to have been their wedding day.

What if he went to jail? Or what if he just kept on riding and she didn't see him again? What if she waited for years watching the horizon like she had just been doing until wrinkles creped her skin, until arthritis made her knees ache? What if she wasted her life loving a man who had put her behind him?

Something was in the bowl balanced on her hip. She beat it harder than she needed to because it made her angry to have been caught out crying by her renter.

She never cried. Not since the day when she, wanting desperately to please Mrs. Morgan, had burned dinner. Made dozens of people go hungry while her mentor cooked it all again. And she, as ashamed as she could possibly be, ran to the garden to weep her eyes out.

And then, after so many years… "I remember you."

For someone who rarely cried, how was it even possible for Jesse Creed to have witnessed her doing it two times?

She'd done the only thing she could. She'd stood up, smoothing her apron, gathering what dignity she could while she gazed down into Jesse's face. Then she'd fled, just as she had all those years ago.

Now her humiliation was complete. She stared at the bowl, thinking it might be a cake she was preparing or cookies that she had made too thin.

All she needed was for this to be the moment Johnny finally walked into the kitchen. He'd see her hair straggling out of its bun, her clothes rumpled and dirty from kneeling in the garden and dried tear tracks on her cheeks.

Would he look inside her and know that she had doubted him?

No. She doubted that Johnny would look so deeply into her.

Now that her emotions were beginning to settle, she tried to see things more reasonably. Johnny was coming home. Nothing could keep him from the future they had planned.

Chapter Eight

In the end, the stuff in the bowl could not be salvaged. Besides, she would make better use of her time by fixing her hair.

If she didn't want Johnny to look too deeply inside her when he finally got here—and how much longer could it be really—she would need to keep his attention focused on her outward looks.

It should not be hard to do since Johnny always took pride in her looks. She always went to extra care to please him by making sure every detail of her dress was attractive.

Since she had been living at the ranch, she'd become more casual about her appearance, letting her hair fall free and not wearing a corset every hour of the day.

From now on, all that was changing.

Didn't she owe her fiancé, the man who had handed her a dream come true, that much? From now on, she would show her loyalty to him by looking a proper lady.

Jesse and Bingham ought to be busy in the paddock with the horses until later this afternoon. There would be plenty of private time for her to see to her appearance.

About the time she set her curling iron in the fireplace to heat, she noticed the light dim in the parlor. Within moments of mixing a cup of molasses and water, she had to light a lamp.

Rain must be coming…again.

Sitting on the raised hearth, she brushed out a narrow section of hair, dampened it with the water-and-molasses mixture, then wrapped the strand around the hot iron. When it was good and set, she unwound it. What had gone in wavy and unruly came out like in an orderly spring. No matter how many times she stretched it out, it bounced back into a perfect coil.

It would take a long time to complete the process but the results would last for days. Johnny would appreciate the effort.

By the time she had made ringlets of one half of her head, rain let loose on the roof sounding like thousands of tapping fingers.

Apparently it was going to be a cozy afternoon. Perhaps when she was finished with her hair, she would reread the *Ladies' Home Journal and Practical Housekeeper*. Or she would have another go at baking something. Now that she was back in control of her emotions, she would find comfort in the process.

Food was what Jesse would appreciate. When he came in from tending the stock, dripping and cold, he would sniff the air. One side of his mouth would tip slightly higher than the other when he smiled. The corners of his eyes would crinkle in happy anticipation of what he was going to eat.

Maybe she should not take so much pleasure in cooking for him, but she did. It didn't lessen her devotion to Johnny…no, not a bit…but Jesse was her renter and she rather liked his appreciation of the effort she went to.

In fact, she was looping a strand of hair around the hot iron and daydreaming about his crooked smile when the front door opened.

Turning, she answered the very smile she had pictured in her mind. "Don't forget to wipe your feet," she said.

"Your hair is smoking!" He dropped an armload of firewood in the bin. "What the blazes are you doing? Is that gingerbread I smell?"

"Not smoking, steaming. And the scent is molasses. It sets the curls in my hair."

He sat down on his chair and slicked damp hair back from his forehead with his palm. "Why? Seems like a bit of work to go to when your hair looks so pretty hanging loose."

"You must be a rare man. Most fellows like to see that a woman has gone to the trouble of looking attractive."

"I reckon, but—"

"Jesse Creed, if you make an unkind comment about my hair, I'll set the iron to *your* hair."

He clapped his palm on top of his head. "Got enough trouble going on up there as it is. I'm just saying your hair is pretty just the way it is…was."

"Anyway, I'm styling it for Johnny, not you. My fiancé might be a cowboy but he has a fine sense of fashion. When he comes, I don't want him to find me unkempt. Will Bingham be here for dinner?"

"I sent him home… We've been living together for a while now, Laura Lee. You've never looked anything but beautiful."

She might take that as a compliment if he weren't frowning. As it was, the statement was probably meant to criticize Johnny more than to admire her.

"One day soon, Johnny is going to walk through the front door and you will be sorry for what you thought of him."

"I would be sorry if—" He hung his head, staring at the floor. When he looked up again, it was with that gaze that wouldn't let her look away. "You look lovely, Laura Lee. You could shave your hair clean off and still be the most beautiful woman for miles around."

He probably shouldn't say such a thing to her. She should not enjoy hearing it…and yet…

"I remember you, too." She set a curl free of the iron, watched it bounce into place out of the corner of her eye. She readied another strand of hair for the iron. "From back then, in the garden of the Lucky Clover."

"I'm surprised." He arched both brows.

"Well, it's not you I remember so much as the boy who came upon me at a very low moment in my life."

"Burning dinner wasn't such a horrible thing. No one went to bed hungry."

"The thing is, I wanted to prove myself in the worst way." Finished with the last curl, she set the iron aside to cool off. "Mr. Magee took me in, gave me the first home I ever knew. I wanted so desperately to prove myself worthy."

"I think," he said while raindrops pattered against the windows, "it was yourself you needed to prove things to. You were only a little girl. No one expected perfection."

"I thought about you over the years." There was no harm in confessing that truth. "I used to wonder what you were doing. If you ever got your wish for a ranch."

"Here I am. Wish fulfilled."

"And here I am, wish fulfilled, also. I wonder which one of us—" No, she didn't! How could she without doubting Johnny's honesty? This was her home… Jesse Creed was her renter. "What did you do before this, Jesse? Have you always been a rancher?"

He shook his head. His eyes darkened before he slid his gaze away. "Do you consider us to be friends, Laura Lee? Even with this house to come between us?"

"Yes, I reckon I do." It was the truth. When the time came to part company, she suspected she would miss him.

"I'd like to tell you…confess maybe, who I became a few years after that evening in the garden at the Lucky Clover. I suppose you have a right to know who you're living with, even if it means you won't see me the same way. I'm not a man most women would consider for…anything really. I've lived hard, Laura Lee. In fact, if you want me to rent a room in town until the judge gets here, I'll do it. But you need to know who I was in order to know how much this ranch means to me."

A part of her yearned to run to her bedroom and close the door. Another part yearned to hear everything about him. Which was a risky thing. She already liked him. Knowing his secrets might plant the seeds of a bond between them that should never grow. It was unlikely that what he revealed about his past would make him unworthy of being anyone's husband, because surely that was what he meant to say.

"I won't judge you."

Or send him to live in town. Facing the fact that she would miss him was not easy because what exactly did that mean about her feelings for Johnny? How could she miss Jesse when the man she loved would be with her?

"I didn't get my ranch right off, like I wished for that night in the garden." He looked at her with a smile, small and quickly gone. "Being a kid, I thought it would be easy, but life's a bit more complicated than we thought back then. Well, I worked a couple more years for the folks who adopted me. I stayed for the horses more than any kind of family ties. Running off, I was still young enough to think life would be easy, with no one telling me what to do and when to do it.

"Sure didn't take long before I got hungry and cold. I saw a handbill tacked to the sheriff's door one day. It offered a reward for some outlaw, can't even say I remember his name now. It was a bit of good luck that I'd crossed paths with him only the day before. When I turned him in, it was easy money. All of a sudden, I had food and shelter. I hunted down another outlaw and another. After a while, I was a dyed-in-the-wool bounty hunter. I forgot about my dream of owning a ranch during those days. My mind was set on turning in criminals and making a lot of money doing it."

"You make it sound sinful, what you were doing. I see it as an honorable thing to bring in outlaws, Jesse."

"The thing is, not everyone with a price on their head is guilty. I thought maybe some of them were not, but I handed them over anyway. That was my job. It was for the court to decide guilt or innocence. I…my conscience, my sense of compassion…became hardened in ways I didn't like. But the money was good. If a man cried a bucket of tears while I dragged him to the marshal, well, that wasn't my concern. I learned to turn a deaf ear. Just did my job and moved onto the next criminal with a price on his head."

"I don't know what else you could have done." Discreetly, she scratched her scalp where dried molasses began to itch. "What made you quit?"

"Shame. Straight-out shame." She heard the slow exhalation of his breath. "I've never told anyone before, Laura Lee. I did something. It caused a great deal of tragedy."

He closed his eyes. His fists clenched.

"There was a boy, fifteen years old, is all. He was wanted for robbery. I apprehended him and spent the better part of three days with him on the trail. Along the way, he claimed his innocence just like most of them did. But he was so young.

Vowed his only crime was running away from an orphanage and taking his bedding with him, that and a dollar fifty. Since I'd been an orphan, too, I felt some sympathy. When he begged me to let him go, I did. I hoped he'd turn his life around, his crime didn't sound so awful. Still, it wasn't my job to decide if he was guilty or not. Only to take him to the marshal. That's all I had to do. Hand him over and collect my money."

Jesse hung his head, shoulders slumped while he stared at the floor. The poor man looked perfectly miserable, considering all he'd done was show a child a bit of kindness.

She touched his shoulder, felt a tremor run over the swell of firm, tense muscle. "I'm sure he was very grateful."

"No. No, Laura Lee, he was a killer." In the face of her stunned silence, he held her gaze, agony still fresh in the green depths. "The day after I let him go, I heard he robbed a family. He killed the father, left the mother bound to a wheelchair."

"I'm so sorry, Jesse." She cupped his cheek with her hand, shook her head. "You had no way of knowing."

"Which is why I should have done what I was supposed to. I'm no one's judge and jury. That afternoon, I booked a hotel room. Didn't come out for a week, just sat in the dark thinking of who

I was…and wasn't. On the fifth day, I felt the rancher I'd dreamed of becoming come back to life. On the sixth, I laid the bounty hunter to rest, so to speak. The first thing I did when I came out from that room was to begin searching for a quiet little town with a ranch for sale. When I found it, I bought it and put my guns away in the attic."

He shook his head, shrugged his wide shoulders. "So here I am. Here we both are."

She hadn't noticed the tear trickle down her cheek, but she did when Jesse stroked it away with his thumb. For someone who never cried, she was becoming a weeping ninny. It was she who should be comforting Jesse, not the other way around.

"I'm so sorry, Jesse."

His mouth tugged down at one corner, the only indication that he withheld the emotion weighing his heart.

She touched his lip, but then…she leaned forward and kissed the spot.

It was wrong, she was wicked. But sometimes an affectionate touch could cure what nothing else would.

Drawing away, he gazed at her mouth. She swore he was kissing her with his eyes. After a heart-stilling moment, he stood up, his gaze remaining on her lips.

"Shall I move to town, Laura Lee?"

"No." How could her lips feel so titillated by a kiss that never fully happened? "Please don't."

Jesse walked toward the general store, coffee mug in hand. Golden sunshine stroked his shoulders through his coat. Fall was in full glory. Cool air and warm sunshine, leaves twisting in a glorious display of yellow, orange and red. A sense of excitement in the air. At least that's what it felt like to him.

Confessing his past to Laura Lee, seeing that she did not judge him for it, in fact had pressed a kiss to the corner of his mouth, made him feel lighter of step.

It could also be the pumpkins on porches putting him in happy frame of mind. For some reason, he'd always enjoyed them. His adopted parents used to complain that he wasted time he could be working while carving them.

A spray of golden leaves raced around his boots and up the road. The arrival of autumn always put a smile on his face.

The last week at the ranch had been a good one, with friendly conversations and comfortable silences while he and Laura Lee sat in front of the fireplace of an evening.

Once in a while, a thought sneaked into his brain. The prickly thing made the suggestion that it wouldn't be so awful if the judge took his time getting back to Forget-Me-Not.

He'd have to catch himself in those moments, give his mind a good shake. The longer his renter lived under his roof, the more natural it was to imagine her there permanently. The day was coming when he was going to look up from his nightly reading and miss seeing her, head bent and nimble fingers busy with needlework.

Opening the door of the general store, he shook his head. This line of thinking would lead to a sorry end.

It broke his heart thinking of it because she was destined for grief however things worked out. He was beginning to suspect that her heartbreak would be his own.

"Morning, Jesse." Thomas stood beside the stove feeding a log to the glowing coals. Even though it was warming up outside, the building held the cool of the night. "How's Bingham doing at the job? From what he tells me, he's the best cowboy to ever ride the range."

"I can truly say he's the best I've ever had." Jesse dug into his vest pocket, fished out some of the money he'd withdrawn from the bank. The rest was to be wired to the woman he'd widowed and put in a wheelchair. "I've come by to pay him."

"I'll take that praise to heart even though we

both know he's your first. This means quite a bit to me, Jesse. I ought to be paying you." Thomas took the money, set it somewhere under the counter while shaking his head. "You've spent time with him so you'll know how eager he is to please. How he tends to worship his heroes."

"Sure hope you don't mean me. I'm a thousand regrets away from being a hero. That boy of yours works hard. You can be proud."

"I have been, since I first saw him squealing in his mama's arms. But if he hadn't gone with you? It wouldn't be pride I'd be feeling now. I've heard something…about the Underwoods. I'm more relieved than I can say that he's not with them."

"What was it you heard?"

No doubt the Underwoods included Hell Dog in their number. For Laura Lee's sake, he hoped her fiancé hadn't done something too horrible. At least not more horrible than he'd already done by giving her a false deed.

"A traveler stopped in, oh, only half an hour ago. He said that they robbed a store in Gilmore Crossing and shot the storekeeper. It was just a matter of time—we all knew it."

"Just them, no one else?" he asked, but it was a vain hope that Johnny Ruiz had come to his senses and parted company with the criminals.

"I believe the fellow said there was one more. A handsome cowboy who practically charmed the ladies out of their purses. Called himself Hell Dog, of all the crazy things."

Jesse hadn't put his sidearm away so long ago that instinct didn't make his fingers twitch. He had buried the gun in the bottom of a trunk in a dark corner of the loft, never thinking to use it again.

But would he? It was unlikely that Ruiz was coming back to Forget-Me-Not, but what if he did and tried to force Laura Lee to go with him?

It made no sense that he would. If he wanted her, he would have married her in the first place. As far as forcing went? It made Jesse sick at heart to think it, but no doubt Laura Lee would go away with the fool of her own free choice.

In his opinion, the criminal was well gone.

If only the secret Jesse now carried was gone as well. It wasn't, though, and what was he to do with the damned thing? Tell Laura Lee and see her heart break…or harden because she didn't believe him? Not say anything and let her continue to live with false hope?

He bid Thomas Teal goodbye and stepped outside. Once again, wind blew leaves about his feet as he walked. The pumpkins waiting on porches to be carved into jack-o'-lanterns with snarling grins no longer gave him the contented feeling he'd experienced looking at them the first time.

Gossip could travel fast. In half an hour, the

news could be all over town. Jesse quickened his step.

In the distance, he spotted Laura Lee placing a cup of coffee in a woman's hand, then curling her fingers about the payment. Her neatly arranged curls, her declaration of faith in her fiancé, bobbed about her face.

He'd like to lay Hell Dog flat for leaving it up to Jesse to break her heart. It made him half sick, wondering how he would tell her, if he even could.

The market was crowded today. People stood in groups talking. It was possible they discussed the weather or the last pumpkins on the vine. But at some point, if it hadn't already, talk would turn to the Underwoods' crime. The name of Hell Dog would come up as sure as sunrise.

Only ten feet away from where Laura Lee stood, a woman covered her mouth with her hand, looking shocked at what someone told her. The speaker shook his head while delivering the message. The woman spun about, then hurried to three other women. Within half a second, more heads were shaking, more hands covering open-mouthed shock.

Jesse recognized the spread of gossip when he saw it, had witnessed it often when he'd delivered wanted men into the hands of the law. The news about the Underwoods was spreading far too quickly.

He sprinted forward, praying he would reach Laura Lee before the scandal came to her ears.

Her eyes flew wide at the pressure of his fingers gripping her elbow when he spun her away from the group of people she had been cheerfully approaching.

"We need to get back to the ranch." Even while he spoke, he tugged her back toward her pastry and coffee stand.

Dang it, a customer stood there waiting to be served.

"I'm not finished here yet." She tried to wriggle free of his fingers. "Jesse Creed, what's gotten into you?"

"I'm sick."

"You don't look it."

"You can't see a fever." She probably could see a lie, though.

"You don't seem flushed." She touched his forehead with the backs of her cool, smooth fingers.

"I am…on the inside. If we don't leave now, I'm going to pass out at your feet."

"There's the doctor buying a jar of jam." One of her fair brows arched, ripe with suspicion. "Let's call him over."

A rabbit in a snare couldn't be more caught. If he did faint, it would draw the doctor over for sure.

It would also distract folks from discussing the Underwood robbery.

Chances were he couldn't pull it off but—

Moaning, he flung both arms about Laura Lee and slowly slipped down the front of her into fake unconsciousness. By the time he pooled on the ground, his eyes were peacefully closed.

His insides were churning, though. Laura Lee had some sweet curves. Only a man who cherished her should be allowed to savor them.

He thought maybe that man might be him. Sure as blazes wasn't Johnny Ruiz.

"You owe me for the wasted coffee and the pastries I didn't have time to sell, Jesse Creed."

"Ugh…"

Shifting her weight on the slats of the wood seat while taking a tighter grip on the reins, Laura Lee glanced behind her at the wagon bed where the groan came from. Jesse lay among half a dozen bright orange pumpkins he had insisted upon bringing home, his arm flung across his eyes.

For all that he looked miserable, she doubted he was sick. A great, virile man like him fainting for no reason whatsoever? She shook her head. Even the expression on the doctor's face while he'd bent over Jesse had been skeptical.

Some men did exaggerate illness because they

enjoyed being coddled, but she hadn't guessed him to be one of them.

"How's your belly ache?"

"Worse," he moaned.

"Ha! It was a fever! You distinctly said fever."

He eased onto his elbows, glanced about. "I did. It's gone and left me with a bellyache."

"Well, then, that's a shame. I thought I'd take one of those pumpkins and bake a pie, but if you're feeling so poorly, I'll save myself the trouble."

From one second to the next, Jesse's grimace turned to a smile. He scrambled up from his autumn nest and joined her on the bench.

"All of a sudden I feel better."

"Do you often fake illness?"

He started to say something, then shut his mouth. "I reckon I wasn't very convincing."

"Why would you do such a thing?"

"I had a reason, a good one. I reckon I might tell you about it when the time is right." He looked steadily at the horizon where the trees had gone a blaze of red, yellow and orange. She wondered if he was afraid to look her in the eye because she might guess whatever he was hiding.

"What's wrong with right now?"

"A few things."

"Name one."

"There's something I've discovered…about a person."

"Who?" Perhaps it was not her business, but she did deserve more of an explanation of why he dragged her so suddenly from the farmers market.

"Just someone in town. When I feel I can, I'll tell you about it."

He touched one of the curls that had bounced loose from its pin with the jostling of the wagon. With molasses to give it stiffness, it sprang back into place when he let go. For some reason, that made him frown.

"Are you going to cut out little dough leaves for the top of the pie?" he asked, then pulled the curl again.

This time she batted his hand away. "Trunk and branches, too, if you'll behave yourself."

He stared at her lips while she spoke. Shame on her for imagining a bit of mischief.

Chapter Nine

The next evening, the one after he'd faked that ridiculous illness, guilt drove Jesse outside. Shoulders hunched within his coat against the cold, he crossed the bridge. Coming to the paddock, he braced his arms across the fence rail while watching the sun slip below the distant hill.

If he wasn't feeling like a lowdown worm for not telling Laura Lee what he knew, he'd have smiled at the sight. Pink-and-orange clouds floated up from the horizon, then disappeared into the darker sky. Fingers of sunshine streaked between them with brushstrokes of fading light.

The tranquility of sunset was one of the reasons he'd longed for a ranch of his own. Most of his life he'd dreamed of standing just so, the work of the day put behind him, a warm fire and a good book ahead.

Turning away from the darkening promise of evening, he gazed back at his house.

The soft flame of a lamp burning steadily behind a lace curtain warmed one window. An orange glow from the hearth flickered in two more. Even with the doors closed, the aroma of dinner cooking trailed across the yard and over the bridge.

His stomach growled in anticipation. Laura Lee was a cook in a million.

Even though the air was crisp and fresh, the house looked inviting and the scent coming out of it was a step short of rapture, for him there was no peace or tranquility inside.

Nor was it out here where he'd expected to find it either.

He wondered if Laura Lee thought the secret he kept had to do with simple town gossip. Probably not. It was a stretch to believe she thought he faked passing out to keep her from learning a stranger's secret.

Even so, she would not likely suspect that the secret had to do with her.

All day long, she'd been singing while kneading bread and smiling when she swept the floor. The only time she looked anything but cheerful was when she gazed out the window looking for a man who, she must begin to suspect, was not going to come.

At least, the criminal wouldn't if he valued his freedom. While Jesse was done with tearing apart families by putting their loved ones behind bars, he felt a whole different way about Hell Dog.

And that was because he felt a whole lot different about Laura Lee.

Day by day, something was changing within him. She—the girl in the garden, that is—had always held a sweet place in his memory. The woman, though, she was walking right into his heart. As risky as it was, he found himself holding the door wide open.

The screen on the front door squeaked. With the night so still, he heard the faint screech. She descended the steps, her figure half hidden in twilight.

One day soon, she would leave the ranch. It was no lie that he was going to miss the way his heart warmed whenever he looked at her.

Crossing the bridge, she waved her arm. He'd bet his last bounty there was a smile to go with it, but it was nearly dark and he didn't know for sure. He hoped there was a smile because Miss Laura Lee Quinn had one of the most bewitching ones around. He couldn't imagine there would be a time he'd grow tired of seeing it.

"It's breathtaking!" she announced, coming to stand beside him at the fence. "There's nothing quite as spectacular as sunset. You'd think the Creator spent years designing each and every one."

"Who's to say He didn't?"

"Not me. I've got nothing against sunrise, mind you. But sometimes I'm too busy take notice and, I'll admit, too sleepy."

"Were you raised in church, Laura Lee?"

"I couldn't say I was raised at all, really. I imagine my father fed me when I was small or I wouldn't have survived, but as for guidance... toward church or anything else? I watched what other folks did, not my father. At the tent we lived in most of the time, Sunday morning was for nursing Saturday night's hangover."

"Funny how my growing up years were so different than yours and yet...not. You're shivering, darlin'. Why didn't you put on a coat?"

"It was hot in the kitchen and I thought to just call out that supper was ready. I never expected to get caught up in the sunset."

It was nearly dark now so the stars began to pop and twinkle. Guess that's why he didn't suggest going back inside. And why she didn't either.

"How were they different and not?" she asked.

He opened his big coat. "Room for a friend in here."

Would she come close to him? Share his warmth without suspecting he was feeling more than friendly toward her?

"Thank you. It is getting bitter out. I wonder if the weather is going to turn."

She stepped inside, her back toward his chest.

Her hair smelled like fresh-baked bread. The lapels of the coat fit neatly around them both. He tugged, pulling the curve of her backside against him. She brushed his hands away, then held the coat closed herself.

She would do that, of course. It was the proper thing to do, no matter what was going on in his mind.

He let his arms fall to his sides.

"It's the end of October so I reckon it will," he said, curling his fingers into his palms to keep from caressing the curve of her hip. "From what people have told me, you can't know what to expect with the weather this time of year. It can snow one day and melt the next…or the wind can pick it up and blow it to the next county."

"So." She tipped her head. The faint scent of molasses reminded him that she was waiting for another man to claim her. "Tell me, how was it different for you and yet the same?"

"The ladies, they coddled me for the first six years, spoiled me like I was a little prince. But I didn't go out into the real world, especially not to church. Naturally, that all changed when I was taken to the Children's Aid Society. No coddling, not with so many to be cared for. Later, the farmers who adopted me and the other boys taught us how to work hard. It never did feel like a family, though. Just like you, I feel like I raised myself.

You and I, we had parents, but at the same time, we didn't. We both had to figure things out on our own."

She sighed. Her posture shifted so that her back rested against his chest. He wondered if she noticed how his heart suddenly slammed against his ribs.

"Different but the same? Yes, I can see how."

"It wasn't until I came to work at the Lucky Clover that I learned how things ought to be," he said. "Folks there were family."

"That's how I felt, too. They were kin, even if they weren't blood related. It's why I told my father I was staying. I hoped to be a part of that."

"I reckon it's what we both wished for that night in the vegetable patch. Someplace like that of our own."

Her stiff curls brushed his chin when she nodded. "When we made that wish, I vowed I'd work my fingers raw to have my own home."

"Not exactly your own."

The scents of bread and molasses faded with the cushion of heat building between their bodies. The fragrance of her sweet breath and heated flesh filled his senses.

"No. Not until Judge Benson returns."

"What I meant was…you plan on sharing it with your new husband."

Just saying the words made him feel sick.

"Oh! Yes, naturally."

He thought her back stiffened slightly, or perhaps it was only his hopeful imagination that she had begun to suspect the truth. Herding thoughts around in his mind, he tried to corral the words to tell her that her Johnny was a criminal and not to be trusted. All he got was a lump in his throat.

"Dinner will be getting cold." She stepped out of his coat. Frigid air invaded the space.

Tomorrow would be time enough to tell her. Or the next day.

"Well, Miss Saffron." Laura Lee adjusted her boots in the stirrups, then stood up to get a better view of the land. No, not *the* land, *her* land. "I can't imagine what took me so long to go exploring."

Gazing upon the gently rolling hills, golden in the autumn afternoon, she found she actually could imagine. In the beginning, she'd had to make the house livable. That had taken hours upon hours.

At times, the weather had prevented her from taking stock of her land.

Then there had been money to earn, lots of baking and selling to make sure she had the funds for her first payment. A payment that was surely coming up soon. She would have expected to have received some communication from Corum

Peterson or a mortgage lender by now. It worried her that she had not.

Not to be forgotten among her duties was the fact that she had a man to cook for. That was a time-consuming chore she had not anticipated.

"But to be honest, what I didn't expect—" she glanced down at Chisel, who trotted beside the horse, swinging his tail "—is to—" could she say this aloud, even to the dog? "—I didn't expect to like it so much. But you see how he appreciates every bite that goes into his mouth."

Chisel stopped suddenly, lifted his nose to a hawk making lazy circles in the sky. He sniffed the air, then growled low in his chest.

"It's not like it's going to swoop down and carry you away."

It wasn't as though she expected an actual answer either, so when he trotted along without so much as a glance up her, she wasn't offended.

She ought to be more like the dog. Appreciate the beauty of the hills and autumn-hued trees, to rejoice in the babble of the stream flowing on the other side of the dense brush. To take pleasure in the chorus of tiny birds flitting merrily in the branches.

Here, she believed, was the same spot she had stopped on the way home that first night...or close to it. Things did look different in daylight.

Despite last night's bone-chilling cold, the sun

shone down warm this afternoon. A rest beside the stream would be in order.

After tying Saffron to a bush, she followed a break through the shrubbery and made her way to the stream. Squatting down, she drew her skirt back from the lapping current, then scooped up a handful of cold water. She drank half, then patted her face and neck with the rest.

Brush rustled behind her. With a start, she remembered the cougar from her first night on the ranch, but luckily, it was Chisel who trotted up beside her.

As much as she loved each and every one of her three hundred and twenty acres and felt at home here, an unexpected sense of unease tickled the back of her neck. The rustle of the breeze through the brush, each crack of a twig put her senses on alert, made her heart thump. She had the distinct sensation of being watched.

Which was foolish. It was hard to imagine the stealthy creature that could come close to Chisel without him being aware of it.

"I'm just going to sit here for a while and be calm. I can't live here and be such a ninny about every shifting shadow."

Chisel stood up, peered across the stream at a stand of trees growing on the hillside. The grove grew close to water where it turned east, toward home.

"Don't you dare go chasing off after anything, though." She dug her fingers into his fur to make sure he understood.

A crow cawed from a tree growing on the opposite bank. Something small, rabbit-sized, scuttled through the grass. Really, what could sound more peaceful?

She would have to trust the dog and his acute senses that all was well. It was too lovely an afternoon to allow unwarranted worry to have its way.

She lay back on the ground, arms spread, and watched thin clouds whisk across the sky. There was still time before she needed to start supper. She could close her eyes and drift into a delightful doze if she chose to.

It wouldn't hurt to take a few moments and dream of the man she loved.

Or at least try to. For some reason, his image wouldn't come. No doubt it had to do with the fact that Jesse Creed's image kept shoving him out of the way. It was Jesse who gazed down at her with love, asking for the same back.

Green eyes along with a smile that lifted in humor made her feel languid inside…made her stretch her arms over her head, sigh and wonder what his kiss would be like.

This wasn't the first time Jesse's image had shoved Johnny into a corner.

She could only wonder why. If she loved Johnny

the way she thought she did, how could she let it happen? A dutiful fiancée would never dream of another man and enjoy it so.

"But I do, Chisel. And that's the plain truth. What could it mean?"

Probably nothing since the imaginary Jesse wooed her without fail. The flesh and blood Jesse had never acted in a way that was inappropriate.

"Do you know—and I'd never admit this to anyone but you, Chisel—I've never daydreamed overmuch about what it would be like for Johnny to touch me? I had a pretty good idea since he was always trying to insinuate his fingers into places he shouldn't. What was there to imagine really?"

But Jesse? Even when she was awake, she'd catch herself watching his hands stroke the neck of a mare, his fingers slowly tracing the words down the page of a book he was reading...and she'd wonder.

Surely it was because of the close company they kept. Once Johnny came back, all would be right again. Jesse would go away and she wouldn't think of him...often.

"I'm wicked." She loosened her grip on Chisel's sun-warmed fur and began to stroke him. "You're a far more faithful creature than I—"

She felt the rumble of his growl an instant before she heard it.

Sitting upright, she glanced about. She didn't

see anything. Nor hear it either. Coming slowly to her feet, she backed out of the shrubbery.

The last time the dog had growled in this spot, a mountain lion leaped out of a bush. This time, Chisel was not looking at shrubbery but across the stream.

One moment, he was still, his big body tense. The next, he flew into the water, bounded out in a leap, then bolted through the dense growth of trees on the other side. The sound of his barking, and not in a friendly *nice to see you* way, grew fainter with the distance he covered.

She rushed for Saffron, stepped into the stirrup, then swung onto the horse's back. According to the dog, her odd, uneasy feeling had not been without reason.

She waited, straining her eyes at the hill, watching for Chisel to return. Praying that he would return.

What she wanted to do was run home to Jesse, but she had no idea what the dog had gone after. A bear? A wolf? Whatever the creature was, it might turn on him.

She could not possibly ride to safety and leave him wounded and alone.

"Let's go, Saffron." She led the horse across the stream. If Chisel was mortally injured, he would not die alone where he lay.

Deep in horrid thoughts, she urged her horse

uphill. Before she reached the crest, she spotted him, trotting happily toward her, his great hairy tail swinging. He dragged something in his mouth, looking so very proud of his catch.

"What on earth?" she said, bending in the saddle to peer at his prize more closely.

It was a man's coat. Chisel relinquished it willingly when she tugged at it. A weight in the pocket made it sag. Reaching in, she drew the object halfway out.

A whiskey bottle, and half empty!

Of all the strange things. The coat was far too small to be Jesse's or even Bingham's. She bundled it in front of her on the saddle.

Urging her mount quickly toward home, she thought about something and it was unsettling. Looking back on how frightened she had been when Chisel launched after the intruder, she'd had one thought. To run to where it was safe. But it turned not to be to where, but to whom.

To Jesse. Not Johnny.

Jesse sat on the porch steps enjoying the last hour of sunshine with a hollowed-out pumpkin braced between his knees.

He glanced east, watching for Laura Lee. She'd gone exploring, which he didn't feel good about. Neither had he been able to forbid her to do it. She was not his to forbid.

Assuming a man could forbid his woman to do something. Oh, he knew some who had managed it, but only because they ruled their marriage with a closed fist. In Jesse's opinion, they were no better than criminals.

Gazing at the lumpy pumpkin, he set his knife to it, cutting the bottom of a jagged-toothed grin. It didn't turn out to be his best artistic creation because he kept wondering about marriage…and what a good one ought to be.

Friendship between a man and woman ought to be first thing, he figured. That and trust. Lust he reckoned would come on its own with no effort at all.

He glanced up from the pumpkin again, staring down at the narrow road that ran beside the stream. Laura Lee was usually fixing supper by now. If she didn't come by the time he'd carved a pair of eyes, he'd saddle his horse and go looking for her. The ranch wasn't massive like some were, but that didn't mean things couldn't go wrong, out there all alone like she was.

He worried about her. Not only because it was late in the afternoon and she was not where she normally was at this hour of the day, but because of what the future held for Laura Lee.

Something in his gut told him that Hell Dog was the kind of man who would rule his wife. Not love her as his dearest friend. Unless Jesse was able to convince her that her fiancé was no good, she would end up worse than brokenhearted. He felt the dark truth of it to his bones.

He'd just slashed an eyebrow across the jack-o'-lantern's face when he heard Chisel's deep bark. A second later, he saw Laura Lee's horse keeping pace with the dog as they trotted down the road.

After seeing her safe and whole, he wondered what she was going to make for dinner. He even grinned in anticipation.

Eager anticipation vanished when he noticed the unease creasing her mouth and eyes. Setting the pumpkin aside, he stood, then crossed the yard to give her a hand down from the saddle.

"Something wrong, darlin'?" The frown line cutting between those fine brows didn't look natural. Most of the time, Laura Lee smiled.

"Why do you call me darlin'? You shouldn't do that."

"You don't like it?"

She stared up at him for a silent moment. "I like it, Jesse, and that's why you shouldn't do it."

With a swish of her hand, she dismissed the direction of that conversation. But there was no way in hell that he was going to let it lie.

"I think someone has been on our property." Blushing, she dangled a man's coat from her fingers. "My property, I meant."

He took the jacket from her, turning it this way

and that. It belonged to a man. Not an overly large fellow. Not overly clean either. The thing smelled like sweat and alcohol. Maybe vomit, too. There was a rip in the pocket. A half-empty bottle of whiskey sagged out of it.

"How close did he get to you?"

"Not so close, I don't think. Chisel ran off, then came back with the coat a few moments later."

Much too close. Ten blasted miles would be too close.

"Walk with me to the barn while I brush down Saffron," he said. It was time to tell her about Johnny Ruiz. He snagged up the horse's reins and led it toward the barn.

Laura Lee walked beside him. "I wonder who it was."

"A drifter, maybe, looking for a place to rest."

Or one of the Underwoods looking for a way to steal his horses. He'd suspected as much in the beginning.

Worse, it could be that no good Hell Dog…not coming for horses, but for his fiancée.

Any one of those possibilities set him on edge. In the end, whichever it was, Laura Lee needed to know what her fiancé had been up to.

"It happens now and then. Someone just passing through," he said, putting off what he needed to say because she looked so worried. She walked close to him, so he caught up her hand, squeezed her fingers, then held them lightly. "Isn't that right, Chisel? You chased off a common drifter?"

All of a sudden, Laura Lee stopped walking, her smile returned. "You talk to animals as if they're folks. I heard you doing it to one of the mares, too."

"Reckon I do." He shrugged.

"I do it, too." She returned his squeeze, added one of her wide, sweet smiles to go with it. "I reckon that makes us kindred spirits."

"The way I see it, critters listen better than some people do. Even if they don't know most of the words you're speaking to them."

"I'd like to have a house full of dogs and babies." She sighed deeply. "I'll have to do some fancy talking to convince Johnny, though. He doesn't like dogs."

"Not babies either?"

"I'm sure he likes babies—everyone does. It's just that he wants me all to himself for now."

Hell, her and any woman who blinked her eyes at him. Not that he would tell Laura Lee so. To see her heart break would break his.

The other business, though. Her intended was a wanted man. She needed to know it.

While he searched his heart for a gentle way to deliver the news, she said, "I've an idea, Jesse! After dinner, let's finish carving those pumpkins.

I can set a couple of them out with my coffee and pastries at the farmers market on Friday."

"Good idea. It will be Halloween."

Carving with Laura Lee would be a fine thing to do. Unless he wanted to ruin the fun, he'd have to wait with his confession.

The trouble was, the longer he waited, the more difficult it would be to do. He had to tell her soon because in a few days, they would be making the trip to town. Having passed out one time already, he was out of ideas to keep her from discovering the truth from someone who didn't care for her deeply, the way he did.

Chapter Ten

A row of bright orange pumpkins set on the dining table. Three large ones with grimaces and sharp teeth and three smaller ones with hearts for eyes, all smiling.

Pumpkin carving had been more fun than she'd expected. Back at the Lucky Clover, life had been too busy for such frivolity. This time of year, the kitchen girls had spent every spare moment making candy and baking treats for the children's Halloween party.

Tonight, it seemed that years fell away. She felt carefree. So young at heart her cheeks hurt with smiling. She and Jesse had laughed and carried on as if they were still those children in the garden.

Funny, but she couldn't recall laughing with Johnny. Most of the time, they had discussed the future. How happy they would be…one day.

For all the levity of the evening, once in a while she would catch Jesse staring out a window or at the front door. His hand would rest on his thigh and his fingers would pluck at his wool pants.

On the surface, he was engaging. Charming. But she knew he was making an effort to appear cheerful.

Yes, he'd smiled and had a brief conversation with Chisel about the unruly amount of hair he shed. He'd again wanted her opinion about which mare would suit which stallion.

On the surface, everything was friendly, as it should be.

Of course, many things went on below the surface of a situation. Unless she was very wrong, Jesse was more than a bit concerned about the stranger on his land. Given the way he had been following her about with his eyes all evening, did he fear the man might be a threat…to her?

She had to chuckle discreetly, under her breath. Did he expect the trespasser to burst through the window and carry her off?

Perhaps he did. Why else would he be watching her so intently?

Oh, she would be flattered to think such a big, handsome man had a bit of an interest in her, but he didn't. Jesse Creed was a protector. Given that he believed her to be his renter, in his mind, she was his to watch over.

For all that she considered herself to be strong and independent, something of a modern woman even, she didn't mind knowing he watched out for her. Yes, in the same way she didn't mind Chisel watching out for her. She couldn't deny sleeping more soundly because they were in the house.

"Those are right friendly-looking pumpkins, darlin'." Jesse leaned back against the oven door, pointing at her creations. "Can't see how it will scare even a timid goblin."

A reminder for him not to call her darlin' was in order, but the endearment touched her. The voice of her conscience, growing ever softer these days, warned her it should not. What was it in his smile? The way it tipped up on one side more than the other made her stomach flutter.

It also made her wonder if he did feel something for her that was more than friendly.

The idea gave her heart a thump. Would she betray Johnny? How could she when he had been working hard for their future?

"Well, we'll have to leave your jack-o'-lanterns at home on Friday. They'll frighten the children to tears."

He nodded, shrugged.

She had expected him to answer her challenge, not to simply stare at her in silence, his playful expression fading.

"You're worried about that man." She went to him across the kitchen, placed her hand on the spot where his arms tucked one under the other, gave him a reassuring squeeze. "I imagine Chisel gave him a good enough fright so he won't come back."

Uncrossing his arms, he caught her hand, grazed a quick kiss across her knuckles.

It was wrong to wonder, so very faithless of her...but what might it be like if he kissed her lips instead?

An image of Johnny's face, his expression shocked and betrayed, flashed in her mind as clearly as if he had caught her in the act.

She snatched her hand away and fled to her room.

The voice of her conscience roared to life again. She could not erase her fiancé's stricken gasp from her imagination.

Nor could she make her lips quit tingling, thinking of Jesse's kiss.

Three hours had passed since Laura Lee had gone into her bedroom and closed the door. During that time, Jesse read a book, ate pie, drank coffee and stared at the fire dancing happily in the hearth.

Worried about a lot of things, too.

When he tired of that, he went outside and stood on the front porch. Gazing out at the night, he narrowed his worries to one. Who was the stranger on the land? Not likely Johnny Ruiz. If it had been that fool, Laura Lee ought to have recognized his coat.

Unless Ruiz had just purchased it. In that case, Jesse could not safely assume it wasn't Ruiz. About the time Jesse changed his mind and figured the coat wasn't the dandy's style, he noticed the chill begin to make his nose run. It was turning cold as old bones out here.

Going back inside, he added a log to the fire. Given there was only the one fireplace in the small house, he and Laura Lee each kept their bedroom doors open to allow the heat in.

After three hours with her door shut, the room had to be good and chilly. Went to show how devoted she was to Ruiz, that she would close the door because he'd merely kissed her hand in friendship.

That was a blamed, blasted lie. There was far more to his lips on her knuckles than that. In his mind, he'd been kissing her lips…slowly, deeply and unreservedly.

He stared at her door for a full minute. It was time. No good could come of waiting to tell her what he knew.

His feet felt like hundred pound weights as he crossed the floor, his arm even heavier when he lifted it to knock.

Something dropped on the floor, fabric rustled, followed by complete silence.

"Open the door, darlin'. It's got to be freezing in there."

"Go away, Jesse. I'm not presentable."

"Better cover up then. I'm coming in." He waited ten seconds to give her time, then cracked the door open bit by bit.

"Laura Lee, I've got something to tell—what's all over your head?"

No wonder she hadn't wanted him to come in. She sat upon her bed, legs crossed under her flannel nightgown, twisting something—rags, that's all they could be—in her hair.

He knew ladies had secrets to keeping their hairstyles, but to him, never having had a woman of his own, they were a mystery.

Laura Lee did look a bit like Medusa but he thought it best to keep that thought to himself.

"I'm wrapping my curls to keep them fresh. No woman has the time to use the hot iron every day, I'm sure. Please leave my room and close the door."

In spite of the distraction, he had come to say his piece and he was going to do it. Since there was not a chair in her room, he sat at the end of her bed. It wasn't appropriate to be in her bedroom…or to sit on her mattress…but somehow, it didn't feel wrong.

It felt like home. Even though he was already home.

"You're angry." He didn't need to see her narrowed eyes and pursed lips to know it was true.

"Oh? Why would I be?"

"Because I kissed you."

"No, you kissed my hand. That's not a kiss. At least not one that means anything."

"I think we both know what was really going on. You have every right to be angry with me. And I do apologize."

"Go away." She dropped the rag, shoved his shoulder.

He moved even closer. The bedspring squeaked with the shift of his weight. "Can't think why you want to do that when your hair's so pretty hanging loose."

"If you had any care for fashion, you would know why. My Johnny knows. He appreciates the effort I go to."

"Since he's not here, why go to the trouble?"

She picked up the rag, did some sort of twisty twirling movement that ended in her hair being wound in a knot on her head. "Because he will be here. I don't know when it will be, but I don't want him to walk in and find me looking frumpish."

"First of all, you could never look frumpish—"

"Says a man who knows nothing about good form. Get off my bed."

"I would but there's something I've got to tell you." If he didn't say it now, he now he might not ever do it. "It's about Johnny...and him coming back."

"What is it?" She anchored a blond ringlet in a knot at her temple. "You know something about where he is?"

Her eyes did not light up like he expected them to. He wondered why, given that she must think he was about to deliver good news.

"I don't know where he is now. Only where he was."

"Someplace close? It's a good thing I'm keeping up my hairstyle, then. I'll need to look my best. Get off my bed."

Maybe she was right and he didn't know much about good form, but he did know there was a world of difference between needing to look one's best and wanting to.

"About fifty miles away, in Gilmore Crossing. But it would have been more than a week ago."

"He could be here anytime!" She clutched his hand and squeezed. He wasn't sure why she did it but was relieved that she no longer seemed angry at him—at least she wasn't for the moment. "We won't send you out into the cold, Jesse. I just want you to know that. When things are sorted out about the ranch, you and your horses don't need to leave in a day."

He wondered if she didn't want him to leave any more than he wanted her to.

He didn't want her to leave...

The truth of that didn't hit him as hard as he

thought it might. For years, he'd figured it would be only him and his herd, all peaceful on the ranch. But now, he wanted to share it with Laura Lee. When the time came for her to move on, this place...the tranquility he'd longed for...he might not want it that way anymore.

Gazing at her sitting in her worn and stitched up flannel gown with knotted rags all over her head, he was certain she belonged here with him.

Forever.

The problem was, he was not who she wanted. Johnny Ruiz was. For the next thirty seconds anyway. After that, she might hate the man.

Which did not mean she would accept Jesse in his place.

He had to think, though, that their friendship was real. The bond they had formed over the past weeks meant something to her.

"Darlin', do you remember when I faked that faint?"

He had to force the words out. The last thing he wanted was to break the heart of this precious woman. And that, he knew, was what she had become to him. Irreplaceable and precious.

She nodded, her brows sliding to a frown.

"I told you I found something out...about someone."

"You went to a lot of trouble to keep me from hearing about it."

"Still wish I could." He started to reach for her but snapped his hand back, curled his fingers tight in his fist. "But that news has to do with the Underwoods—and your fiancé."

She covered her mouth with her hand, her eyes squeezed tight.

"They got him into mischief!" Suddenly her eyes popped open, her cheeks blushed a furious red. "Was he injured?"

"Not that I heard, but the thing is, they robbed a general store and someone was shot. They're all wanted men."

"Not Johnny!" A tear slipped down her cheek. "They must have forced him."

"I know it's hard to hear, but that's not how it happened. From what's been told, he was willing."

"But…" Her shoulders sagged. He slipped his arm across them, drew her close. "I can't believe it. There must be a mistake. I never thought he… He could not have… No."

He kissed her temple, felt soft strands of hair and the coarse fiber of rags graze his lips. "I know it's a hard thing to hear, darlin', but you don't have to face this alone. I'm right here. I've got you."

"What if you heard wrong?" He felt tears soak the shoulder of his shirt. "How do I know you aren't making this up in order to—"

He tipped her chin up with his thumb, kissed

her cheek and tasted the salty tracks of her silent weeping. He touched his forehead to hers.

"You know, Laura Lee. You know."

She did know. In that place in the mind that knows truth for what it is, she did know that Jesse would not lie to her.

"Leave the door open, please," she said when he stood up to leave her room.

She had begun to shiver and needed the warmth of the fireplace to take away the chill. She also needed to see Jesse as he sat in his chair and picked up his book. To feel the solid presence of her friend while doubt grabbed her, shook her up and spun her about, as out of control as a dust devil.

He glanced up at her once, then back at the page.

Snuffling silently into her nightgown, she wondered if Jesse could have misheard. He would not lie to her, but that didn't mean everything he'd heard was true. It could be wicked gossip.

But even if the robbery had happened, perhaps Johnny hadn't been there. The man she thought she knew would not have done such a wicked thing.

Then again, the man she thought she knew would have married her already. The man she remembered would have worked side by side with her to see their dream come true.

Her Johnny was—

Not here.

There had been moments of doubt, when she thought maybe she did not know him as well as she supposed. She had ignored those moments. But the look on his face when he rode away with the Underwoods? That should have made her question him. What logical woman would not? But then he had given her the ranch and she was too happy to question anything.

Perhaps this was all her fault. If she had given him what he wanted, her body before the wedding, he might not have gone with the Underwoods that morning.

Men were men, Johnny had tried to explain to her. Their needs more demanding. If what Jesse said was true, the blame for what might have happened could fall a bit on her shoulders.

If each time he'd tried to sway her she had not put him off with a kiss on the cheek and a promise of their wedding night, maybe he would be with her now.

But perhaps the gossip was not true. Wagging tongues often were only about drama. If so, she was being beyond faithless to Johnny. She owed it to him to know the truth before she judged him.

Before she suspected robbery was the way he intended to pay for the ranch.

Getting up, she shut the door. She needed to be alone, to sob or curse or whatever it took to make it through the night.

As much as she would like to crawl into Jesse's lap, feel his arms around her, this was something she had to deal with alone. No person, no matter how good a friend, could face the truth for her. Accepting what was fact and what was not might be the most soul-crushing thing she ever did.

It could mean that Johnny was an outlaw.

It also could mean that the ranch was not hers.

From the far side of the door, she heard Chisel scratching and whining to be let in. But she could not throw her arms about her furry friend any more than she could her strong muscular one.

In spite of what Jesse said, that he was here for her, she felt completely forlorn.

On the way to town Friday morning, Laura Lee had resolved two things in her mind, which led directly to a third.

First. There was no point in more weeping. Either Johnny had committed the crime or he hadn't. Until she knew for sure, she was honor bound to wait for him. To trust in his innocence until the facts were verified.

Second. The ranch may or may not be hers.

She did believe that Jesse thought the ranch to be his, but if she could be duped, why couldn't he?

Third, and this was why she got out of bed before dawn this morning, trundled to the kitchen in her slippers and lit the stove. Whichever it turned out to be, truth or gossip, hers or not hers, she needed to make a living.

"Looks like there'll be a storm before nightfall," Jesse said, pulling the team to a halt in front of the library. He helped her down from the wagon. "A big one, I think."

She'd tried to convince him not to come with her to the farmers market today. Her emotions were scattered every which way and she barely knew what to say to him. For the most part, she hadn't said anything, remaining deep within herself, trying her best to keep a steady keel.

Here he was, though, still uneasy about who had been on their—the—property and why. Until he did know, he was adamant about her not going anywhere by herself.

The truth was, she didn't mind having him nearby, even though they hadn't had much to say. Not because of any strife between them, but more that they were caught up in their own thoughts.

Taking the smaller of the boxes out of the wagon bed, he placed it in her arms. After he unloaded everything, he told her he had business

at a few places in town and would be back to collect her in a few hours.

Going inside, she was grateful to find the library already warm. Auntie June spotted her and
bustled over to Laura Lee's table beside the fireplace.

"I'm glad you came! I'm half surprised anyone
did with the weather on the way." Auntie June's
comfortable arms wrapping about her brought
tears close to the surface again.

Straightening her shoulders, Laura Lee vowed
she was done with that. If Johnny Ruiz had de-
ceived her, she would face it. She was hardly the
first woman to be tricked by a man and she would
not be the last. Whatever the case turned out to
be, she still had a future to make for herself.

People entered the library, gathered in front
of tables, near the windows, but not in front of
the fireplace. They spoke in unusually hushed
voices. They might be talking about the weather,
but guarded glances in her direction led her to believe they were not.

Folks did love to talk. It was a sorry fact of life
that would never change. And truly, she did not
believe they meant any harm by it. For the most
part, they were kind folks, no doubt concerned
for her welfare and hesitant to speak about a subject that would cause her pain.

There was but one way to put her confusion to rest. And that was to discover the truth.

She crossed the room to Auntie June, who was handing a jar of her preserves to a customer.

"Would you mind watching my booth for a moment?" Laura Lee smiled at the departing customer and he nodded back.

"Not a bit," Auntie June said. "Take care if you're going out of doors, though. Keep an eye on the sky. Everyone's talking about Thomas Teal's aching knees. Last time they both ached at once, we had horribly wicked weather."

Laura Lee nodded. She took a step toward the door but spun back around. "Auntie June, do you know that my deed is fake?"

"Are you unhappy living out there with Jesse?"

"No." In fact, she could not recall when she had been less unhappy. Not even when she and Johnny set off in search of their future together.

"All I know is that it will all get sorted out once Judge Benson returns," Auntie June said with a firm nod.

Going outside, Laura Lee turned right out the library door and walked a block and a half to Sheriff Jones's office. Wind snapped her skirt every which way. A button-tipped hat pin pulled loose from her hat and pinged across the boardwalk. She slammed her palm on top of her head to keep her lace-and-feather hat from taking flight.

Going inside the office, she found the stove glowing and a pot of coffee on to brew. The sheriff wasn't there, but she heard noises coming from the back room where the cells must be.

She glanced about at the tidy space. It smelled masculine, like leather and wood. Behind the desk, wanted posters were tacked to the wall, some old and faded, some so new she thought she smelled fresh ink.

Johnny's likeness was pinned on top.

She sat down with a thump on the sheriff's chair. She should not have been so bold, but it was that or the floor. Her knees felt liquid and her stomach upside down. With her mind spinning, she braced her forehead in both hands.

It was one thing to suspect something to be true but quite another to find that it was.

The door leading from the cells opened, then closed. She glanced up to see the sheriff setting an empty lunch tray on a side table.

"Good day, Miss Quinn." She started to rise but he motioned for her to stay seated, then reached behind her and snatched the sketch of her faithless fiancé off the wall. "I'm sorry. I understand you are engaged to him."

She nodded, then shook her head. Words were a thousand miles away.

"What can you tell me?" she finally asked while

the sheriff poured a cup of coffee and handed it to her. "All I've heard is gossip."

Pouring himself a cup, he sat on the desk, his hip braced on the edge. He didn't drink the coffee, just held it and watched steam rise from it like a whirling spirit.

"The gossip is true, I'm afraid…as far as it goes. But there's more."

"Was it Johnny who shot someone?"

"George Wilton, the storekeeper, got shot defending his customers whose purses were being rifled, though. It wasn't Ruiz who fired the shot, if that gives you any comfort."

"I suppose it ought to but no, it doesn't much. Did the man survive?"

"Time will tell." Sheriff Jones shook his head and she feared time would tell something she dreaded hearing.

"You said there was more?"

"With everyone's attention on the store, they robbed the bank on the way out of town. The bank crime and the shooting together is what put a good-sized price on all their heads."

Sheriff Jones hadn't sipped his coffee and neither had she, but she stood, thanking him for it just the same.

"May I keep this?" she asked, pointing a half-steady finger at the wanted poster.

"Can't see that it would hurt anything." He

picked it up and handed it to her. "Everyone here will know it if the Underwoods come home."

She didn't go back inside the library. How could she and still be strong among all those people? They would see she knew the truth and pity her. She sagged down on the bench outside the library door, watching black clouds scuttling across the top of the distant hills.

Pity was not something she deserved. She had been blind when it came to Johnny Ruiz. While he hadn't been a criminal when she left the Lucky Clover with him, she ought to have recognized something about him was not as it should be.

He was far too charming for one thing. No one came by that trait naturally now that she thought about it. How many times had she ignored the way other women fawned over him? And the way he'd been so impatient with her refusal to allow him liberties? A man who respected a woman would not.

It cut her to the soul to think it, but had he faked a deed, thinking that in her gratitude she would lie with him? For the first time, it hit her that he might have intended to take her virtue and then desert her.

Had he intended to marry her at all?

Who was Johnny Ruiz, really? Was her intended truly a deceitful man, or had he been caught up in circumstances that he was too weak of character to resist?

Her head was spinning to the point she thought it might fall off.

"Darlin', what are you doing out here in the cold?"

"Jesse!" The bench gave with his weight when he sat down beside her. She wanted to fling her arms about him, hold tight to this solid, dependable man. Since anyone might see her, she clenched her fists in her lap. "Will you take me home?"

Chapter Eleven

Laura Lee sat on the fireplace hearth, watching the land beyond the window blanch with lightning. The storm had blown in during dinner with great gusts of wind and rain pelting the house.

It was a good, solid structure. There were no leaks in the roof, and cold air did not seep through the window frames. Whomever this home belonged to was a lucky person.

With a sigh, she reached for a curling rag and slowly wrapped a hank of hair.

She wasn't sure why she did it. Out of habit, maybe. Or some misguided hope that Johnny was not so guilty that he could not be redeemed.

Not that it mattered. The truth was, she would not marry him now. Even if he hadn't committed that crime, even if the deed he gave her turned out to be real, she could not marry him because… because she couldn't see him sitting in Jesse's chair.

Why then, did she continue to wrap and roll?

She'd always been a loyal person. Even as a child, she had remained with her father far longer than she ought to have. Perhaps she was doing the same thing with Johnny. Holding on for no other reason than that it was in her nature to do so.

How terribly foolish. There was every reason to believe he had never wanted a future with her. Or if he had, had he lost interest when she would not surrender to his blatant lust? Looking at it now, she wondered how she could have mistaken his desire to have his way as affection for her.

She also wondered if he was a weak and impressionable man who had fallen in with her dream of marriage and a home. When the Underwoods came along offering a life of adventure, he'd followed that.

In any case, Johnny Ruiz was not the man she believed him to be. The man named Hell Dog was very far removed from the hero who had saved her from a mad coyote.

Strange how she could hurt with the loss of someone whose true character only existed in her heart.

Stranger still, she no longer felt like crying over him. That was odd. She ought to have a dozen hankies wet by now.

"Why are you doing that, darlin'?" Jesse rounded the corner of the kitchen with a pastry left over from this morning in his hand. Crumbs dotted his lip.

Why did that look so appealing? She was grieving over a loss and shouldn't notice Jesse's mouth.

"I wish I knew."

He sat down beside her. The warm glint of the flames shimmered in his hair.

"You had a dream, one you cherished." He caught her hand when she lifted a rag. "They aren't so easily let go of."

He cupped the back of her head, gazed at her with something that was not quite a smile but not a frown either. It most certainly was not pity, even though he was doing his best to comfort her.

He untied one of the rags binding her hair. When the corkscrew curl bounced free, he did the same to another. "Changing one's mind about... well, things isn't easy," he said, continuing to free her head of its bindings.

She ought to stop him because...

This act of curling her hair had been her declaration of faith in Johnny. It was her belief that he would stride through the door of their home, perhaps bring the preacher along with him. She was performing a demonstration of hope that, in spite of what she knew, things would be as she had planned them.

Except that would mean seeing Johnny in Jesse's chair.

A lump swelled in her throat at the vision.

With her hair liberated of rags, her head felt lighter, but the ringlets bobbed about her face like corkscrews.

Jesse cupped her temples with his palms, caressed her scalp, then slid his fingers through the strands of her hair. He did it again and again until the curls began to loosen.

"It won't always hurt like this, darlin'. Heartache fades."

"Yes, so they say." The freer her hair became under Jesse's tender touch, the more clear something became. "But the thing is, I wonder if I actually do love Johnny. I really don't miss him so much as I miss loving him. I loved being in love. And I grieve the future I saw with a home and a husband...babies creeping about the floor."

"You wouldn't want that with someone who wasn't right. It would only turn your dream into a nightmare." His fingers stilled in her hair. "I don't want to sound cruel...the last thing I'd do is hurt you, Laura Lee. But I think that going away with the Underwoods was the best thing that fool could have done for you."

She looked down at the curling rags scattered over the hearth. She picked one up and tossed it into the fire.

Jesse grinned. She couldn't see him grinning because she was staring hard at her lap, but she knew him well enough to know that he was.

Following her example, he scooped up a handful of rags and tossed them in. One by one, they tossed them in until the last rag lay on the hearth between them. Reaching for it at the same time, they pitched it in. With a flare, it burst into flame, then in a moment turned to ash.

"You are a brave woman and I admire you."

If he knew what was going on inside her now, how she wanted to go to her bedroom and never come out from under the covers of her bed, he wouldn't think so.

"Jesse." Her voice cracked. She took one of his big, rough hands and squeezed it with both of hers. "Is this your ranch?"

Nothing she asked could have anguished him more. He couldn't lie. Neither could he plunge a dagger in her heart.

Thunder rolled closer to the house while he searched for a way to answer that would not flay her soul. In the end, it didn't matter what he did or did not say. She already knew the truth.

"Yes." The word ripped his throat. He lifted her chin with his finger because she was looking intently at a fold in her skirt. "Yes. It's mine."

Seeing the grief in her eyes, he wished it wasn't his. He wished that Hell Dog was her Johnny and that he'd given Laura Lee the ranch as a wedding gift.

Except…oh, hell…her lips were inches from his. Her breath puffed warm and sweet on his face.

And blame it, she was no longer bound to a castle in the sky offered by a fraud.

"I believe you, Jesse." Her whisper quavered. A tear slipped down her cheek and she dashed it away. "I never used to be weepy."

"I reckon no man has ever been fool enough to break your heart before, darlin'."

"Well, I won't say it isn't breaking, but I wonder what over." A lock of wavy hair fell across her cheek. He brushed it behind her ear and she caught his hand, drew his knuckles to her heart. He felt her deep intake of breath. "I like it when you call me darlin'. Even when I thought I loved Johnny, I liked it. So what is it that I'm so broken up over?"

"You did love someone. Just turned out he wasn't real."

It was impossible to read the odd look she gave him. But she closed her eyes and said, "I wonder?"

Before he had a chance to puzzle out that remark, she blinked them open and shook her head. "I'll move to town as soon as the weather clears."

"Your rent's paid for another week and a half."

"I can't stay—you know I can't. I've invaded your home long enough."

"No, darlin'. Not only my home." He tapped his chest where his heart thumped in burgeoning soreness. No…her leaving was the last thing he wanted!

He wiped the tear from her cheek with a swipe of his thumb. Another tear welled and slid down her face. He kissed it away.

"Stay." He skimmed the word across her cheek, tasted salt and felt dampness under his mouth.

She ducked her chin, then slowly lifted it again.

He turned her face, only an inch but it brought her lips within a fevered breath of his mouth. This could not possibly be the moment he should kiss her. But what was it she had wondered about? Him?

So he kissed her. He felt a tremor shiver under his fingertips when she leaned into him.

Her mouth was soft, as warm and as loving as he'd imagined it would be.

His thought had been to ease her pain, to give her something else in its place. Hell, that was a lie. He knew it the instant she lifted her arms, placed them around his neck. Knew it before he even tasted her lips, felt heat ignite his senses.

It might have lasted only an instant, clinging to each other, or it may have been forever. It didn't matter how long since the kiss rolled on and on inside him.

"Jesse?" she whispered. He pressed her tightly to him, feeling the quick rush of her breathing. "I've never... I mean, it's never been..."

"Like that before," he finished for her. "I know. Not for me either, darlin'. Don't go, Laura Lee. Stay."

"I've got to." She pushed against his chest so he let go of her.

"After—" She touched his bottom lip with the tip of one finger. "Well...you see why I can't stay."

Three hours later, she wanted nothing more than to open her bedroom door and sit across from Jesse watching the fire. No, not that so much as she wanted to settle into his lap and feel his great, strong arms wrap her up.

This storm was unlike any she had ever been through. Lightning hit the ground close to the barn. Another strike skittered across the yard in front of the house. Thunder shook the walls, rattled them in the foundation.

Chisel, apparently not concerned with the feral weather, slept peacefully beside the bed. She nudged him with her toe. He continued to lie there like a great lump of dough while she sat on her bed, still fully dressed and ready to... well, she wasn't sure what she was ready to do. Certainly not flee the shelter of the house.

If the dog wasn't alarmed, perhaps she should not be either. Perhaps she ought to put on her sleeping gown and get under the covers.

She'd rather live Jesse's kiss over again...for the hundredth time...than sit on her mattress half quaking in fear.

She could honestly say that she had never been touched with such pure, tumultuous passion before. It shocked her to find that Johnny's kisses had been child's play by comparison.

Just as she was settling into her imagination, smelling Jesse's warm skin and feeling his heat ignite hers, the dog jumped up with a start.

From sleepy to snarling in the space of a second, he padded across the room, braced his paws on the windowsill and growled. Coming to the window, she touched his neck to reassure him that the weather would pass and all would be well. Not that she completely believed it.

She spotted a light near the barn. Staring, she watched it bob about in the darkness like a giant firefly. All of a sudden, two more lanterns floated toward the first. They drifted away from one another, circling the barn.

Dashing for the bedroom door, she tossed it open.

"Jesse!" she called.

The only answer was a great rush of wind under the eaves and shivering the door in its frame.

He was not in his room, not in the kitchen either. That could only mean he'd gone outside to confront whoever carried the lanterns.

One man against how many? Three at least.

The only weapon she had at hand was standing at the door scratching to be let out.

She turned the knob to let Chisel out. A strong gust snapped the door out of her hand, allowing the storm to blow inside. Rain blew in sideways and soaked the floor.

It didn't matter. She ran after the dog without a thought for what would happen to the hardwon shine.

Chisel crossed the yard in long, swift strides. She tried to keep up but he was far faster. Crossing the bridge, she felt something sting her scalp. All at once, a deluge of hail battered down.

Lifting her arm, she covered her face and ran, half slipping toward the barn.

She huddled under the only shelter to be had; the two-foot-deep eaves of the barn wall.

The lanterns were no longer visible. The invaders must have gone inside.

Jesse had been a bounty hunter—he was a capable man. Still there were three of them, possibly more. Oh, there was Chisel, to be sure, but if the invaders were armed with guns—

"Don't think it! Do not let fear make you useless!" she whispered, creeping toward the small door in the back of the barn. She was forced to press flat against the wall, and splintered wood pricked her dress. Marble-sized hail punched her skirt.

With her hand on the door latch, she heard chaos inside. The vibration of shrieking horses and shouting men shivered under her hand. Hail and rain slammed the roof with such force she doubted the shingles would hold.

She drew the door open. A jagged shard of electricity exploded in the dirt a hundred feet out in the paddock. It bleached the barn in blazing light. She was nearly blown inside with the force of the thunder.

She stifled a scream, but even if she'd let it out, no one would have heard.

There was a stall to the right of her, so she ducked into it, then crouched behind a mound of straw. There had to be a way to help Jesse. She just needed a second to figure out how best to do it.

With so much shouting, with the horses panicked, rearing and prancing, she couldn't tell where Jesse was. Or who the intruders were.

"Get ropes around their necks!" someone yelled. "They'll scatter otherwise!"

"You get ropes around their necks!" another one called back. "I ain't getting trampled on! This was your blamed idea in the first place."

"Shut up and do what you're told!"

"Shut your own self up," was what she thought the other voice said, but over the cacophony it was hard to be sure.

But she was certain that she didn't hear Jesse's voice. She glanced up in a quick prayer that they hadn't already done something to him and that was way why she couldn't hear him...no, nor Chisel either.

"We should have robbed the bank in Beaumont Spur like I wanted to!"

She heard that clearly. The man must be close to her. She peeked over the straw to see the speaker dodge a kicking hoof. He backed closer to her to avoid being stomped upon.

Water dripped from the ceiling in a few places. At the highest point of the roof, a shingle caved in. Hail and rain poured inside, dousing another man who had just smacked a horse hard on the rump.

"Serves you right," she mouthed while glancing about for some sort of weapon. There was a shovel in a stall on the opposite side of the barn, for all the blamed good it would do her.

The fact was that the second she emerged from

the stall, she'd be spotted. Since that would not help Jesse, she hunkered down behind the straw, desperately trying to concoct a plan.

"Hey, baby doll. Sure have missed you."

No! She spun on her knees. Johnny grinned down at her over the wall of the next stall. He pulled himself over, then then leaped down to crouch beside her.

"What are you doing here?" she asked. Somehow, having him so close to her, leaning forward as if to kiss her hello, made her feel half—no, completely sick. She scooted away, pressing into the low wall for all she was worth.

"I came to get you like I said I would." He reached for her.

She swatted his hand. "What happened to you, Johnny?"

"The better question is, what happened to you?" He reached for her, as though he would fondle her hair. She swatted his hand again.

"You look—" he tilted his head this way and that, evaluating her "—dowdy." He blew on his knuckles. She was glad to know that the second whack smarted. "Turned into a shrew, too." He lowered his brows, studied her for a long moment. "I don't mind, though."

"You don't mind!" Her voice was shrewish but she didn't care. If it drew a cohort's attention, she'd give them an earful, too. "I mind! You gave me a fake deed and left me on our wedding day!"

"Don't mind that, honey. Didn't mean any harm. I still meant to come back for you. We'll start over fresh."

"I'm out of here!" yelled someone from somewhere. "Stealing horses ain't worth getting killed over!"

"Me, too! I got a bad feeling." This from the voice of the one who insisted on roping the horses a moment ago.

"Time to git." He latched onto her arms.

She bit his hand.

"Hey! What was that for?" He tightened his grip instead of letting go. For the first time ever, he actually caused her pain.

A face peeked around the corner of the stall. The man's long beak-shaped nose pointed at the floor. She recognized him from the day Johnny rode away.

"That's the woman you've been talking about?" The man studied her with a puzzled frown.

"Sure is, but she was a lot sweeter as I recall." Johnny lowered his face to hers. He did not mean to kiss her, she was certain. A rush of heated, angry breath smelling of alcohol grazed her cheeks.

"Don't know why you want that one. Not with

Dulsie and the others so willing. Come on, let's get out of here."

"I'll be along." She'd never heard Johnny's voice sound so harsh.

"Don't expect us to wait for you." With that, the man disappeared. The others must have already gone. She no longer heard shouting voices.

"You've been with other women, Johnny? While I waited and watched for you?"

All of a sudden, his demeanor changed. Not threatening but sheepish. "Aw, they didn't mean nothin', baby doll. They were just whores. They didn't count."

"Who are you?"

"It's me, still me...your Johnny. I'm taking you to the preacher, just like we planned. I promise we'll get married, the first thing we find a safe town. I've earned a bit of money so I can buy you a little home, all your own. You'd like that, wouldn't you?"

A town like Beaumont Spur? Where they would probably rob another bank because it was safer than taking Jesse's horses?

"Earned it? That's not what I heard, you low-down thief! What have you done to Jesse?"

"Jesse?" He looked puzzled for a moment. "The fool who owns these horses, you mean? Don't rightly know where he is. Expected him to be here to defend what's his. Curl in those cat claws of yours, baby doll, and come along."

"You can't be serious?" She yanked backward, trying to get free of his biting grip. "I'm not going with you."

"No? I say you are!" He stood and hauled her to her feet.

The man she had known slipped away as easily as that, to be replaced with the one who had likely been there all along. Sadly, she had been too starry-eyed to recognize it.

"I say she's not." The voice, deep and commanding, made Johnny flinch.

Jesse stepped out from behind a horse, rifle in hand, barrel nose to the floor. His expression might be all the weapon he needed. Steely green eyes locked on Johnny as though they were the sights of the rifle.

Johnny's fingers snapped off her arm.

Laura Lee dashed beyond his reach. She stood equal distance between the men.

Johnny appeared to gather his wits, fluff up his pretty feathers like a bantam rooster.

"Don't know who you are, mister, but this lady is my fiancée and I've come for her."

"Not unless she's willing to go."

"She's willing. Come now, Laura Lee." He crooked his finger at her.

She spun about and ran for Jesse, taking shelter under his arm.

Jesse lifted the rifle nose out of the dirt. "Better get a move on if you want to catch your friends. They're halfway to hell by now, I reckon."

Johnny—no, not Johnny—Hell Dog backed toward the small barn door. "You and me, baby doll, we could have had a good life."

"Damn fool outlaw," Jesse muttered.

Johnny would not have heard even if Jesse shouted. He bolted after his gang in the blaze of a lightning strike.

By the time Jesse and Laura Lee got the animals calmed, the lightning had moved on. That still left a lot of rain. It came down in pelting sheets. Luckily, the broken shingle was in a spot where it would not leak on the animals.

The run back to the house left them cold and drenched. Laura Lee went straight for the fireplace. He knelt in front of it, poking the embers and adding a log.

Seeing her shivering in front of the flames, watching the way the glow cast her pretty, worried-looking face in a soft orange blush, he wished it would rain until the area flooded.

Earlier, before the Underwoods tried to steal his horses, she'd told him she was going away.

Try as he could to remember how good he used

to feel about having a ranch with only him and his horses, he couldn't. Now he couldn't imagine his ranch without Laura Lee.

Her shoulders hitched, she hid her face in her hands. He watched her shake her head but couldn't figure out if she was hiding tears or… or he didn't know what.

Rising, he stood behind her, then curled his arms about her waist. For all that he shook with cold, the contact shot instant heat though him… and her, he hoped.

"I'm glad you didn't go with him, darlin'."

As much as he wanted to beg her to stay, he did not. The way Johnny kept trying to get her to leave, if he did the same but trying to make her stay, she'd only end up feeling like a reed tossed about in the wind.

If in the end she did choose him, he wanted her to know they were right for each other without a single doubt to shadow her decision.

Blame it! They were right for each other and had been since they were children. That night in the garden, neither of them had understood it, but in raising hands as they did, they'd joined destinies.

Sure couldn't say that out loud, though, because it sounded fanciful. And yet he knew it to be true.

"I'm going to undo the buttons on the back of

your dress, darlin', but only because you'll catch a chill unless you take it off. You don't need to worry."

"I trust you," she said simply.

All of sudden, he wondered if maybe she shouldn't. It wasn't that he didn't want to warm her by touching her…holding her body to him and—

And nothing. If one day she did him the honor of standing with him before the preacher, then he would do what he dreamed of with her. But that time was not yet.

Tonight, he was going to divest them of their icy clothing so they could warm up by the fireplace before bed.

And he was going to kiss her one more time because he couldn't not do it.

He didn't linger over getting it done because that would be risky business. Soon, she stood, her back still to him wearing nothing but her wet shift. He stood behind her in his damp red underwear, his arms rigid at his sides. He kept his gaze strictly on the flames.

"You warm yet?" he asked.

She shook her head. "No."

Turning her slowly about by the shoulders, careful to look only in her blue eyes, he bent forward and kissed her. For a long time.

"Now?" he asked.

"All of a sudden." She nodded her dripping head. "Quite warm."

He kissed her again but this time on her brow.

"Better get along to bed. You can leave the door open for the heat. I won't bother you."

Chapter Twelve

Not bother her?

That would depend upon what Jesse Creed considered bothering.

Because he bothered her, quite intensely. Why, she was afraid to put her feet on the floor for fear that she would walk right over common sense and straight into his bedroom.

She could see him from where she sat upright on her mattress. He appeared to be sleeping but fitfully. At odd moments, he turned, pounded his pillow and muttered under his breath.

It was unthinkable that she would turn from dreams of Johnny's embrace and rush directly into Jesse's real one.

Wasn't it? Well…maybe more foolish than unthinkable.

She cared for Jesse deeply. More than cared. It was hard to imagine how she would ever smile again after she left the place she had come to think of as home or the man who was at the heart of it.

He was handsome, caring, brave and everything a man ought to be. Everything she had believed Johnny to be.

And he was more. Much, much more. Jesse respected her. Clearly he desired her. She felt the yearning in his touch, saw it in glances that he didn't realize she noticed and heard it in his voice when he called her *darlin'*.

Even given that, she knew beyond a doubt that he would never dishonor her.

Oh, yes, she did more than "care" for him.

He "cared" for her, too. Even though nothing had been declared, her heart knew what it knew. Feelings between them had gown past casual affection.

Which meant she needed time to sort things out, for more reason than her heart being raw over her fiancé's betrayal.

The ranch stood between her and Jesse.

Not like it had before, with each of them claiming ownership. It stood between them because she needed to be sure her affection for Jesse went beyond these walls.

She had to know if she could separate him from this place and still feel the same way about him. This time, she must be certain that she was in love with the man. With her flawed judgment, she might once again be in love with her dream of happily-ever-after in a sweet home of her own.

The thought of her and Jesse continuing on as they had, the two of them in their chairs by the fire but as a married couple, was completely beguiling. But it had been that way with Johnny, too.

How could she trust it?

Because Jesse was not at all like Johnny, the voice of longing suggested.

Given that the voice of longing had recently led her astray, she ignored it.

But what was she to do? Run home to the Lucky Clover and hope to get her old job back? If she did, she would have four solid walls over her head. But they would not belong to her.

A home of her own was still what she wanted. Her feckless beau was good and gone, but the dream remained. The only thing to do was begin again. One day, she might love a place the way she loved this one.

As much as it hurt, this was Jesse's home and always had been. Going away was the only way to know anything for sure.

She gulped down a sob, and it was not over Johnny.

Jesse sat on top of the barn roof, nailing on a new shingle. It was surprising that only one had torn off. A few others had come loose so he crawled about replacing them.

Light rain tapped on his hat and coat while he knelt with a nail between his lips. Looking into the distance, he could see puddles of water dotting the land to the horizon.

Mud would keep the horses confined to the barn for the time being. It would also keep Laura Lee with him a bit longer. Which was going to be a torture as much as a blessing.

They would sit by the fire and chat, and she would cook for him…food. Only food.

But they would not bring up what was most on their minds because there was nothing to be done about it.

For his part, he was ready to sweep her up and carry her to the preacher, promising to love, honor and cherish. But of course he could not. It was doubtful that she still held any affection for that worthless Hell Dog, but he could hardly read her mind.

Her body was another thing. He had read quite a bit into that. She had not kissed him like a woman pining for someone else.

Then again, she was going away.

There was not a single damn thing he could or even should do about it.

With the last nail hammered in place, he climbed down the ladder. The scent of something roasting in the oven carried from the house. Glancing over his shoulder as he went into the barn, he saw smoke curling out of the fireplace. It whisked away west, caught up in rain and wind.

Several horses lifted their noses in greeting. Others serenely swished their tails.

"Mighty glad you all are safe," he said while going from animal to animal, stroking one and hugging another about the neck. "Those fools might have killed you by taking you out in the storm."

He turned to a workhorse when it bumped his elbow looking for attention. Or food. "You're right, Whittle. Maybe I ought to have gone after Hell Dog. He had a price on his head."

The situation sat uneasy on his nerves, had left him tossing about on his bed last night, sleepless and cussing under his breath.

He'd sworn off bounty hunting and for good reason. All he could hope for…pray on his knees for…was that this time, allowing a criminal to walk away would not result in tragedy to an innocent person.

Even if he'd been of a mind to chase the gang down, there had been Laura Lee to consider and the horses to calm. His duty as a friend and a rancher came before that of his former occupation.

Let some other bounty hunter collect the reward. He was finished with that life.

Unless the fool got near Laura Lee again. That event would change his mind in a hurry.

With her in town and him on the ranch, he couldn't look after her as easily as if she stayed here. But she had made her decision. The choice was out of his hands.

"The thing is, Whittle, I plan to be in town quite a bit since I intend to start courting."

He hadn't known that was his plan until he told it to the horse.

Courting Laura Lee! It was a course of action, something to set his sights on instead of wallowing in loneliness.

He reckoned he'd need a new suit, which would mean a trip to town. He'd need a few excuses for going to Forget-Me-Not in order to keep an eye out for Laura Lee. Making sure she was safe was upmost in his mind.

Not only that, the sooner he got to courting, he figured, the sooner he could woo her back home.

Tonight, after she was asleep, he would make a list of things to go to town for, one each day. He might have to ask Bingham to put in extra hours. Jesse still had a ranch to run, a home to keep up.

But damned if he didn't need Laura Lee in it.

Bleak.

The room at Auntie June's hadn't seemed depressing the first time Laura Lee had stayed here.

The same ruffled curtains hung on the window, the same frilly coverlet lay across the bed. The same tree swayed in the breeze beyond the glass.

The tree was the one thing to have changed. Cheerful autumn leaves had blown away, exposing stark bare limbs and twigs. Had she been in a different frame of mind, she might have thought the mottled bark lovely, but not today.

No doubt it was not the room that was bleak, but herself. The darkness was in her heart. It colored everything in a way that was not natural to her.

Where was the Laura Lee who smiled and laughed so readily? Perhaps she would return one day. Even though at the moment it didn't seem likely.

She sat down on the desk chair with a thump, kicked the toe of her boot at the edge of the rug.

What was Jesse doing now? He'd dropped her off at Auntie June's a quarter of an hour ago and she missed him already. She could watch for him to walk by on the boardwalk.

But no, she'd spent too much time in the recent past watching out of that very pane of glass.

A hand tapped lightly on her door. Before she could rise to open it, Auntie June bustled in carrying a platter with tea and what looked to be a sandwich.

"Here you are, my dearie." She set the tray on the desk, then instead of leaving Laura Lee to rue her situation, she sat down on the mattress. "You must keep up your strength. No man is worth losing your health over."

Laura Lee had to assume Auntie June meant Johnny Ruiz. The truth was a bit different.

It was true that she was deeply disturbed by what Johnny had done and it would take her some time to get over it, but she did not miss him. In fact, she would be relieved to never see his treacherous smile again.

"You know, Laura Lee, any woman can be duped by a smooth talker, and that dandy was one of the best I've seen. Even better than the one I was duped by."

"You were duped?" She'd have thought Auntie June much too wise for that.

"There was a time when I was as young and dreamy-eyed as you were."

"Well, maybe there is hope for me, then. I feel like such a fool."

"Drink your tea." A waggle of fingertips brooked no argument. "It will make all the difference."

Taking a sip, Laura Lee did feel stronger, but it probably had to do more with Auntie June than the Earl Grey. The woman had a motherly presence that made one feel wrapped in a hug.

"You knew, didn't you?" Laura Lee set the cup on its matching saucer.

"About the deed, you mean?"

Laura Lee nodded. The sandwich smelled more appealing by the second. Perhaps she would survive after all.

"Of course I did, dearie."

"But why would you say you'd forgotten?"

"Why, to match you up with Jesse, naturally."

"But I was engaged to another man!"

"Oh, I saw well enough who he was. Not a man but a male full of cock-and-bull and feathers." Auntie June shrugged. Her bosom lifted in a sigh under her flowered apron. "Now, our Jesse? That one is a man."

"I'll agree that he is. But, Auntie June, he wasn't my man."

"No, he wasn't…then." Auntie June cocked her head, her gaze probing. "I was so sure my plan would have worked."

"But here I am."

"As you should be. We all need a safe nest now and again in order to heal."

"What if I don't heal? I could end up a spinster boarding here with you for the rest of my life."

"There are worse fates than being without a man. You'd be better off that way than having poppycock to answer to." Auntie June stood up, reached into her pocket, then crossed the room.

"You, a spinster? Oh, Miss Laura Lee, I think not." Auntie June stroked Laura Lee's hair, a quick maternal caress, then pressed a note into her palm. Leaving the room, she didn't close the door, so her laughter carried down the hallway, bright as morning birdsong.

Laura Lee thought it wasn't the best time to get a bill for her rent, but renting she was. She opened the invoice, wondering if the cost had gone up in the weeks she had been gone.

The words were written in a bold, masculine hand.

Dear Miss Quinn,
Would you do me the honor of having dinner with me three nights from tonight? Yes,
I am courting you. I've never done it before,
so please don't break my heart. As you are
reading this, I'm probably buying a suit for
the event.

She smiled. How could she not smile? He'd signed it:

Your good…very good friend,
Jesse Creed

Courting? Well, she didn't recall ever being courted before either. Johnny hadn't courted. He'd simply taken her over, as she now saw it.

Once she had been Laura Lee Quinn, and within a day, everyone knew her as "Johnny's girl." Not a bit of proper wooing ahead of the fact. She chastised herself for not seeing the difference between courting and conquering.

All she could think of was that she had wanted someone and someplace all her own so badly that it had blinded her.

Dinner with a friend wearing a new suit? In the moment, she could not think of a single thing she would like more.

Jesse opened a can of beans, dumped them in a pot. He set it on the stove, watching to make sure they didn't burn like they had last night.

He'd only wandered away to stare out the window for a second but that's all it had taken. The second had turned into ten minutes of a daydream about Laura Lee. The house had smelled bad all day.

When the beans started to bubble, he dumped them in a bowl and grabbed a spoon. He took his meal into the parlor to sit by the fire and eat because that's how he used to do it when Laura Lee was here.

Lifting a spoonful of dinner to his mouth, his jaw hung open. The spoon sagged in front of his chin. He couldn't figure how he was going to eat when all he did was stare at the chair she used to sit in.

A man could starve to death, remembering the way her hair trailed loose over her shoulder or other times sprung up and down in absurd curls. He could forget to chew and swallow, recalling the way her mouth looked when she smiled. How the expression made her eyes light up.

A great canine sigh woofed up near the hearth rug. Chisel gazed up from between his paws with sad eyes. At least that's how Jesse read it.

The dog had tried to go with Laura Lee but she would not allow it. A boardinghouse room was no place for a beast of an animal.

"I miss her, too, big fella." He reached down to comfort the dog and himself. "You can come along tomorrow night. We'll court Laura Lee together."

The heavy tail thumped one time, then Chisel closed his eyes.

Jesse wished he could pass the time so easily.

Looking away from the chair, he managed to finish the beans. He picked up his book beside the table, but even the antics of Tom Sawyer couldn't hold his attention.

All he saw when he read a sentence was Laura Lee standing in the wagon bed, skirt rucked up, mud up to her knees, gripping a pitchfork in her hand. The chore of tossing hay to the herd had never looked so entrancing.

In Jesse's opinion, dinner with Laura Lee in front of the fireplace at Cowbell's Steak Corral had been a polite affair with nice conversation suitable for overhearing by other dinners.

They spoke of the horses and Chisel. The dog waited outside on the boardwalk, no doubt eager for Laura Lee to come out and scratch him on the forehead.

If any curious ears had been listening, they would have been disappointed. The name Johnny Ruiz did not come up. No doubt folks did wonder if their renting situation had developed to something more than a business deal.

Which it had…and had not.

No one would guess a thing, though, by the proper way they spoke to each other.

He reckoned that was what courting was about. Taking time, chatting and slowly wooing one's ladylove.

With dinner finished, they began the short walk back to the boardinghouse. It was a fine cold night with a full moon lighting the road. Lanterns placed on shop walls illuminated the boardwalk. Chisel trotted beside Laura Lee, making sure his neck was under her hand, his fur tangled in her fingers.

It wasn't right to be envious of a dog, but there it was, nipping at his heart.

"I miss you, darlin'." Saying so at this point in an evening wasn't out of line, he guessed. If it was, no one but Chisel was close enough to hear.

Her silence meant something. He wished he knew what.

"I've been eating beans and canned peaches all week," he admitted, hoping to bring back the conversation.

Her mouth twitched. She glanced sideways at him, the laughter in her eyes reflecting a beam of moonlight.

"No wonder you looked like you were in rapture when you were chewing your steak. Don't you know how to cook more than beans?"

"Reckon not. The truth is I've still got the stench of burned pork and beans in my nose." He hooked out his elbow, longing for her to take it. This, he figured, was a proper way to touch her during early courting.

"You poor staving man," she muttered, then set her hand demurely on his arm.

Seeing this, no one would guess that he'd once had his fingers in her hair, his mouth on her lips or that he'd worn her nightgown.

Too soon, they stood in front of the door of the boardinghouse.

He didn't kiss her because he figured a gentleman wouldn't. But in his mind… Sure wasn't proper courting going on in there.

"Good night, Jesse," she said, reaching for his cheek but then snapping her hand back. "I had a good time."

He touched the doorknob to open the door but hesitated to turn it.

The silence between them sizzled with things he figured they both wanted to say but did not.

"There's a Harvest Dance next Saturday, darlin'."

"I've heard. I'm bringing pecan pies."

"Pies?" He clutched the shirt over his heart. "I think the Harvest Dance might be a slice of heaven. May I be your escort for it, Miss Quinn?"

"I'd like that, Jesse. You can't imagine how much."

With that, she turned. He opened the door and watched her walk inside through the parlor and toward the stairs.

"Good night, dear." Auntie June walked into his line of sight. "Have a safe ride home." She closed the door with a click that echoed across the street, all the way to the bank.

Chisel whined. Jesse thought he did, too, because it was on this very porch he'd seen Laura Lee for the first time in so many years. Yes, this very spot.

She'd been wearing a wedding gown. His heart

had tripped over itself then. Not now, though. Now it was a big swollen ache in his chest.

Courting was a damn slow process.

If a week had ever passed more slowly, it was not in Laura Lee's lifetime. Even baking a dozen pies in Auntie June's kitchen had not made the minutes tick-tock by faster.

At last, here she was standing in front of the long mirror in her room on Saturday. Pivoting left, then right, she judged the color and the fit of the gown she had sewn for the Harvest Dance.

She'd picked a fabric the color of a pumpkin because she knew how Jesse liked them. The swirl of the material would be just right for dancing. It resembled a gently rolling cloud when she spun about.

Looking out the window, she watched the sun slip below the peak of the bank's roof.

Funny, but watching for Jesse through the window glass didn't make her stomach turn in apprehension. The opposite was true. It turned in anticipation. Her stomach still churned, but it was a lovely and exciting feeling.

Since Jesse wasn't due at her doorstep for another ten minutes, she sat down at her desk chair to wait for Auntie June's knock announcing his arrival.

She traced her fingertip along the shape of the

vase on the desk. It had been a gift from Jesse. Bingham had delivered it one night on his way home from the ranch.

Never had she seen an arrangement of hay and straw look so beautiful. Perhaps because she had never seen an arrangement of hay and straw before. Given that there were no flowers this time of year, Jesse had made do with horse feed.

No rose or lily could have touched her as deeply. Inhaling, she smelled…home.

Try as she might to face the fact that the ranch was not her home, at times it was difficult. She had stitched the curtains and polished the floor… prepared meals for a man who sighed over every bite.

She shook her head, felt her loose hair sway down her back. No doubt many women would attend the dance with their locks done up in stylish curls, but Laura Lee doubted she would ever put an iron or a rag to her head again.

Pleasing Jesse was proving to be an easier thing than pleasing Johnny had been. Johnny had been about appearance, how someone would view him with a stylish woman on his arm.

Jesse, she felt, cared for her however she looked. He'd seen her muddy, dripping wet, with flour on her face and even with those funny-looking rags on her head. Never, not one single time had he ever made her feel less than desirable.

Living away from him over the last two weeks had not dulled her desire to be with him. She was beginning to suspect that her feelings for him had nothing to do with wanting a house, with the dream she'd carried over the years.

A light knock rapped at her door.

Finally, counting the minutes ended. Jesse was here.

Walking into the livery, Laura Lee was delighted by what she saw. The big barn looked nothing like it had when she had purchased her team and wagon.

Not a horse, cow or half-constructed wagon remained inside. They must have been moved to neighbors' barns. Old straw had been swept away and new put down, making the rustic walls and weathered floor smell fresh.

Lanterns hanging from rafters and sitting on tabletops cast the livery in a cheerful glow. The effect was enchanting. She half expected to see fairies peeping out from behind one of the many barrels turned upside down for sitting upon.

Each barrel was covered in a quilt, some with bright flower patterns and others with delicate rose stitchery.

"Looks like we're the first one's here," Jesse announced with a longing glance at the food table.

The table was made up of doors supported by

sawhorses. A dozen tablecloths that were probably their owners' finest stretched across the length. Pumpkins and ears of corn accented such a bounty of food that Laura Lee figured she would burst her stays by evening's end.

But evening's end was the last thing she wanted to think of at the moment. There were still several hours to spend with Jesse.

"Do you think anyone will care if I fill up a plate now?" he asked.

"Jesse Creed." She stood in his path because he'd focused his gaze upon a bowl of mashed potatoes. "Someone will make an announcement when it's time. Sit down over here and be patient."

She plucked his sleeve, drawing him toward a pair of quilt-covered barrels.

A side door squealed open and a woman bustled in carrying a bowl of steaming gravy.

"Good evening, folks!" She gave them a sociable smile, then set the gravy beside the potatoes. "Looks like there will be snow before the party ends."

The door squealed again when she left.

"Be a shame to let that fried chicken go cold, though."

"Don't even look at it. I know how much work the ladies put into this feast. You'll just have to wait."

"I reckon you attended a lot of parties at the

Lucky Clover." He wrenched his eyes off the food table and looked at her. The expression of longing didn't leave his eyes. Still, she shouldn't hope that it was because she was sitting scant inches away. More likely, he was having lingering thoughts of fried chicken.

"Not as a guest. But yes, I was there setting out the food. The ranch was known for its big parties and barbecues."

"I remember. I watched from a bush one night that summer. All the fancy folks dancing and laughing...eating. I remember seeing you carrying a plate of cookies past my hiding place. You sneaked one off the plate and gave it to one of the hand's children."

A pair of men with fiddles came inside the livery. They nodded in greeting, then went to a plank stage set up in a corner.

"You can't possibly recall that," Laura Lee said. "You're making it up."

"I told you, darlin', I remember you. The barbecue was only a week after we made our wishes in the garden. I guess I was watching for you. Wanted to make sure you weren't still remorseful over the burned food."

"I was, but I was relieved to be given a second chance, too. Mrs. Morgan could have sent me to do laundry, had she a mind to."

"Mighty glad she didn't. I can't say how much I miss your cooking."

If pork and beans from a can was what he had been eating, it was no wonder. Still, she hoped he missed her for more than her cooking.

Gradually, people wandered in, alone and in pairs. No children, though. The Harvest Dance was an event for adults. Little by little, the noise in the livery increased. The sounds of folks laughing and talking blended with the fiddle players tuning their instruments.

"You warm enough, Laura Lee?"

It had been chilly when they first came in but someone had lit stoves placed near the doors. With so many people coming in, the space warmed quickly.

She nodded, cherishing the sound of his voice. Truly, she missed hearing it since she'd moved to town.

He helped her out of her coat, then carried it across the room to the coat table.

She'd missed seeing him walk, too. Tall and graceful but in a strong, manly way. He made her heart sigh.

Humph! Apparently he made another woman's heart do the same thing. She stood beside him, setting her coat next to Laura Lee's while watching in great admiration as Jesse's shoulders rolled and flexed when he took off his own coat.

Amazingly, he didn't seem to notice.

Johnny always appreciated the attention women paid to his looks. As much as other women's attention toward her former fiancé had troubled her, it hadn't bothered her as much as this woman's doe-eyed gaze at Jesse.

Then he smiled. But it was not at Miss Fashionably Coiffed Hair. It was at Laura Lee. He hadn't returned the woman's interest in the slightest way.

It felt like her heart slipped right out of her chest and flew across the room.

She wanted nothing more than to keep falling deeply in love with this man. He was more than any woman had a right to hope for. She did not doubt him in any way.

It was her own judgment she still doubted. Having followed her heart once and found it to be unreliable, did she dare do it again?

Probably not.

Maybe.

How could she?

But then he sat down beside her and held her hand. There was every chance that a decision was beyond her control.

A dinner bell clanged.

"Now?" he asked, eagerness giving him the look of a starving adolescent.

"Now."

Like a racehorse bolting from the starting line, he hurried across the room.

Oddly, he took his time looking the offerings over. With great thought, he placed a few things on a plate, then carried it back to their barrel seats.

For as starving as he was, she expected he would need three plates to settle his appetite, not the one.

"I hope this is what you like." He extended the offering to her.

"Jesse...this is perfect...but I could have served myself."

He shook his head, sat down, then looked longingly at a chicken leg on top of the assortment. She picked it up with a napkin and handed it to him.

"I'm courting you," he said. "Doing it as properly as I know how. I'm no expert but I reckon making sure you eat first is the gentlemanly thing to do."

"It's the thoughtful thing."

She was reminded that Johnny had never truly courted her. He'd paid compliments to her appearance, given her kisses and false promises, but he had never served her a plate of food when he was the one who was hungry.

Love was blind, she'd heard. Maybe so, but she had been blinded by a dream. Devoted to something that made a faithless man appear to be her one true love.

Her starving beau—she guessed she could think of Jesse as that since he was courting her—all but breathed in the chicken leg.

"This is perfect," she assured him, then sent him off to get his own food.

Two minutes later, he returned, his plate heaped in a four-inch mound of mashed potatoes with gravy dripping down the fluffy sides.

"I've got a fondness for potatoes."

"Yes, I know." When she used to ask what he wanted for supper, it was potatoes every night. Mashed, fried, roasted... He looked like he wanted to lick the plate.

"I sure do miss your cooking. I think I've lost a few pounds." He set his fork on the plate, the bite ignored while he gazed at her in the way that made her feel like she could crawl right into his soul. "The thing is, I miss your smile more."

"That's a very courtly comment to make."

"No, darlin'. That's right out of my heart. I miss everything about you."

He missed her. She missed him.

It's what she wanted. It's what she feared.

Something about knowing he missed her made her smile deep inside. The fact that he thought about her when they were apart made her feel cherished. This was what she wanted.

The problem was, she missed him, too. All day long, she thought about his laugh, his smile…his kiss. This was also what she feared because every time she imagined those things, they were happening in the house she so dearly missed.

How was she to know anything for sure?

He must have noticed her distress because he said, "So does your dog. Chisel mopes about day and night."

"What?" she asked, hoping to restore the lightness of the moment and the fun of the evening. "He likes me better than Whittle and Bride?"

"You're prettier," he answered, grinning. "And you smell better."

Finished with eating, he took their plates away. When he came back, they sat for a while watching couples polka about in front of the fiddlers. They didn't speak but leaned shoulder to shoulder while listening to the music.

She tapped her foot. He bounced his knee.

"You know how to do that?" he asked.

"I've never learned to dance. I was always too busy serving and tending to folks' needs. Do you?"

"Don't know a single step. I spent all my time trailing criminals. Wasn't much call for that kind of entertainment around the campfire at night."

"It looks like fun."

"Doesn't seem so hard to do either." He stared

at a couple prancing by, laughing and appearing to be having a fine high time. "It looks like you touch my shoulder and I put my hand on your waist, then we hop and spin about."

She thought there was a bit more grace to the movement than that, but folks sure were hopping and spinning.

Grinning for all they were worth, too.

After ten more minutes of toe tapping and knee bouncing, Jesse caught her hand. "Let's give it a try!"

"What if we look as foolish as a pair of loons?"

"I'm partial to loons."

"Have you ever actually seen one?"

"Three times, in fact."

"Well, then, let's see if we can do them proud."

Chapter Thirteen

"Ouch!"

"That was your foot? Sorry, darlin'."

Laura Lee laughed out loud when he spun her suddenly left. "I'll get yours next if it's in my way."

"You'll have to get lucky since there's no telling where it's going to stomp down next."

To his relief, his boot hit the solid floor of the livery. He'd lost count of the number of wrong steps he'd taken. The odds were better than even that he was the clumsiest fellow to ever lead a partner about a dance floor.

Not that his lady seemed to care. No matter how many times they tripped over each other, she came up laughing.

Of course, they hadn't toppled to the floor yet. A mistake like that could lead to a ruined evening. He could see it now. They would go down, then another couple on top of them, another, then another. The vision was nearly enough to convince him go sit back down on a barrel.

But that would mean taking his hand off Laura Lee's waist and he wasn't about to do that. Touching her like this was something he'd been dreaming of day and night. He was more grateful to be able to do it and call it dancing than he could express.

"What are you laughing at, Jesse?" She was flushed, breathless, her cheeks the prettiest shade of pink. He wanted to lean down and kiss one of them...or both...and her mouth in between, but the room was filled with folks bounding here and there. It wouldn't be appropriate.

He admitted to her his vision of boots and skirts, tangled in a heap and kicking.

She lifted her hand from his shoulder, covered her mouth. "You have a wicked imagination, Jesse Creed." She put her hand back on his shoulder where it belonged.

No doubt about that. Good thing she couldn't read his thoughts because it wasn't only kissing her lips crossing his mind.

All of a sudden, her steps faltered. She gazed up at him, not smiling, but not frowning...quite... either.

She might not have read his thoughts but he

had a feeling down deep in his belly that she'd read his eyes.

He quit hopping. She quit jumping. Slowly he turned her in a circle to give the appearance that they were dancing. A moving embrace was what it was and he could tell she knew it.

Slower, then slower. He got lost in her blue eyes. Other dancers, the music and the scent of pie faded away.

The only thing in the world of any importance was the woman in his arms. Only a fragile, nearly vaporous sense of good manners prevented him from scandalously kissing her in front of everyone.

He was shocked back to propriety, to decent courting, when someone danced into Laura Lee, bumped her flat against his chest. He thought it might have been Judge Benson finally come back to town.

"Jesse," she whispered. He recognized the unspoken desire to be kissed when he saw it.

"I know, darlin'," he answered.

Taking her hand from his shoulder, he tugged her along to the coat table. He grabbed up her coat but his was out of sight under a couple dozen others. He left it there even though the woman carrying in gravy earlier in the evening had said it was going to snow.

With urgency, he wove a path through a mass

of folks, pulling Laura Lee behind him. Proper courting rules required a slow process, but his feelings for Laura Lee outpaced his desire to be mannerly.

Once outside, cold air hit his face with a slap. He held up the coat for Laura Lee to shrug into.

She did but didn't bother to button it up.

"This way." With an arm about her waist, he took her to the back side of the livery, to an alcove that would not be noticed except by the most cold-hardy of folks.

He backed her up, braced his hands on either side of her against the wall. Wood vibrated under his palms to the thrum of the music.

Neither one of them spoke, only looked into one another's eyes in that way they had between them. The way that said there was nothing in the world beyond what they could be to each other.

Needed to be to each other.

A single snowflake drifted down and landed in her hair.

Leaning in, he pressed his mouth to hers because words could not say what was in his heart. He could explain until his last breath but he needed to make her feel it. He wanted to make her sigh under him, to snatch away her breath and make her pretty little toes curl in her shoes.

Rising on tiptoe, she made *him* sigh, snatched his breath and curled his toes.

He released her lips but took her hips in his hands and drew her belly to his.

"You know what I'm saying to you, darlin'."

She glanced away, but he touched her chin, drew her gaze back. The heat of her breath misted in the space between their mouths.

"I know, Jesse, but—"

He cut her off with another kiss. "The thing is, I don't know if I'm cut out for courting. It's a damn slow game for a fellow who's already in love."

"You shouldn't say—"

"Come home?"

"Don't say—"

"I love you?"

He cupped her face in his hands when she tried to look away.

Her head jerked, nodding.

"I love you, Laura Lee." Her mouth sagged in clear astonishment, although he couldn't figure why she ought to be astonished since he was courting her for all to see.

There was nothing for it but to kiss that pink circle of lips for a long, hot time.

He had to pull back when his mouth began to blister and good sense went on a holiday. The last thing he wanted was for Laura Lee to feel forced to marry him because he'd taken liberties.

She was a fine, respectable woman and that

was how he would treat her. Even if it was blamed painful to quit touching her. The effort to put her at arm's length left him short of breath.

Snow drifted gently down, landing on his shoulders and Laura Lee's eyelashes.

"I love you, darlin', but you don't need to say the same back. I understand why you need time. But I'll be waiting. Come tomorrow you'll find me courting again, nice and polite as pie…and then when you're ready, I'm going to ask you to marry me."

"Oh, Jesse!" She touched his hair, drew the strands through her fingers with a gentle tug. Moisture glittered in her eyes. That along with the dusting of snow made them look like blue crystals.

He slid his hands down her ribs, anchored them at the dip where waist flared to hip.

"If I said I love you, it wouldn't be a lie," she murmured. "But love…that's an emotion I can't say that I trust. Not so long ago, I planned on spending my life with Johnny…believed I loved him. And now I don't. How can I possibly trust anything?"

"You can trust me."

She dropped her hand from his hair, stepped away from him and out of the alcove.

"Yes, I can. But you can't trust me!" Her voice sounded ragged, ripped from a place of pain. She spun about, ran in the direction of the boarding-house.

He followed a distance behind, watched heavy-hearted while she disappeared into the first swirl of heavy snow.

Laura Lee stared at the snow sifting down like a white wall beyond her window. It had been snowing on and off for six days.

It was a lucky thing the Harvest Dance had not been scheduled for a week later or no one would have been able to come.

Turning away from the sight, she crossed the room and sat down hard on her bed. At least the little bounce the mattress gave was something fun to do.

Well, not quite fun but better than staring at the relentless white outside. It was far better than sighing because she hadn't seen her beau in a week.

Foolishness had a grip on her, made her wonder if it was the weather keeping him away or her behavior the night of the Harvest Dance.

A reasonable person would know it was the weather. At one time, she had been a reasonable person.

And weren't there a million women who would call her a fool? The best man in the world had declared his love, his honorable intentions, and she had not been sure. And not because she doubted him. She was the one with the upside-down heart.

Getting up from the mattress, she paced a circle on the carpet until she grew dizzy looking down at red-and-yellow wool roses.

There was the *Ladies' Home Journal and Practical Housekeeper* that she could reread, but what was the point? She no longer had a home to put all the wonderful ideas to work in.

She had spent the best part of the week—after she quit weeping into her mattress and feeling absurdly sorry for herself—wondering what to do about her current situation.

Wait was one thing. Given enough time, what Johnny had done to her would not take up so much space in her heart. In time, with the damage the criminal had left behind weeded out of her heart, her love for Jesse would have room to grow deep roots.

The thing was, how long was Jesse willing to wait? The world was full of…no not only the world, but right here in Forget-Me-Not…women who would adore having Jesse Creed as a husband.

Another thing she could do was ignore the doubts she had about herself.

Going to the desk, she picked up the vase of hay and straw, cupped it to her heart. She also snatched up the wanted poster of Johnny, which she kept in plain view as a reminder of her bad judgment.

She held the poster at arm's length, seeing again the vain and wicked man Johnny Ruiz had turned out to be. Perhaps he had been like that from the beginning and she hadn't noticed, believing him to be the one to make her dream of a home come true.

Then again, maybe being weak of character, he had simply succumbed to the influence of the Underwoods.

It was entirely possible. Weakness and vanity might have been his only flaws when they met, but those could have led him to embracing the life the Underwoods offered.

The more she stared at the likeness of him, the more she resented what he'd done and the angrier she became. How could he have claimed to love her and been with other women? And worse, claimed it didn't matter because of who they were!

The truth was that he hadn't respected her any more than he had them. She'd lost count of the number times he had urged her to cross an indecent line.

Oh, what she wouldn't give to lay into that man with a switch, to flay him with a piece of her mind. In a small way, she regretted that she would never see him again.

Anger, in some odd way, was making her feel better about things.

She cupped the vase of precious straw to her chest. The more she felt the tickle of it against her fingers, the more she thought of Jesse. Thinking of him didn't rile her temper in the least.

What a different man he was from the one she came too close to marrying.

She prayed that it was only the storm keeping Jesse away. She could hardly blame him if he'd changed his mind about his feelings for her after what she'd said about him not being able to trust her. She'd cried all night over the hurt she'd seen in his eyes when she'd vowed her love, then disavowed it all in a single breath.

And here she went, slipping into the murky turmoil of her mind as readily as tears slipped down her cheeks these days.

What she needed was to be around people. Yesterday's farmers market had been canceled because of the weather. She'd dearly missed baking, selling and socializing.

Since she was not the only person in the house, she decided to go downstairs where she could both socialize and bake. If Auntie June hadn't already prepared dessert, perhaps she would allow Laura Lee to do it.

* * *

"You young fool!" Laura Lee heard Auntie June's scolding coming from the parlor as she came down the stairs. "Brave and handsome, I'll give you, but foolish as they come. I'd never have thought it of you. I suppose you had good reason, though."

A voice answered but in a hushed tone. She did not recognize the speaker or the words. It would be good to have company from the outside, whoever the offender of good sense turned out to be.

Rounding the corner, she nearly tripped over her feet.

"Jesse!" She rushed toward him but stopped short of flinging herself into his arms. "What are you doing here?"

"I scorched the last can of pork and beans and got hungry. I was hoping you might feed me."

"Fool boy," Auntie June said again. "You could have been—well since you weren't, I'll just go read a book in my room." She shook her head. Before she mounted the stairs, she cast a wink over her shoulder. "I'll see you both at dinner."

"What are you really doing here?" Laura Lee caught Jesse's coat when he shrugged it off his shoulders. She carried it to the hall tree where the heavy layer of snow could melt onto the towel Auntie June kept by the front door.

"You know what. I'm courting you."

"In this weather? Jesse, you shouldn't have."

"A man can only take so much of talking to dogs and horses."

"Did you bring Chisel with you?"

"He's keeping Whittle and Bride company for the day."

"You cared enough about the dog to make him stay home," she scolded while she led him to a pair of chairs in the bay window. "But not about yourself."

Sitting, he scooted his chair closer to hers. Reaching across, he held both of her hands in his.

"It's been a long week, darlin'. A man can learn a few things sitting in silence."

Yes, and so could a woman.

"How are the horses?" she asked, distracting him for a moment from the deeper conversation that was surely coming. She wanted to sit and simply look at him before she had to think of anything else.

"They're getting restive after a week pent up inside the barn. Another one like this and I reckon they'll stomp down a wall to get outside and run."

"I feel the same way," she admitted. "There's only so much baking to do. I finished everyone's mending three days ago. It's like I'm waiting for a seam to rip or someone's stomach to growl, just for something to do."

"My stomach's been growling since the Harvest Dance." He slapped it with the palm of his hand and arched a brow at her.

"You poor man. Come with me."

Taking him by the hand, she led him to the kitchen. This was her favorite room of the big house. It always felt warm and welcoming. She swore the scents of cinnamon and ginger lingered in the walls.

She prepared him a plate heaped with three cookies, a slice of apple pie, two squares of fudge and a sweet roll. It was a lucky thing she had made more than the renters could possibly eat.

"I hope this is worth the ride to town." She pulled out a chair, indicating with a flip of her fingers that he should sit down.

He caught her hand, kissed it, then sat down in front of the dessert plate. "You were worth the ride."

She sat across from him, but he shook his head. "Over here, darlin'."

There was only one chair on that side and he was sitting on it. Smiling, she came around the table. He put his hands on her waist, then drew her down to his lap.

"I'm blocking your food, Jesse."

"All of sudden I'm not hungry. I told you I've

been going over some things in my head this week."

Learn was what he said the first time. She had learned a few things, too.

"I'd like to ask you something," he said.

"All right." She rested her cheek against his hair. It smelled clean, like snow and fresh hay.

"You told me that you love me, and you also said I shouldn't trust you. Why would you say so, darlin'?"

"I said it because I thought I loved Johnny. Why should you trust a woman who is not capable of telling love from an illusion of it?"

"If that were the case, you'd have gone with him when he came for you. You didn't. That tells me something."

"What? That I at least have the sense not to go off with a— Well, there's more to it than that."

"What?" His eyes looked at her with more tenderness than anyone ever had...the same he had the night in the garden. "Tell me."

"You know more than anyone does how I wanted a home of my own. So when Johnny came along, I added him, part and parcel, with it. He'd saved my life. How could he not be meant to be a part of my future? My feelings of love got all tangled up with the house I wanted."

"That's understandable."

"Is it really, Jesse? I don't understand how I

could have been so blind. And now, I love you…
but you have a home that I also love. How do I
know if I'm not making the same mistake? You
and the house, one and the same thing?"

"Say it again."

"How do I know—"

He silenced her with a finger to her lips. He
shook his head.

"I love you, Jesse," she whispered so softly
that she barely felt the words cross her lips. "But
I—"

This time he silenced her with a tender kiss.
At last, he said, "I reckon you need to know you
can love me without the ranch." He brushed away
a loop of hair that slipped over her brow.

"Yes. I need to know that."

"All right, then. I'll sell it. If you still love me
after, will you marry me?"

She leaped off his lap like it had caught fire.

"That's not a bit funny, Jesse Creed. You will
not sell an inch of it."

"I will, the whole damn thing. This week was
the loneliest I've ever been. I nearly took down
your curtains and slept with them."

"Don't sell it, please!" Standing in the doorway, she pinned him with what she hoped was a
firm glare.

If it was, it didn't keep him from rising from
his chair. "If it's the ranch coming between us, I

don't want it. If selling the place is the only way to know how you feel about me, you won't talk me out of it."

"What about your herd?"

"I'll leave the horses with the new owner if he wants them."

"But you love those animals!"

He approached her, step by slow step. Cautiously, as if he believed she would flee to the sanctuary of her room.

Sell the ranch! She could not let him toss his dream away because of her. It was unthinkable.

"No, darlin'." He drew her close, then wrapped her tight to his heart. She thought she might be drowning in him. "It's you I love. Only you."

"I don't love you, Jesse." The whispered lie hung in suspended silence between them. "Don't sell your dream for no reason."

"Is that so?" He traced the curve of her bottom lip with his thumb. "Your eyes say you do."

"Eyes can't speak."

"No? What are mine telling you?"

More than she could bear. She would not be the one to ruin his future. She shoved out of his embrace, fled for the stairs. Halfway up, she spun about.

Blame and curse it! The man was grinning.

"Don't sell the ranch! I really will not love you if you do."

* * *

The next morning, the scent of frying bacon drew Laura Lee to the breakfast table. She hadn't come down for dinner and so she was now famished.

"Ah, there you are!" Auntie June set a plate of scrambled eggs on the lace tablecloth and motioned her to sit down. "We missed you last night."

"Oh, well… I was sleepy." But only after she'd spent most of the night turning from front to back, side to side on her mattress. And only after she'd gotten out of bed, lit the lamp and glared at the wanted poster for an hour.

"What a shame."

Auntie June placed eggs, bacon and toast slathered in butter on a plate and set it in front of Laura Lee. She made another for herself, then sat down in the chair beside her.

"It was a pleasant evening. Jesse stayed for dinner and then we had a nice chat in front of the fireplace. What a shame you slept through it."

"Is he here?" She glanced about. They were alone. Apparently no one had heeded the call to bacon as quickly as she had.

"I believe he didn't trust himself not to sneak up to your bedroom so he spent the night at the livery."

"Auntie June! Jesse is a decent man. He wouldn't do that."

Her landlady arched an eyebrow, cocked her head to the side. "He's also a man in love, Laura Lee. You cannot predict what a fellow will do in his state."

Oh, she could do that well enough. He was going to sell the ranch.

There had to be a way to keep him from doing it. A couple of ideas had occurred to her last night while she stared up at the dark ceiling.

One, she could claim to have seen the light, now understood her heart and could love him without the past making a muddle of her.

Naturally, he would not believe her sudden change of heart any more than he believed her when she said she didn't love him.

Two—

"Jesse told me about the unwelcome visitors the night of the thunderstorm."

"They were after the horses."

"And one of them was after you, he told me."

"It was only Johnny. As you can see, I refused him."

"I imagine he wasn't happy about it."

Laura Lee crunched a bite of crisp bacon, surprised that it tasted so good. This conversation ought to rob her of her appetite. "I imagine he'll get over it quick enough. No doubt there are half a dozen women in Beaumont Spur to ease the rejection."

"Beaumont Spur?"

"One of the Underwoods mentioned the town. I got the impression they were going there to commit a crime."

"We ought to send a telegram so the sheriff can be on the alert." Auntie June stood up.

Laura Lee patted the chair cushion. "Finish your breakfast, Auntie June. I've already visited Sheriff Jones. He said he'd take care of it."

"You are well rid of that Ruiz fellow, Laura Lee."

She was, but not as well rid of him as she would be a week from now.

Now that Jesse was going to sell the ranch because of her, the second idea that had occurred to her seemed a very good one. It glowed in the pit of her belly like a slowly simmering fire.

Truly, it could be a brilliant plan for a couple of reasons. She had even been able to sleep for an hour after she'd considered it.

It had to do with the wanted poster lying on her desk next to the vase of hay. The generous reward had been staring at her for days without her recognizing its worth.

Now that she did, she thought it could solve her angst over Jesse and also send Johnny to the place he deserved to be.

With the reward money, she could purchase her own home. Living within her own four walls, she would discover whether or not her love for Jesse could stand alone.

Most important, Jesse would have no reason to sell his own ranch. She would find out what she needed to, without him having to go to that extreme.

Chapter Fourteen

Jesse stood on his front porch, gazing out at the midmorning sunshine glinting off the snow. He sipped a cup of coffee but didn't really taste it. With the early morning chores finished, he had a moment to stand here and reflect on things.

He couldn't say he liked reflecting on things these days. This porch, these acres that used to bring him such satisfaction, no longer did.

All he could think about was Saturday, when he could go to town and visit Laura Lee. Give another go at convincing her that they were meant to be together.

He had his argument ready in his mind and it was a good one.

That night when they were kids in the garden, they had made wishes for their own place to belong. What he'd turned over in his mind was that maybe the place would not be four walls. He wondered if the place was more of an in-the-heart sort of thing. That it was simply being together, wherever that turned out to be.

It was a valid way to think of things. He only hoped she saw it the same way. He figured she didn't, given she was so confused about where home really was.

An unexpected smile brightened his outlook. Yep, thinking of ways to press his point with kisses and tender words made him see things in a better light.

He didn't want to sell the ranch, but if he gained Laura Lee over it, it was worth the price. When he went to town on Saturday, he'd ask around, see if anyone was interested in his property.

Parting with the horses did give him pause, but it wouldn't shatter him. Not like losing Laura Lee would.

Rousing from his thoughts, he spotted a rider in the distance. It was a woman bouncing about in the saddle like she wasn't used to riding.

Auntie June? Coming to visit on a weekday morning?

Something had to be wrong. He set his coffee on the rail, then ran down the road to meet her.

"Is Laura Lee here? I don't suppose she is but I do hope so," she said without greeting.

"No." The fine hairs on his neck prickled with alarm. He hadn't felt this sense of misgiving since he'd quit hunting bounties. He gave Auntie June a hand down from her horse.

"She's not at the boardinghouse or anywhere in town that I can tell."

"Go inside while I put your animal in the barn. You can tell me what you know." He snatched the reins, his mind in a hundred black places at once.

"I'll walk with you."

"How long has it been since you've seen her?"

"Yesterday. After the noon meal, she said she had a headache and went to her room. When she didn't come down for breakfast this morning, I got worried and knocked on her door, but she was gone."

"She didn't say anything?" Damn, he should not have told her he was selling the ranch. She'd been shaken by it. She might have run off to keep him from doing it.

"She left a note, but it was vague… Here, maybe you can make something of it." Auntie June reached into the pocket of her coat and retrieved a small sheet of paper.

He read it once, then again out loud. "I've gone but will keep my room. Don't let Jesse sell the ranch."

"She left a month's rent," Auntie June said. "Are you selling?"

"Yes. I told her I was and she wasn't happy about it."

"Don't sell the ranch. I can't imagine why you said such a foolish thing, but don't do it."

"We can talk about it later. Did she say anything at all? Mention a place in conversation?"

"She did mention Beaumont Spur, but that was last week."

"That's almost a hundred miles from here. Why did she mention it?"

"She said the Underwoods and that awful Johnny Ruiz blurted out that they were going to commit a crime there. She told Sheriff Jones about it and he said he'd send a wire to the sheriff there."

He clenched his fists, ground his jaw. "The sheriff of Beaumont Spur is a cousin of the Underwoods." He was acquainted with Hank Underwood, having turned over a criminal to him once.

Lawman or not, in Jesse's mind, he wasn't a whole lot better than his kin.

The town of Beaumont Spur was a dirty place. Tawdry compared to sweet Forget-Me-Not. Paint peeled off clapboard walls and dust filmed many of the windows. For the most part, folks passed one another on the street without greeting. Without smiles either.

Was there even a church or a school?

There was a bank. She'd spotted the place

Johnny and his friends had talked about robbing first thing after getting off the train.

There was also a hotel that turned out to be a run-down, cheerless place. She checked into a room but wasn't sure she wanted to sleep on the bed for fear she would not be the only living creature in it. Just looking at the faded coverlet made her hair itch.

Shutting the surroundings from her mind, she reminded herself that as a child she had stayed in worse places than this. Besides, it wasn't the hotel room upmost in her mind but the bank.

As far as she could tell, it had not been robbed. She had no way of knowing for sure, but the folks she'd seen passing on the street did not seem to be speaking of anything dramatic.

Hopefully she had gotten here in time because two things had to fall into place before she could execute her well-devised scheme.

First, she needed Johnny—no, Hell Dog—to be here. Then if he was, she needed to trick him into meeting with her. Craftily convince him that she was sorry for not coming with him in the first place.

It was unlikely that he would suspect a trap, especially if she flattered him enough. Unless she missed her guess, he would not see past his ego. There was nothing he liked better than fluffing and preening. It shamed her that she hadn't seen it from the very first.

Praise the good Lord that she now did.

What was clear was that he deserved to be in jail. It was only right that he paid for his crime. Not the crime of betraying her trust; revenge was not what she was seeking. But he had harmed innocent people and that was what she believed he ought to account for.

She also believed that he owed her a home. He didn't know it yet but he was going to give her one as soon as she collected the price on his head. That, in her opinion, was not revenge, but clear justice.

Her scheme involved a bit of deceit, but she didn't feel so horrid about it.

The man was a thief to his bones. Not only had he stolen the goods of innocent folks but he'd ravaged her dream. She counted her lucky stars that she'd got away with her virtue unblemished. She'd lost count of the number of ways he'd tried to seduce her with a vain promise of marriage.

Never one time during intimate moments with Jesse had he ever attempted such a thing. And those times had been far more heated…more scalding to her heart and her body than they had come close to being with Johnny.

When Jesse asked her to marry him, she had

no doubt it was a sincere proposal and he intended to carry through with it.

She shook her head, clearing her mind of everything but the reason she'd come to Beaumont Spur. The sooner she dealt with the taint of treachery Johnny had left in her soul, the sooner she could sort out where her heart lay with Jesse.

First thing, she needed to discover for certain whether or not the bank had been robbed recently.

To that end, she visited the café across the street. If the crime had been committed, folks would be talking about it over breakfast. Hopefully it had not. If Jesse had come and gone already, she didn't know what she would do.

Coming inside the front door, she was relieved to find the small restaurant clean. The windows sparkled and the embroidered curtains smelled freshly laundered. The floor was free of dust and crumbs. Even the tables had been buffed to a high shine. The café was an oasis of cleanliness in a dilapidated town.

For the first time since she'd stepped off the train, Laura Lee was greeted with an engaging smile. She ordered coffee and cake. It was impossible not to when it crossed her mind that Jesse would sigh over the chocolate perfection.

She would eat it on his behalf and imagine his satisfied grin as she did so.

She missed him more than she could have

imagined. Memories came upon her at unexpected moments. Just now she saw the two of them stomping on each other's feet at the Harvest Dance. And then there Jesse was, faking illness and curled around a pumpkin in the wagon bed. And always he sat in his new chair reading a book beside the cheerfully snapping fire in the hearth.

She smiled, although she had not at the time, at the vision of the scene in the library when they had spilled coffee over everything. That was the time Auntie June convinced them to become each other's renters.

All the visions she held dear made her miss him desperately.

While she did miss the house—the solid stone hearth, the shine on the floor and her handmade curtains in the windows—it was not what she longed for.

She clinked her fork on the plate, swallowed the lump of chocolate cake swelling in her throat. Perhaps refuge and a sense of belonging could not be found within four walls but within the heart of another person.

If it was the ranch she cared for as much as she did Jesse, she ought to be pining for land and trees.

Well, figuring all this out was why she was in Beaumont Spur. She picked up her fork. She

would make herself finish the chocolate cake...
if only for Jesse's sake.

"I hope everything is to your satisfaction,
miss," said the young waitress. Laura Lee suspected she might also be the cook and owner of
the business.

"Oh, yes...this is wonderful, ma'am. You've
certainly got a talent for baking."

The young woman blushed at the compliment,
her blue eyes a sparling contrast to her lush black
hair. "Thank you. I haven't seen you before. Are
you new to town?" She tilted her head in asking.
"Or just passing through like most folks?"

"I am looking for place to settle, but I haven't
decided where. Is this a good town, do you
think?"

She shrugged, cast a glance back at the
kitchen. "It used to be, before the railroad spur
was built. Now there are strangers coming and
going, mostly off to somewhere else...and saloons
being built to entertain them on their way. We
still have some good farmers and tradespeople,
but you can see what the town looks like. No one
cares about it like they used to. And now I'm sure
I've discouraged you from settling here."

Clearly, no one did care. With the exception
of this well-tended place, Beaumont Spur did not
resemble pretty Forget-Me-Not in any way. But
she didn't say so aloud.

"Would it be safe to visit the bank, keep my money in it? Like you say, the town connects to a railroad spur and strangers do pass through."

"Oh, I would think so. The bank hasn't been robbed in nearly a year."

"Well, then, that's good."

It meant that the Underwoods and their accomplice had not yet committed their crime.

She dearly hoped that they were already in town because she truly dreaded every night she would have to spend in the questionable hotel bed.

It was snowing again by nightfall, heavily enough that people were saying that the train would not risk the trip along the spur.

Standing beside the window of her hotel room, Laura Lee looked out at the gently whirling flakes. At least a fresh coating would cover the dirty snow underneath.

Three men came out of a saloon only to lumber unsteadily toward the next one. One of them slipped on the ice and was scooped up by his fellows.

As far as she could tell, they were not Underwoods.

She didn't mind the weather so much, except that it might keep her prey...her quarry...from getting here if they were traveling by train.

But no, they would not be. What criminal escaped by train?

Then again, if snowfall delayed a train, it would delay a horse even more so.

"Please let them be here already." Her whisper fogged the glass, so she wiped it with her sleeve. She picked up her coat from the bed and put it on. With a resigned sigh, she took it off again.

Her intention had been to hide in the shadowed doorway of the café across the street and watch for Johnny, but it was far too cold for that. Instead, here she stood, gazing out the window like a proper voyeur.

Luckily, lamps along the boardwalk illuminated the passersby. At this hour, they were all headed for one of three saloons.

Pulling the desk chair across the floor, she sat down to watch. Glory if she didn't feel like the old Greek goddess Nemesis she'd read about as a child, full of indignation, eager to deal retribution for evil…for undeserved fortune.

Dramatic? Highly, but she needed some distraction from this dreary room.

An hour went by with no sign of her feckless former fiancé. Another ticked by and then another. Her eyelids sagged. She popped them open with a start. The last thing she wanted was to miss seeing him.

After more time, although she had no idea how

much, she spotted a man walking along the board-walk. He was visible, then not as he walked in and out of lantern light. Snow swirled around him, but she recognized his long stride.

All at once he stopped, glanced up at her window as though he knew she'd been watching. He lifted his hand to her. She knew those long mas-culine fingers...had been touched by them. Green eyes cut the darkness. The half-crooked smile that was unique to Jesse melted her heart.

Her head jerked, startling her awake. The dream whisked away in a wisp, like the snow drifting past her sleep heavy eyes.

Yawning, stretching, heartsore, she wondered if Jesse was looking out a window tonight, think-ing of her and watching snow blow past. If he was, was it with affection or bitterness? Given that she had gone away so suddenly, the marriage proposal barely out of his mouth, he might very well feel betrayed and bitter.

Knowing the man as she did, he'd be angry, too, if he guessed where she'd gone and why.

How could he, though? She'd been careful not to reveal anything.

Hopefully he would come to understand why she was doing this. She'd tried to explain how she felt about him and the house and Johnny, but wasn't certain he understood.

She didn't know if she understood it herself.

Her fear was that in trying to discover what it was she wanted most, she may have lost it.

Snowfall came down heavier now. Men continued to go in and out of the saloon but their silhouettes had become vague, like disembodied shadows out for a walk.

Turning from the window, she fell upon the bed, face-first and arms wide.

How could she not wonder if she had made the biggest mistake of her life in coming to Beaumont Spur?

But no. She had to deal with Johnny. Until she put the past to rest, she could not deal with the future. When she came to Jesse, it would have to be with a clear mind and heart that was not befuddled by recent heartache.

She would not love Jesse in the way she had once loved Johnny—for a place, for a dream—and not the man himself.

Jesse banged his fist on the stationmaster's window. If the man didn't open the door soon, glass was going to shatter.

The train he'd stepped off moments ago waited on the tracks, the great engine rumbling. Billows of black smoke curled into the afternoon sky while steam hissed across the platform of the Smith's Ridge Depot, disappearing into the frigid air.

A porter, shivering in his coat, called in a deep, rich voice for the passengers to continue to come aboard.

Jesse was continuing—but not to where the train was suddenly heading.

Frustration built inside him as hot and boiling as what was powering the steam engine. If the stationmaster didn't open the door soon, folks collecting their baggage would see steam shooting from his ears, too.

All at once, the door swung open. He grabbed his fist back in time to avoid hitting a man's narrow, red nose.

"Mister, I'll tell you the same as I did the last fellow. The train's not taking the spur to Beaumont Spur today. By the look of the weather, not tomorrow either."

"I've got to get there."

"Unless you want to get a shovel and clear the tracks yourself, the train's not going that way."

The door slammed in his face with a bang so loud it made a woman standing ten feet away turn and look.

He pounded on the door again.

Yesterday, after hearing what Auntie June had to say, he'd gone to town right off in order to catch the early morning train. The only things he'd taken the time to bring were the gun and holster buried in the loft. That and Chisel, who waited to be fetched from the baggage car.

He'd made a firm vow that he was done with a life that required deadly tools. Just went to show how life could take a turn. He hadn't expected to dig them out of the loft any more than he'd expected to fall in love.

He sure hadn't expected Laura Lee to go after Ruiz. What did she intend by doing it? Auntie June didn't know and neither did he.

He'd spent the whole of last night in a spare bedroom of Auntie June's, puzzling over it. Never did come to a satisfactory conclusion, only a suspicion or two. Mainly he flopped about on the bed like a fish landed on a stream bank with a hook in its mouth.

If even one of the things he thought she was doing turned out to be true—hell, he just hoped she wasn't. But if she wasn't, then what? Why would she go someplace she thought Ruiz was going to commit a crime?

The door swung open again. "The tracks are covered with snow. It's a fact. No trains are going to Beaumont Spur. Beat your knuckles on my door until they bleed, it won't change what is."

"I appreciate that, sir." He did, for all that he denied it. "But there's a woman involved."

The old fellow's expression softened. "Should have guessed, good-looking young fellow like you."

"The thing is, I've got to get to Beaumont Spur. The lady might have gotten herself into some trouble."

"This wolf belong to anybody?" a man's deep voice bellowed over the activity on the platform.

Looking toward the baggage car, Jesse spotted Chisel straining at a rope leash tied around his neck. The dog turned out to be the stronger of the two. The baggage man dropped the leash.

Chisel charged toward Jesse. Folks dove out of his path, no doubt fearing a raving beast had been set loose among them.

Before anyone drew a weapon, Chisel lay down at Jesse's feet as docile as a lapdog. Things on the platform settled from outright fear to wariness. One boy, apparently teased into action by friends, crept up and touched his tail. Chisel licked the child's hand so the crowd relaxed.

"Do you know where I can rent a horse?" Jesse asked.

"You've nearly got one, far as I can tell." The stationmaster cast a glance at Chisel, arched a brow. "But rent? Check the livery is all I can say. Though I doubt Granderson will let any of his animals out in this weather. Treats his animals like they were his children."

"Buy one then? You know anyone willing to sell?"

Scratching his gray head, the old man simply stared at him.

Hell, it was going to be one long walk to Beaumont Spur.

Laura Lee awoke to sunshine streaming on her face. She covered her eyes with her arm to hide from the glaring light. Lying still, she waited to see if anything itched. She had tried to sleep on the chair but after a while, a bug bite seemed less risky than a sore neck and tweaked back.

Her plans for the day would require having her wits about her. It wouldn't do to be distracted by aches and pains.

She sat up, shook out her hair, then waited another moment to clear out last night's dreams from her head. They had been lovely and at the same time, strange. One moment she had been kissing Jesse, then the next she had been kissing Johnny.

She'd gone from blissful delight to a sense of being trapped. In Jesse's embrace, she felt…at home. Secure, with a sense of life being right.

The opposite was true when it was Johnny holding her. His arms had given her a sense of doom. It was as though she had to be with him even though she didn't want to. Even in sleep, she had looked down the years of her life with dread, knowing she loved one man but was bound to another.

Getting out of bed, she dressed in the plainest garment she had, all the while beyond grateful that dreams vanished with the light of day.

The bad ones at least.

Kissing Jesse… The warmth of that image lingered. She missed him terribly and was nearly sorry she had run away. But something here needed doing and she could not leave this town until it was accomplished.

She was no longer sure of what she would do after she turned Johnny over to the sheriff.

Her intention had been to take the reward money and buy a home of her own. Only by fulfilling that dream would she truly understand her feelings for Jesse. Or so she'd thought.

But this morning, sitting in the chair and bending down to put on her boots, she was pretty sure she already knew. For all her dreaming, both awake and asleep, she hadn't once dreamed of the ranch, longed for the land or the curtains she had left behind.

All over the country, there were homes with curtains and shined floors, but only one Jesse.

Only one strong, green-eyed, former bounty hunter turned rancher stirred her. Made her want to smile at the future, run forward and embrace it.

She dropped a shoe on the floor. All of a sudden she knew for sure that she would rather live from tent to tent with him than alone in her own home, as sweet a place as it might be.

As wonderful as the realization was—how it made her heart leap and dance—she could not go running home.

There was still Johnny to be dealt with. She could not move on, or go back as the case was, until he was.

She picked up the boot, shoved her foot into it, then laced them both up. Standing, she went to the window and looked southwest, toward Forget-Me-Not. As soon as this ugly business was finished, she would go home.

To the man, not the place.

As long as he would still have her. She wouldn't blame him if he wouldn't. She'd treated him horribly. He'd declared his love and what had she done? Claimed to love him, too, but turned on the declaration by saying she feared it to be a false feeling and that he should not trust her.

And then she'd run off without a word. If he never looked her way again, it was no more than she deserved.

She walked to the window, braced her fingers on the sill and watched sunshine glitter off the thick deposit of fresh snow.

It was lovely, but she knew what was underneath. Dirt. She could not help but be reminded of Johnny. Under his handsome swagger, he was really Hell Dog.

Across the street, the restaurant door opened. The young woman who had been so pleasant stepped outside carrying a shovel. She cleared the snow off the boardwalk in front of her establishment, then went back inside.

Smoke curled into the clear blue sky, not only from the chimney, but the stove flue as well. If Laura Lee was lucky, the cleanest place in town would be open for breakfast.

Somehow, getting her mind and her heart in agreement with each other over her feelings for Jessie made her appetite blossom.

"Good to see you again." The waitress's voice sounded as welcoming as it had yesterday, her smile as genuine.

She set aside the broom she had been stabbing at a corner. Looking as graceful as a willow wisp, she walked in long strides toward the window table where Laura Lee had seated herself. The spot gave her full view of anyone out walking.

Although, when she thought about it, it was unlikely that Johnny or anyone with him would be up this early. Not after a night of carousing, which if he were here, he'd no doubt been doing.

"It looks like you survived a night at our lovely hotel."

"As far as I can tell, I only got bit once and that was on my knee."

"Easy to scratch." The waitress winked, then flicked her thick black braid interwoven with a pink ribbon over her shoulder. "What can I fix for you?"

As Laura Lee suspected, she was both the cook and the waitress. "Eggs, bacon…coffee?"

"It'll be ready in a swish." With another wink and a nod, she spun about, walked back into the kitchen. After a moment, the scent of bacon seeped into the dining room.

So did the urgent cry of an infant.

"Hush, now, darlin'." The woman's voice carried into the dining room, gentle and soothing.

Whatever had troubled the child no longer did. The only sounds coming from the kitchen were a whisper-soft lullaby and the sizzle of frying bacon.

Moments later, the woman returned, balancing a plate on one hand while carrying a baby on her hip. She set the plate on the table.

"My daughter." She inclined her head toward the child. "Seems like she always gets hungry at the same time as my customers do."

"She's adorable." She truly was. All babies

were but this one seemed especially sweet with the whirl of dark brown curls circling her head.

"I'll be within earshot if you need anything else."

There were a few things, but they had to do with information. "Do you know what time the train pulls in today?" Laura Lee was beginning to wonder if perhaps Johnny was not yet here.

"Oh, I doubt if it will. The railroad doesn't bother with shoveling deep snow off the track to Beaumont Spur. If the sun stays out to melt some of it, the train might come tomorrow or the next day."

"I'm meeting my…my brother. I don't know if he's already in town or not." Laura Lee sipped her coffee, sighed out loud. "This is delicious."

"Even I can make coffee." The waitress laughed and moved the baby to her other hip. "What does your brother look like? If he's been here to eat, I'll remember."

"You should give yourself more credit in the kitchen. Your food tastes delicious." How could she not know that? "My brother has black hair and brown eyes, not overly tall. He dresses with style so some women find him attractive. But he's fallen in with a group of friends who are a wild bunch. He could be with them."

Most of what she said was true. She ought not

feel bad about the part that was not since she was working toward a better good.

"I'm sorry, I don't believe I've seen him. If I do, I'll send word to the hotel."

"Would you mind if I sit here for a while and watch for him? It's cleaner here than in my room."

"Stay as long as you like. You wouldn't know it now, but there was a time when the hotel was known for its elegance. That was before it got fleas and bedbugs. I'll be by to refresh your coffee."

Sitting in this spot gave her a better view of the people coming and going than there was in the hotel room…with the added benefit of coffee.

Cowboys with jangling spurs walked past the window. A man with a silver star pinned to his coat strolled slowly by, his gaze lingering on one of the saloons for a moment before he moved along.

As soon as she located Johnny, she would need to find the lawman.

A woman walked past with a grocery basket hanging on her arm. She seemed nervous, casting glances over her shoulder before turning aside into the milliner's shop. Perhaps even the presence of the lawman did not make her feel secure.

Time crept by as slowly as a turtle running a race.

The waitress came from the kitchen, gliding

toward the table with another baby hugged to the crook of her hip. She held a coffeepot at arm's length to keep it out of the squirming baby's reach.

"More coffee, miss?"

Laura Lee lifted her mug. "Your son?"

The child was clearly a boy.

"Yes and no. He's my nephew but I've adopted him."

The young woman bore a good bit of responsibility on her slender shoulders. No doubt she had a good, solid husband to support her.

A husband like Jesse would be. Thinking of him, she became even more anxious to get this business with Johnny finished. The image of that wonderful man grieving because of her fickle heart made her want to pound the table and weep.

She fixed her eyes on the coffee being poured into her cup, watched the deep brown swirl and the steam rising and made a vow that weeping was something she was done with forever.

"Juliette!" bellowed a man's voice, sounding impatient, demanding, from the kitchen. "I'm hungry, girl!"

Juliette held the hot coffeepot away from the baby, rolled her dark-lashed eyes. "My father-in-law."

Chapter Fifteen

By noon, many of the shopkeepers had roused themselves and cleared enough snow to make it possible to walk along the boardwalk.

Laura Lee stood in front of the restaurant, gazing north toward the Suzie Gal Saloon and south toward the Saucy Goose. There was the Fickle Dog on the other side of the street, but she would have to walk through six inches of slush to investigate that one.

Her feet were only half warmed from when she had crossed earlier this morning.

The Fickle Dog, being only a couple of doors up from the hotel, could wait until later. If it was late in the day by the time she returned, it made sense to look there last.

North then, if for no other reason than she liked the name Suzie.

The Johnny she knew had never been a late riser. Of course, he hadn't been a thief either.

Whichever way she went, it wasn't likely to matter since the saloons were only beginning to show signs of life.

Johnny Ruiz could be anywhere…or nowhere.

Her only reason for choosing this town to search for him was that during the raid on Jesse's barn, the criminals had mentioned it.

All of this might be a great waste of her time.

Yes, a squandering of precious hours that she could be sharing with Jesse. There was so much she had to make up for where he was concerned. Her mind was all in a twist, thinking of ways to convince him that, when she next told him that she loved him, she'd mean it with a clear and sincere heart.

Impatience to get back to Forget-Me-Not gnawed at her. There was so much she wanted to say and it was not as if she could shout it across the miles.

She walked slowly past the Saucy Goose, giving it sidelong glances because it didn't seem proper to outright stare at it. A bit of activity stirred inside, but there was no sign of Johnny or any of the Underwoods.

Along the way, she'd spotted the sheriff a time or two but she could not approach him yet. Not until she had her criminal spotted. If she ever did.

When she finally crossed the street to the Fickle Dog, impatience at not being able to locate Johnny made her nerves spark. Frustrated, she felt like going into the saloon and "bellying up to the bar," as her father had described it on numerous occasions, and outright asking.

Since she hadn't been inside a saloon since she was eleven years old, she decided a peppermint stick from the general store would better suit to settle her insides. In order to get to the general store, she would have to navigate the slush that had not been cleared away from the saloon's front door, but peppermint was peppermint and would be worth the risk of a fall.

Many were the times she'd consoled herself with the treat while sitting in an alley behind a bar, waiting for her father to get drunk enough so she could lead him back to their tent.

Would Johnny ever fall that low? she wondered. Had he already? But maybe he was lower. To her knowledge, her father had never robbed anyone.

What a relief that Johnny Ruiz was no longer hers to worry over. She shivered even with sunshine on her shoulders because she had come so close to living a life worse than the one she had escaped from her father.

She might need two peppermint sticks. One for now and one for later when she was in her grungy room with nothing for company but her thoughts.

Opening the door of the general store, she

wished she had been able to bring Chisel with her. She would not have been lonely like—

And there he was. Her foot paused midstep. She could not put it on the floor for fear he would hear, turn and see her.

Everything would be ruined if he did.

Even though his back was to her at the counter, she knew his posture. The whisper of his voice was too familiar not to recognize even though she could not hear his words.

In utter silence, she lowered her foot.

The odds of making an escape were in her favor because Johnny was not alone. He stood hip to hip with a young woman, one arm slung across her shoulder.

"Thank you, sir," the counter attendant said. "I'm sure your young lady will treasure it always."

"More than always," said a young voice, sweet and ripe with innocence.

Johnny shifted his posture, dropped his arm and began to turn.

Spinning, Laura Lee fled outside, but where to? Glancing about, there was no place to hide. It would only be seconds before he and the girl stepped out behind her.

Around the back of the building! It was the only place to go.

She pressed her back against the wall, trying to listen over her heavy breathing.

"Back here." Johnny's voice sounded close. He could only be feet away from rounding the corner.

No time to run. She glanced about for something to slide into or hide under.

There! On the back porch sat a large overturned pickle barrel. She skidded for it, arms windmilling. She bumped against the oak slats, regained her balance, then lifted the mouth of the barrel and squeezed under.

The rim hit the porch with a loud thump. Anyone not focused on seduction would have easily heard it. No sooner had the rim settled into place around her than she heard the woman giggle.

Have mercy! Her voice sounded only feet away.

The barrel was tight and smelly. Laura Lee had to pull her knees to her chest and rest her head on them in order to fit inside.

Luckily, there were gaps in the slats that let in light and air enough to breathe. Not enough air to displace the stench of strong vinegar, though.

Blast—oh, blast! Her skirt hadn't fit all the way inside the barrel. A great wide ruffle of brown plaid lay in full view. *Please, please, please don't let them see...or if they do in their distracted state, let them think it's mud.*

"You like it, baby doll?"

Baby doll! Indignation made her forget about the exposed ruffle.

"Oh, Johnny," the young voice cooed. "It's the most beautiful brooch I've ever seen."

Purchased with stolen money! She felt the urge to shout the sordid fact from her cramped hiding place. In spite of the weather, it was growing hot inside.

"How about a little kiss to say thank you?"

Laura Lee heard the quiet smack.

"Those are the sweetest lips I've ever tasted, not that I've tasted more than a couple, mind you."

"I like kissing you, too." The admission sounded shy, awkward.

"You know, baby doll, I've never felt like this before about anyone, but… I feel like I'm falling in love with you."

Truly, it was hotter in this barrel than the outside temperature accounted for. Sweat was popping out on her brow. She would end up with embarrassing stains under her armpits.

"I… I feel the same way. I know it's fast, but will you come and meet my parents?"

"Oh, yeah, honey, yeah. But right now, I'm… Well, a man in love has got needs and you are the—"

"Only woman in the great, wide, beautiful world," Laura Lee mouthed silently.

"—who can satisfy them. Please, baby doll, do you know someplace we can go that's private? It won't take long and then we'll go directly to your parents. I'll ask them for your hand."

Laura Lee had to bite down on her bottom lip, clench her fists tight against her mouth.

"Yes, I know a private spot and it's not far from here. No one will disturb us."

The urge to burst from the pickled oak and rip the victim from the snake's embrace roared in her veins. If indignation had the ability to make noise, Johnny Ruiz's eardrums would be blasted out of his head.

But she was trapped, stuffed inside here same as the pickles had been.

If she made one little noise, a sigh or a shiver of disgust even, he would hear and everything would be ruined.

She owed it to womankind to put this man away. Sadly it might not happen soon enough for this poor girl.

The only thing for it was to sit tight with her mouth shut, be patient and then turn him in and collect the bounty.

After a moment of having to endure the squishy sound of a long seductive kiss, she heard footsteps crunching away in the snow.

Ha! Jesse's seductive kisses never sounded squishy. Since she had to wait here a bit longer to make sure they were well gone, she thought about them... Jesse's kisses.

How hot could it really get in here?

All of a sudden, cold air hit her. Bright light flooded her eyes.

The man who lifted the barrel set it aside. "Run into a bit of trouble, ma'am? Saw your skirt playing peekaboo."

"How do you do, Sheriff?" she asked, accepting his hand up.

She fluffed her skirt, shook off bits of dirty ice. Breathing deeply through her nose, she expelled the stench of pickled oak.

"You are the very man I was looking for."

Around noon, Jesse figured he'd have been better off to wait for the tracks to clear. At the rate he was traveling, the delayed train would arrive in Beaumont Spur before he did.

Back in Smith's Ridge, he'd spent the better part of an hour trying to rent or purchase a horse. All he'd managed was a pair of snowshoes that the livery owner didn't need.

With his mind picturing the many horrible things that could befall Laura Lee, he'd strapped them on and tromped north out of town.

At the time, walking had seemed a better choice than waiting. He'd traveled a quarter of a mile over the glittering white ground with ease.

Then he'd turned around to see Chisel buried

hip deep and struggling to try to keep up. The dog would be exhausted within two miles.

Since Jesse couldn't rightly leave him behind to face an icy grave, he'd turned around and gone back to town.

The stationmaster had a splintered, rusted sled he was willing to sacrifice, in the name of love, for only three times its value. Since money was the last thing Jesse was concerned about, he had paid the price, only grateful that there was a sled to be had.

Now, four exhausting hours later, he dragged the sled across a vast expanse of blinding white with the hundred-and-eighty-pound dog napping on it.

There was no telling how much longer it would take to walk to Beaumont Spur. With the sun shining down and making the snow slushy, it became harder to lug the sled along behind him. He halfway wished another storm would blow in to turn everything to ice again.

In the meantime, he wouldn't mind stopping to rest with the dog, if only for a moment.

Sure as blazes couldn't do that. The frightened look on Laura Lee's face that night in the barn... It followed him like a shadow, haunted his mind like a demon. Hell Dog had had her by the arms and her eyes had been wide and terrified. It had taken all he had not to batter the criminal into the ground.

But there'd been Laura Lee's safety to ensure first. Then there were the horses to be calmed and Chisel, too. The dog had whined and yipped in the stall where Jesse had stashed him.

Narrowing his eyes against the glare, he hunched his shoulders into the rope straps attached to the sled. He drew his burden along foot by foot, inch by inch.

He didn't know for sure if Hell Dog was in Beaumont Spur. Didn't know for certain that Laura Lee was either.

What he did know was that the lowlife cowboy had tried to force her once. Given the chance, would do it again. This time she would be facing him alone.

Jesse could only pray that he was going the right way.

And that she did not turn to Sheriff Hank Underwood for help. He was more likely to side with his cousins than with Laura Lee.

And so he trudged on, dog in tow, because he was the only one she could count on.

"And why was it you were looking for me, miss?" the sheriff asked once she was seated across the desk from him in his office. "And what exactly were you doing hiding under the pickle barrel?"

The sheriff folded his hands together on his desk, considered her with a half-lidded gaze. Clearly the lawman was bored.

She would rather be explaining things to Sheriff Jones. He listened with a more attentive ear. And he offered coffee. The sheriff of Beaumont Spur had lit a fire in the stove but was clearly reluctant to perform even that courtesy.

"Hiding."

"Why was that, Miss...?"

"Quinn, Laura Lee Quinn. And you are?" she asked because he hadn't formally introduced himself as he ought to have.

"Folks call me Sheriff Hank."

"A pleasure, I'm sure," she said, despite the fact that she was not sure it actually was. In the end, it didn't matter if the man was congenial or not. She was here on business, not to make a friendly acquaintance.

"Tell me, Miss Quinn. Why were you hiding from the man?"

"Because I didn't want him to see me," she answered, suddenly hesitant to blurt out the whole story.

"I imagine there was a reason."

Had the sheriff nearly yawned? His face screwed

up in an expression that only a suppressed yawn could make.

"Until recently, we were engaged."

That got his attention at last. He arched a brow at her and his eyes sharpened upon her face.

"And you want me to arrest him for dallying with another woman? Yes, I did see it happen."

"No. What I want is to turn him over to you and collect the bounty offered for him. And if any of those lowdown Underwoods are with him, you should arrest them, too. They are all part of a nefarious gang. But the only bounty I'm going to collect is for Johnny Ruiz."

All of a sudden, Sheriff Hank blinked, sat up straight.

She reached into her coat pocket, drew out the wanted poster and slid it across to him.

He stared down at it for a moment, then slid it back to her.

"And how is it you aim to accomplish that, Miss Quinn? I doubt he'll walk in here with you of his own free will."

"No, I would not think so." She slipped the poster back inside her pocket for safekeeping. It was her only proof that Johnny Ruiz was a wanted man. "With your help, I'll set a trap for him."

He nodded. "A bit of intrigue? Drama and revenge?"

"Dollars and cents. Doing what is right." His

condescending attitude was beginning to wear upon her.

"All right, then, tell me what you have in mind."

"It's easy enough. I will lure him to my hotel room tonight and the moment he comes in, you will emerge from the wardrobe to arrest him."

"How big is the wardrobe?"

"Bigger than the pickle barrel."

He laughed…or barked maybe. "Let me know when you get this intrigue in order. I'll be there."

Getting Johnny alone was proving to be more difficult than she had expected it to be.

Unless she found a way to pry his new lady-love away from his side, Laura Lee would never be able to lure him to her hotel room.

With the sun going down, she was running out of time. She would need to make sure the sheriff was in the wardrobe a moment before Johnny came in. That meant getting to Johnny before he went to the saloon and got too drunk for her to manipulate.

She'd had a bit of experience at manipulating a drunk man, but it was an unpredictable business and she needed everything to go smoothly in order for her scheme to work.

At least it was proving to be an easy thing to follow Johnny and his new lady. The girl only had eyes for him, and his were focused on conquest.

While that worked in her favor for stalking them, it also kept his victim attached to him every blamed moment.

The sun went down and lanterns blazed to life in the windows of the homes beyond Main Street. The saloons lit up in the same moment the shops grew dark.

From a block away, she watched the restaurant's lamps flicker out, one by one. No doubt this would only be the beginning of Juliette's day. During Laura Lee's vigil by the window inside the café earlier, she'd discovered that she had been mistaken about the young mother having a helpful husband at her side. In fact, she was a widow raising two children, as well as having to care for her late husband's elderly father.

Thinking about Juliette, she nearly missed the lovebirds turning onto a residential street.

She ducked behind a bush that gave little cover. At this time of year, it bore snow-covered twigs instead of leaves.

While she watched, her eyes stealthily narrowed, the pair of them entered a house. Through a large window, she saw the girl happily introducing her new beau to her parents. The deluded family welcomed him, smiling and with arms wide open.

Laura Lee felt half sick. She only hoped that when the girl had taken him to the private place she knew about, Johnny had not left her in a situation that could not be undone.

Kneeling behind the bush, she prayed that he had not.

Rising, she crept slowly toward the house. The wind was rising. With darkness settling in, folks remained inside their homes. Even she could not hear her footsteps, muffled as they were by the scrape of bare branches and sudden gusts racing under the eaves.

Time was up. As much as she hated to boldly knock on the door, it was what she had to do. The girl would be brokenhearted, her parents angry, but in the end they would be well rid of Hell Dog Ruiz.

Her light rap went unanswered. So did her bolder one. Only when she pounded with her fist did she hear footsteps crossing the floor.

The door swung open. Light poured onto the porch along with the warmth from the fireplace. From where she stood, she saw Johnny, the girl cozied up to him, sitting at the dining table in polite-looking conversation with her mother.

"May I help you, miss?" asked a middle-aged man who must be her father.

"I've come for my fiancé."

As she expected, her quietly spoken words had the effect of dynamite being tossed into the room.

"You've come to the wrong house," the man said, his eyes going narrow upon her.

"Laura Lee!" Johnny gasped, leaping from his chair so quickly that it tipped over. In turning, he also knocked his new love's chair. She fell sideways, tumbling onto the floor in a billow of petticoats.

It was no surprise that he paid no attention to the poor flailing girl.

The mother screeched and dashed to the other side of the table to set her daughter to rights.

"I must ask you to leave." The father's mouth tugged down at the corners, quivering.

Laura Lee could not be sure who he was speaking to, her or Johnny.

"What are you doing here?" Johnny rushed past the understandably outraged man and grabbed her elbow.

She would like to explain to the family that she was leading the wolf away from the door, but of course, she could not.

"Me? What are you doing here?" she answered.

From inside, she heard the young lady calling after Johnny, weeping and wailing, her heart clearly shattered.

Leading her by the arm, Johnny led her out of the yard and across the street. The front door slammed. Glancing back while he pulled her along, she saw the three of them through the window, holding each other.

By this time tomorrow, they would discover Johnny had been arrested, perhaps understand they had been saved from disaster.

"What the blazes are you doing here, Laura Lee?"

"At the moment, I wish I hadn't come."

"Why did you?"

"Not to find myself jilted." She yanked out of his hold. "Honestly, Johnny. I can understand why you tricked me about the ranch. I'm sure you wanted to please me, is all. But this!" She wagged her hand at the house now half a block away. "I thought you loved me."

"I do love you, baby doll. But when I came to get you just like I said I would, you refused to come. What did you expect me to do?"

Exactly what he had.

She ground her teeth, curled her toes tight in her boots since he would see it if she fisted her hands.

"I made a mistake, Johnny. Please forgive me." She wiped her eyes with her coat sleeve. Hopefully he didn't notice the absence of tears.

"Hard to believe you changed your mind all of a sudden." He placed his hands on his hips, cocked one to the side while he looked her up and down. She ought to have done up her hair and put on a fancy dress.

"I don't think you understand the appeal you hold for me." She reached a hand toward him, not quite touching his chest. "I've never seen a more handsome man. How could I not have missed you every minute you were away? After you left the barn, I saw the mistake I made. Any woman would give her...her...well, you know...to be with you."

"Will you give it to me, Laura Lee? After all this time, will you finally? It's the only way I'll believe you're sorry. A man does have his pride."

"And a man like you—" she lowered her voice to an intimate whisper, leaned in close to his ear "—so virile, so very desirable, you have every right to be proud." She felt half sick. "Won't you come to my room at the hotel? Let me make it up to you?"

He took her arm again, more gently this time. "Let's go, baby doll, I've waited a long time."

"Oh...not right this minute, please, Johnny. I look a proper mess. Come in two hours. I want to look my best for you. It's what you deserve, isn't it?"

"That's my girl." He patted her on the rump, then drew her in, kissed her hard on her mouth.

It was all she could do not to vomit on him.

* * *

Two hours later, the anticipated, yet dreaded, knock came at her door. Four soft raps, then a pair of quick, solid ones. It was how he always knocked.

Although Sheriff Hank would have heard, she tapped on the wardrobe to alert him that she was letting Johnny in.

Her heart raced, her palms sweated. She reminded herself that this whole thing would take a much shorter time to accomplish than curling her hair and putting on a fancy blouse and skirt had taken.

It would only be an instant from the time Johnny walked in until the sheriff stepped out of the hiding place to arrest him.

Only a few more moments that she would be forced to endure her former fiancé's company.

She opened the door and her prey swept eagerly into the web.

"Hey, baby doll." He wrapped his arms about her, briskly running his fingers over her ribs. "It's you I love and no one else. You know that."

"And I... I..." *Love you, too?* It's what he expected to hear, but some words could not be said. "I know you do. I would never have invited you here if I didn't know it."

Sheriff Hank would have heard Johnny's voice

by now. Why wasn't he leaping from his hiding place?

The warming spell had brought a storm with it. Wind pattered raindrops against the window while Johnny smiled at her, worked the top button of her shirt loose.

"Wouldn't you like some coffee first?" she asked.

There was no coffee brewing. He was bound to notice.

"Naw." He shook his head, sat down on the desk chair. "Take off your dress, Laura Lee."

"I'm sure there's no rush."

Why wasn't the sheriff emerging to make the arrest? She knew he was curled up in there. He could not possibly have fallen asleep.

Casually, she moved toward wardrobe. She pretended to trip. Her hip hit the door. If he had dozed off, he would be awake now.

"Better be careful, watch your step…and hurry up."

Something about Johnny seemed different. She would have expected him to be cajoling, falsely charming in his attempt to get her undressed. She had encountered his attempts at seduction too many times not to know this was different.

The gleam in his eye was cold when it should have been simmering.

"What are you waiting for, baby doll? The preacher to show up and marry us first?"

"I'm not waiting for anything." Her eyes slid toward the wardrobe although she didn't mean for them to.

Rain pelted harder on the glass.

Johnny stood up, walked toward her. "Take it off now, Laura Lee, unless you want me to do it."

"No… I—"

He backed her up by bumping his chest against her, his arms straight at his sides and his fists clenched.

Bump. Bump. Bump. He had her pinned against the wall. His lips twisted in a hard grin, then he grabbed the collar of her shirt. Suddenly yanking, he ripped it. Buttons pinged on the floor. He jerked the sleeves down her arms.

With a nasty chuckle, he drew the blouse from her skirt, tossed it away.

"That wasn't necessary, Johnny! I just hoped to take things slowly. Now I'll have to sew—"

"Slowly, is it? I just figure if you aren't dressed, you won't go running away from me. And I'm not so sure you intend to honor your word."

He slipped one arm about her shoulder. His breath puffed close to her ear. Clearly, he'd had time to get drunk after all.

"Don't look so fretful, baby doll," he said, drawing her firmly toward the wardrobe.

Perhaps she could lunge for the door and fling it open and reveal the sheriff.

"I've had a change of heart about things," Johnny said. His grin made the fine hair on her arms rise.

Something had gone horribly wrong with her simple plan.

Fearing that struggling to get away would further encourage him, she stood perfectly still. In nature, the more panicked prey became, the more likely it was to be captured. And prey was what she was beginning to feel like. She knew this man even less than she had believed she did.

"What things, Johnny?" She turned to him, touched his cheek, hoping to draw out something of the man she thought she knew.

"I'm going to marry you. Give you what you always wanted."

What? Why wasn't the sheriff coming out of the wardrobe? They were standing right in front of it. He had to be hearing every word.

"No." Clearly things had gone beyond her ability to trick and manipulate. "I don't want to marry you."

Beyond the patter of the rain, she thought she heard a dog barking. The sound made her heart ache for Forget-Me-Not...for Chisel, Auntie June, Bingham and most of all Jesse.

"Don't much care what you want at this point, Laura Lee."

Her knee had a clear shot at his groin, but his attention was too intently focused on her for that defense to work.

"You can come out now," he called, grinning at her while he nodded his head at the wardrobe.

The narrow door creaked open. One long leg emerged, then the other.

"Sheriff Hank! I demand that you arrest this man," she said, even though she assumed the sheriff's loyalties had shifted.

Whatever was going on, she was not the one in control.

"He might, baby doll…except that his name is Sheriff Hank Underwood."

Underwood! No wonder the man did not have the good graces to look ashamed of his double-handed behavior.

"That," she said, turning her head to glare at the sheriff, "does not release you from enforcing the law."

"You really thought you could collect the bounty for me?" Johnny asked.

"I intend to." She peered at Johnny's face, so close his nose blurred in her vision. He didn't look so angry at the moment, only amused, a cat toying with a mouse. "Just as soon as the sheriff of Beaumont Spur remembers how to perform his job."

"That's just the thing, baby doll." Had she really never noticed how his amused expression bordered on a sneer? There had been a time when she'd thought it charming. "He's also the justice of the peace. You know, the fellow who can marry folks all legal like."

"I do not consent to marry this criminal."

"Is that what you think of me? I'm some big-time outlaw?"

No doubt he hoped she did, judging by the bragging evident in the twitch of his lips.

"No." Blamed if her right knee was not twitching. "I think you are a common, dime-a-dozen criminal."

"I thought you said she was willing," the sheriff said. The downward tug of his mouth might indicate remorse but she could not be sure.

"There's only you and me here to say she wasn't."

The sheriff scratched his chin, looked at Johnny with contempt. "I may be an Underwood and loyal to my kin. But you ain't my kin, Ruiz. Now, due to your riding with them, I was willing not to arrest you, but you've got problems in your love life? Fix it on your own. I'm not getting involved."

"You're the justice of the peace. Do what we agreed on."

"He also agreed to arrest you, Johnny." She probably shouldn't glare at the only one here who could help her, but he was a better Underwood than he was a sheriff.

Her incensed look went as unnoticed as her words.

"As I recall," said the poor excuse for a lawman, "you claimed this was a simple lover's game and that she would be happy with the surprise. Seems to me she's spitting mad. Can't say as I blame her, Ruiz."

"I won't marry him," she said but still the men ignored her in their rising ire at each other.

"I paid you ten good dollars to perform a wedding," Johnny insisted.

For someone who had always seemed even tempered, affable even, the change creeping over Johnny was frightening. Held as she was in his grip, she felt hot angry waves pulsing off his skin. His breathing turned quick and short.

"And I thank you for that." The sheriff shrugged. "I'll just take that money as a thank you for not putting you in jail and handing over the reward money to Miss Quinn."

"Unless you want her reputation ruined—" Johnny went on to describe the obscene acts he had in mind "—you better marry us good and proper."

With his attention now fully on the sheriff, Laura Lee saw her chance. With a solid jerk, she let her knee fly. Johnny crumpled to the floor.

Sadly, the blow only incapacitated him for a second. But when he scrambled back to his feet, it was the sheriff he went after.

In the second of distraction, she dashed out the door. Fleeing down the hallway, she heard the walls thumping. There was grunting, loud cursing and then silence.

Johnny burst from the room, his expression blazing. Running for the stairs, she was aware of people opening, then quickly shutting their doors.

A door near the top of the stairway opened. An elderly woman gripping a broom motioned for her to come inside.

She could not. Not without endangering her dauntless rescuer. Glancing back, she saw Johnny's face, no longer handsome but dark and furious. He would not hesitate to break down the old woman's door.

Rushing down the stairs, Laura Lee heard a thump. A body hit the floor.

Spinning about, she started back up the stairs but stopped when she heard the old woman laugh, then her door close.

Bless her, she must have tripped Johnny with the broom, allowing Laura Lee precious seconds to flee.

But where to? She could not risk closing herself in a room of the hotel. When he found her, she would be trapped again.

Rounding a corner, she came upon the kitchen, closed for the night. She untied her boots and kicked them off because they were loud enough to alert her pursuer to her whereabouts. She shoved them into a drawer and snatched up a frying pan.

She tiptoed out the back door, closing it silently behind her. Ice-cold rain dripped down her scalp, washed over her bare arms and neck.

If she crossed the street, she could hide behind the saloon. Of course that might be where the Underwoods were carousing. If Johnny sought their help, she could not possibly outwit all of them at once.

She hugged close to the wall outside the kitchen, grateful for the shadow of the deep eves. She could not stay here long. But crossing any of the streets would expose her.

Frigid water sliced shards of pain between her toes, up her legs. In a moment, her feet would grow too numb for her to run without falling.

There were bushes behind the hotel, but they were bare. Rain had washed the shield of snow away. If she lay down flat, she might blend with the mud. But her camisole was white.

Johnny would be able to spot her easily. It was unlikely that he would mistake her for a mound of melting ice. Even if she stripped it off, there was her blond hair. She could not strip that off.

Footsteps pounded on the boardwalk. Listening over the beat of rain on mud, she thought they had come out the front door. If she was right, Johnny was circling the building. She had only seconds.

Mud was her only hope. She raced for the bushes, flung herself facedown. She rolled until she was thickly coated, then lay still, the skillet clenched tight in her fist.

"Laura Lee-e-e." The half-whispered taunt came to her, even over the fat raindrops striking the earth near her ears, pummeling her and probably washing the mud off her hair. "Where are you, baby doll?"

She pressed as close to the earth as she could, squeezed her eyes shut. The breath going in and out of her lungs sounded too loud. She couldn't stop and he was going to hear it.

Footsteps squashed through the mud.

Which way were they going…or coming? She couldn't tell, not with the rain distorting everything.

Slop, smack, squish…

Coming.

A hand touched her hair, stroked it gently before hurtful fingers dug into the strands and yanked her face up.

"You're a mess, all your pretty curls gone."

"What do you want from me, Johnny?"

"You know what I want. To marry you just like we always planned."

She swung the skillet at his head but he snatched it from her fingers and flung it away.

He grabbed her arm, yanked her to her knees, then squatted in front of her.

"You don't love me," she said. "I don't believe you ever have."

He gave a short, hard laugh. "I loved how you looked right pretty on my arm. Other men would see you and think I must be something." He wiped a smear of mud from her nose, then downward over her throat where his fingers lingered, drawing slow circle on her skin. "But you're right. I don't love you."

"Then you can't really want to marry me."

"Oh, that I do, baby doll. But not to love or cherish, naw… None of that nonsense."

She was shivering, unable to stop. Not because of the cold, she thought, so much as the way Johnny looked irrational…insane. In this moment, he was capable of doing anything.

"I'll marry you because you betrayed me, Laura Lee. You thought you could sell my freedom? I'll take yours, make you pay for that every day of your life. Every damn minute."

She shoved him, scrambled backward. He grabbed her arms, yanked her so close she saw red veins in his eyes, water dripping off his nose.

"I won't marry you, ever."

"You, a ruined woman, refusing an honorable proposal? Have a care for your reputation, Laura Lee."

"I'm not a ruined woman. Let go of me!"

"I'll swear you are." He touched the lace trim on the bodice of her camisole, fingered it between his finger and thumb. "You know how gossip spreads."

She heard the dog barking again, held the harsh sound close to her heart. Chisel, like that dog, loved with a pure heart. If she hugged his image close enough, she might be able to make it through the next moment without becoming hysterical, losing any chance she had to escape.

"I'll have what you promised me. That and more."

She kicked, bit his hand.

He let go of her arms, clasped her thighs, scooted her closer. His laugh chilled her more than the freezing mud did. She pushed away with her heels, kicked him in the belly. He doubled over with a grunt.

She scrabbled backward while he lunged for her. For all that she slapped and kicked, she could not get beyond the reach of his grasping fingers or the sneer in his demented laughter.

Metal clicked. A pair of mud-caked boots stepped firmly between her and Johnny. Looking sharply up, she saw the barrel of a gun pointed at her attacker.

Johnny crab-crawled backward. His escape was cut short by a snarling mound of wet dog. Chisel clamped his huge jaws around Johnny's shoulder.

"The single reason your brains aren't blown all over the ground is because your reward didn't say dead or alive."

She tried to stand but her legs, numb and trembling could not support her.

Keeping his gun pointed at Johnny, Jesse extended his free hand down to her.

She tried to stand but slipped again.

Jesse put the gun in his holster. "The dog doesn't know the law regarding dead or alive. Just so you know, he hasn't eaten today."

Jesse squatted down, gathered her into his arms, then quickly stood again.

Pressing her face to his neck, she wanted to weep…to snuggle into him and be home.

"Get up."

Jesse shot a black glower at the man on the ground. If the reward had actually been offered dead or alive, he could not predict what he would have done.

Holding Laura Lee in his arms, feeling how

cold her skin was, the uncontrollable shaking…
he didn't damn know.

In the moment, he and the dog were inclined
to use the same amount of restraint, which was
about a spoonful.

"You have a room at the hotel, darlin'?"

He felt mud smear his neck when she nodded.

"Have him soak in muck until I get back,
Chisel." The dog growled low in his chest. "Good
wolf."

It didn't matter that Chisel was not a wolf. If
Ruiz thought he was, the degenerate would be too
frightened to twitch his nose.

"I'll catch my death out here! Please, Laura
Lee, I didn't mean nothin'. I was just havin' a
bit of fun. You know me. I never would have—"

Jesse felt a tremor shake her. It was a far different thing than shivering from cold.

The dog must have sensed her distress, too,
because Ruiz cried out.

"He bit me! Call him off."

"Funny thing about Chisel, he can spot a liar
from a mile away. Don't forget what I said about
him not eating today. But you sit real still while I
take Miss Quinn to her room and maybe he won't
have you for dinner."

"Not yet, J-Jesse. I want the reward for him.
Will you take me to the sh-sheriff's office?" she
stuttered.

Jesse started in surprise. What? No! She wanted to— "You need to get warm. I'll take him in once I've taken you to your room."

"This is for me to d-do. I have the right."

Looking into her eyes, he saw that she was determined to do this thing. He had no way of knowing what had gone on before he'd seen her fighting him off, so—

"I reckon you do. Hold close, darlin'. I'll take you."

If the sheriff's office hadn't been only two short blocks down, he might have refused, but she had a score to settle with the man and this was her way of doing it.

With the dog now latched onto Ruiz's pant leg, Jesse dashed through pelting rain toward the sheriff's office. He didn't count it as a misfortune that Ruiz had a hard time keeping up with the dog's brisk lope.

Coming inside, globs of mud fell off Laura Lee's dress. Jesse set her on a chair, took off his coat, put it over her shoulders and tugged it tight under her chin. He snatched the set of cell keys hanging on the wall, slipped his gun from its holster.

Chisel let go of Hell Dog's pants. The animal, deserving every bit of the honorable name *dog*, trotted to Laura Lee, nudged her hand, licking mud off.

Jesse indicated with a wave of the gun barrel for Ruiz to go into the back room where two cells were on the other side of the door.

"Been expecting you, Hell Dog," said one of the men in the crowded cell. Hoodoo was his name, the oldest of the Underwood brothers and their clear leader.

It had been the youngest of the gang to confess where Ruiz was and what he was up to. The kid's tongue had been loose with liquor so it only took the smallest bit of encouragement from Chisel for him to talk.

Ruiz went as willingly into the cell as the Underwood brothers had. No doubt the dog had a bit to do with their cooperation. Hauling Chisel across the snow on a sled had been worth the sweat and aching muscles.

Hearing a man's voice in the outer office, Jesse locked the cell door.

In the main room, the sheriff stood near the doorway, rubbing the top of his head and grimacing while he spoke to Laura Lee.

"I am that sorry, ma'am. Ruiz told me you had a lovers' spat, is all. I reckoned it was true after what I saw. He said you'd been wanting to marry him for a long time and you would be pleased at the joke. Oh, hell, the plain fact is…and don't think I'm not ashamed… I'm an Underwood.

Ruiz paid me ten dollars…that and family obligation swayed me."

"Yes, well. All I—I want is the reward f-for Johnny Ruiz." Her teeth chattered worse than they had when Jesse had first picked her out of the mud. The fact that his coat hadn't begun to warm her yet concerned him. "Keep the ten d-dollars."

Sheriff Hank set it on the table. "It's shame money. Have to donate it someplace, I imagine. Come back tomorrow and I'll have your reward money in cash. Sounds like you've got my cousins locked up back there, too. Now that they're fairly caught, there's not much to be done about them. Looks as though you've earned their reward as well."

"I think it was J-Jesse who apprehended them."

"Give the money to Miss Quinn. It was her dog who convinced them to give up." It was right for her to have the reward, even if the money gave her the funds to leave him. A home of her own was what she wished for. She could have it now.

Conversation with the half-principled sheriff having run out, Jesse scooped Laura Lee off the chair, then whistled for Chisel to follow.

Out in the rain once more, he tucked the collar of his coat up about her ears, then he dashed for the hotel. She was still far too cold for his peace of mind. Once inside, he carried her to her room and set her on the bed.

Glancing about, he immediately hated the place. It was dirty, depressing... What had happened to her here?

"Wait here a minute, darlin'. Curl your fingers into Chisel's fur. I'll be right back." Leaning down, he kissed her lips. They felt frigid. "Half a minute."

Chapter Sixteen

It took longer to get back to Laura Lee than Jesse expected it to. When he rushed inside her room, she was laying on the decrepit rag the hotel called a mattress, her eyes closed and her lashes a dark fringe against the bone-white of her face. Kneeling beside the bed, he gently brushed a bit of drying mud off her cheek.

Not so gently that she didn't sit bolt upright, her eyes popping open, wide and startled.

"Don't be scared, darlin', it's only me." He touched her hand, caressed her bone white fingers.

"Yes." Her shoulders sagged. She touched his cheek, perhaps to make sure.

"You're so cold."

She nodded.

"Loop your arms around my neck." Without raising an eyebrow in protest, she did it. He lifted her from the bed. "We're getting out of this room."

She answered with a great sigh against his neck.

Taking the stairs down, he turned right down a long hallway. He half ran past a dozen closed doors.

It wasn't like Laura Lee to have so little to say. She ought to be crowing her pleasure at putting Ruiz behind bars. Tomorrow she would have have enough money to finally purchase a home in her own right.

Transferring her weight to one arm, he opened the door. Blessed warmth washed into the hallway. Chisel, as muddy as his mistress was, rushed inside, then eased his big hairy body down in front of the fireplace.

The owner of the hotel lived in this room, so it was far nicer than the others. For the amount of money he'd offered her to clean it up, draw a bath and build a raging fire, she had been more than happy to move to another room for a night.

It might do her good to live the way her guests did for a time.

He set Laura Lee on the bed, grateful that the linens did indeed look crisp and smell fresh.

Working quickly, he shucked off her soaked boots, rolled down her stockings, then chucked them over his shoulder.

Her eyes were closed again.

"You with me, darlin'?" he asked, rubbing her toes briskly in his hands. He couldn't be sure how much it helped given his fingers must feel like icicles on her skin.

Until this moment, he'd given scarce thought to the fact that he was also soaked and shivering. Blame it, he'd deal with that later.

"There's a bathtub next to the fireplace. It'll warm you like nothing else."

She nodded slightly but with no expression.

"I'll need to take off your clothes. I don't think you can do it on your own."

Her eyes cracked open, and blue orbs peeked out from under the lids. It was hard to tell if she looked worried or not.

In any case, she could barely move, so there was nothing to be done about it.

"You can trust me, Laura Lee. I won't take advantage." He dusted a streak of mud off her eyebrow.

Slowly lifting her hand, she placed it over his, then drew it downward. Brought it to her heart, then tapped her fingers on his knuckles. With a nod, she closed her eyes again.

The simple gesture of trust caught his heart. Giving herself over to him as she did, made him long to—no, need to—protect her from everything for the rest of her life.

He didn't know how she felt about things, though. She'd gone away without a word. Gone to get the money to buy a home of her own. At least, he thought that's why she'd done it.

Lifting her arms out of the coat, he cursed the price she had paid.

"You'll be warm soon," he whispered. His fingers moved quickly over her clothing, unbuttoning this and unfastening that. This was no lover's tender work. Warming her in the bath was his only goal.

Shoving aside the heap of her clothing, he scooped her up. Her thighs and back were as cold as her fingers had been. So pale and fragile-looking, she half reminded him of an ice sculpture.

"Can you stand for a second? Here, hold my arm for balance and I'll help you down into the water."

"I think so."

Hair that used to be sparkling blond sagged down her back and over her shoulders, dark with caked mud.

"I've got you... Just lift your foot and step in."

She managed it but drew her foot back when her toe hit the steaming water. "Hot," she gasped.

"No, darlin'. It's only that you're so cold. It'll feel good once you get used to it."

She stepped in. He helped her to sit down. With a slight moan, she sank chin-deep under the water.

Had this been a different sort of night, he

would have added pretty seductive bubbles to the water along with a dash of sweet-smelling perfume.

Lightning bleached the darkness beyond the window. Seconds later, thunder rolled over the roof. After it passed, rain sluiced off the eaves heavier than it had earlier.

He dipped his hand in the water. Scooping some into his palm, he dripped it on her nose.

Stiffly, he rose and went to the fireplace to bring back the kettle of steaming water. He added some to the bath to make sure it remained warm, then knelt again at the side of the tub.

Gazing down, he was relieved to see that her skin no longer looked so bloodless. Her hair needed washing, but a moment to let the heat seep into her bones was needed more.

She moved her knees, causing water to undulate over her belly and chest.

Laura Lee Quinn was a beautiful woman. His brain could not deny what his eyes saw.

With a groan, he shifted his gaze and watched firelight play across the ceiling, studied the melding light and shadow.

With the woman he loved only inches from his touch, he feared his resolve to remain her protector and not her lover might waiver. Then again, the fact that the woman he loved was vulnerable and under his care would keep him in line.

He would show her respect, no matter how long he had to stare at the ceiling.

"How do you suppose Bingham is doing with the horses, Chisel?" he asked after losing patience with watching the shadows overhead dance and twist in a suspiciously provocative way. "Wonder if the weather is this bad at home."

The dog lifted his head at the sound of his name. Jesse got up from kneeling beside the tub and went to him.

"You got pretty wet yourself." He reached for one of the towels warming on the hearth, briskly rubbed the dog's fur. The great tail thumped. Turning his big head, Chisel swiped Jesse's hand with a big pink tongue. "I'll admit it, boy, I didn't want you in the house first time I saw you. Can't say the same now, though. You're a good dog... Naw, not just that. I'd say you are a friend with four paws. If Laura Lee doesn't take you with her when she buys her new place, you have a home with me."

Steam rolled off his sleeve while he wiped, reminding him of how very chilled he was. He'd been able to ignore it for a time, but now that he'd done what he could to get Laura Lee warm, he was aware that his bones ached.

Jesse took off his clothes and laid them over a chair to dry. He did the same with Laura Lee's underthings. He imagined she had another dress.

At least he hoped so. The one he'd peeled off her might be beyond laundering's best effort.

He hunched in front of the fire for a few minutes, glancing over his shoulder now and again, watching to see if Laura Lee's color was improving. Each time he did, he hoped to see her smiling, looking out him with her usual blue sparkle.

He'd nearly dozed away when she called his name.

"Jesse?" What had happened to her voice? It sounded hoarse, a ragged whisper was all.

What had happened to her bones, muscles and brain? She felt lethargic, as though the slightest movement was not worth the effort.

Her gaze focused on Jesse sitting next to Chisel in front of the fireplace. His knees were drawn up, his arms crossed over them. With his forehead resting on the nest where they crossed, he seemed to be sleeping.

Fire-bronzed skin gleamed over well-cut muscles. Every once in a while, a shiver raced along his spine.

He'd been naked and cold when she knocked him in the head with a skillet the second time she met him, but...no, it was actually the third. So much had changed since then.

She had changed, what she wanted from life and who she wanted it with.

Johnny had changed from vain to violent, malignant beneath a deceptively charming demeanor.

The one who hadn't changed was Jesse. He'd stayed constant through everything. Honorable from the beginning, he remained that way.

Her memory since leaving the sheriff's office was vague. She hadn't been unconscious, but being soaked and smeared with ice-like mud and add in the raging shivers, it all combined to make her withdraw into herself.

Fear had to do with it, also. Johnny had not been "having a bit of fun," like he'd claimed. Looking into his eyes, she'd seen his intent to crush and dishonor her. It had all but consumed him.

A person who would beat the sheriff, a man he knew to be kin to his friends, was someone to be afraid of.

The only thing to bring Johnny out of his rage, return him to a semblance of self-control, was the appearance of a pair of avenging angels who were more fearsome than he was. Coming face-to-face with Jesse and Chisel had left him cowering. Revealed him as the pitiful man he was.

Once he had been put behind bars and her reward money assured, she had let herself go.

She'd succumbed to shivering, her body's attempt to survive it all. At some point, her surroundings grew vague. During those half-lost moments, she clung desperately to her anchor. Jesse Creed was the one man she could trust above all others.

She'd had no fear giving herself over to his care.

"Jesse," she murmured again.

His head jerked up. Green eyes blinked. He smiled. "Welcome back, darlin'. You look better."

With a stifled groan, he grabbed a white towel near his knee and standing, wrapped it about his hips.

There was a kettle on a hook over the fire. He wrapped the handle in the edge of the towel then carried it to the tub.

She didn't need the added water to heat her. Simply looking at him was doing that. His muscular, masculine beauty took her breath away.

"Warmer?" he asked, tipping the kettle and pouring in steaming water.

"Um…yes, a bit." She glanced away because… well, it was the wise and proper thing to do, especially given that she had no idea whether he still wanted to marry her or not.

It would be so easy to abandon what she believed to be right. She was naked…he was nearly so…and the bed was fifteen feet away.

She loved him…and he? He used to love her

but that was before she ran off. Still, he was here, which said something.

But even if she had the strength to follow her desires, she would not. A commitment of that magnitude was meant for the marriage bed. Johnny had not been able to change her mind about it, and Jesse, bless him, would not try to.

He set the kettle back over the fire, then picked up a chair and set it behind her at the head of the tub.

"Scoot down into the water, darlin', I'm going to wash the mud out of your hair."

She closed her eyes and sank farther into the water. Liquid warmth licked her scalp.

Water sloshed around her shoulders, across her chest and belly. Jesse's fingers caressed her head but it felt more intimate. Almost as though he touched her breasts, skimmed his calloused palms along her thighs…but more than that, he walked right into the open door of her heart.

She sighed, wondering how a short time ago everything had been so desperately awful and now everything was warm. Serene. In the moment, with Jesse's fingers kneading her scalp, she rode a wave of bliss.

"I'm so sorry, Jesse."

He swished her hair through the water. "Nothing that happened was your fault."

"I went away without telling you, and I'm sorry."

"Why did you? Not go away without telling me, I don't mean. We both know good and well why you didn't. I'd have told you it was a damn dangerous thing to do. But why did you go away?"

It all sounded so foolish now. It would sound worse when she spoke it aloud.

"I wanted to collect the reward. I know it sounds silly, especially to you, given your former profession. But after the way he tricked me into believing he'd bought me a home, as I saw it, he owed me."

"As far as it goes, I see the logic of it. It was a risky way to get money, though."

It hadn't seemed so foolhardy at the time. Clearly, she had come to know better.

"It wasn't only the money after a while. I watched him intentionally trying to ruin an innocent young girl. He made her believe he loved her, he convinced her to take him to a private place so he could... I only hope she won't suffer lasting...well, heartache would be the least of it, I suppose."

It was natural, easy talking to Jesse, adrift on a sea of peace like she was. Of course, it had always been easy to talk to him.

Especially when times were not peaceful.

He stroked her forehead with the pad of his thumb, then her nose and chin.

"Ah, you wanted to see him put behind bars," he said, "for what he did to her and to you?"

"In the worst way. How many innocent lives would he have gone on to scar if it hadn't been for you?"

"Me? Not me. That night in the barn, I was willing to let him ride away. It was you I came after, darlin'. The fact that he'll face justice is because of you. But what I want to know is… You came for the money. Now you have it. Did you find what you were looking for?"

Him. She'd been looking for him. And yes, she had found him right there in her heart where he'd been since that day in the garden of the Lucky Clover.

The barest pressure of his thumb on her bottom lip made her belly tighten and her heart expand.

"Jesse," she whispered. "I'm sorry, do you… resent me for—"

The chair squeaked when he moved. He touched her bare shoulders, his fingers cool on her warming skin.

She opened her eyes. He'd shifted forward, holding her gaze upside down.

"Darlin', I didn't pull your dog ten hours across slush, three of them through the freezing rain, because I resented you."

Lifting her chin, he kissed her, somehow sweetly and seductively at the same time. And she thought...she hoped...with a promise.

"I didn't think, Jesse!" She sat up all of a sudden. Twisted back to face him. It vaguely occurred to her that she ought to be more embarrassed at being with him. For mercy's sake, she hadn't a blessed stitch on. "All this time, I've been letting you take care of me when you are the one who must be freezing—give me a hand up."

She crossed one arm over her chest, splayed her fingers across one breast. Not that she was any less exposed to him, but now that she was warming up, her sense of modesty was returning.

"Get in, Jesse. How long have you been shivering?"

"I haven't been," he said, standing, then reaching a hand down to her.

Taking it, she stood up, felt water sluice down her belly, drip off her hair. Jesse took the towel from his hips and wrapped her hair up in it.

The cooler air of the room should have chilled her bath-warmed flesh, but how could she possibly feel chilled with the way Jesse was looking at her?

She glanced away because now that the towel was wrapped around her head and not his hips, well...it was time to get dressed.

While she watched Chisel's fur dry, she felt another towel settle about her shoulders.

"Don't be afraid of me."

Turning back, she looked into his eyes, thinking it the safest place to look.

Nothing could have been more wrong. If she had missed, and she had not, seeing his desire for her because of…well, masculine ways, the green fire in his steady gaze declared it even more intensely.

"I set your nightgown across the back of the chair to warm."

"That was thoughtful."

She hurried toward it, lifted it off the chair and felt the row of stiches she had sewn after Jesse ripped it the night she had believed him to be an intruder bent on dishonoring her. She shrugged the soft, worn fabric over her head, thinking about how wrong she had been. Wrong about so many things, in fact.

She heard water splash. It would not be as clean or as warm as when he'd put her in it.

Taking the kettle off the hook, she brought it to the tub. The trouble was, he took up most of the space. There was no place to pour it without burning him.

"Don't worry, darlin', I'll do."

She placed the kettle back on the hook, then sat down on the chair behind the tub.

His shoulders took up the whole space, leaving no room for his arms. His knees jutted up from the water like twin peaks of a mountain range.

"How will you get warm?" she asked.

His eyes shifted toward the bed. "I'll wash off quick, then warm up by the fire. The woman who rented us her room says there's tea."

Us? The word caught her, disarmed her.

She laid her hands on his shoulders, rested her forehead on the back of his hair.

"You really came all this way for me?"

"Hell, Laura Lee. When Auntie June told me you'd gone, I'll tell you, my heart hit rock. Didn't think things could be any worse until she mentioned Beaumont Spur. If you'd only—"

He shook his head, no doubt thinking of a way to reprimand her.

Rain beat hard against the windows, seeming all the louder for the silence that lay between them.

She felt his shoulders hitch. "The spur wasn't plowed. No one had a spare horse. All I could get my hands on were a pair of snowshoes and a sled. I came as quick as I could but—"

Again silence held the room, cut only by rain and the snap of the fire.

"What happened to you before I got here, Laura Lee? Can you speak of it?"

Rising from the chair she rounded the tub, then

sank down, kneeling beside it. His hair, a dripping mass, hung about his face. She brushed it aside.

He clearly feared what she was going say and was going to blame himself for it.

"First thing, I had no right to expect you to come looking for me," she began. "If anything had happened to me, it would be on my own head. But, Jesse, nothing did."

She swept the hank of hair away from his face, saw a wave of relief cross his eyes.

"I was scared, more than I've ever been in my life." Unwinding the towel from her head, she dried his hair while she spoke. "But all he did was threaten. Nothing more than that."

He caught her hand. She dropped the towel. "What did he threaten you with?"

"A marriage of revenge. My plan had been—and before you get upset about it, the way I had arranged it was perfectly safe—the sheriff was supposed to pop out of the wardrobe and arrest Johnny as soon as he came to my room. But I didn't know he was an Underwood. Well, you heard what he said about being loyal to his cousins and their friend with them. So he told Johnny what I was up to, then Johnny gave him ten dollars to marry us. When Sheriff Hank refused, Johnny attacked him. So that's when I fled.

"But then there you were…and Chisel."

"Curse the man. I won't lie, Laura Lee, there's a part of me that wanted to kill him, right there in the mud. I wished he'd given me a reason to."

"I also know you would not have."

"You know more than I do then. If he'd hurt you—"

"But he didn't. Because of you." Finished with his hair, she handed him a fresh towel. "Dry off. We'll sit in front of the fire."

Pushing up from the side of the tub, she walked to a window and watched rain pelt the glass.

For as much as she longed to watch him while he wrapped up in the towel…to touch his skin and feel it warm under her fingertips…she would not. As much as she wanted to share her body with this wonderful and honorable man, she would not play that she was a married woman.

Doing so would dishonor Jesse. He was nothing like Johnny. She would not encourage him to behave as if he were.

Jesse had one death on his heart and had no wish for another. It's one of the reasons he'd quit bounty hunting. Somehow he had to release the anger he felt toward Ruiz. If he didn't, it would fester his soul.

Laura Lee had been frightened, insensible with cold, but not injured in any lasting way.

It was time to look to at the problem that ate at him like nothing else.

He didn't want to bring it up because he feared her answer. The one he hoped for would bless his life forever. The one he dreaded would curse it.

"Take this, Jesse." She handed him a cup of hot tea, then sat down beside him on the floor in front of the fireplace.

Two feet over, Chisel thumped his tail. He stood up, stretched and trotted to the bed. He leaped up on it, circled, then fell asleep. It wasn't a place Jesse intended to sleep. He'd have to shove the dog off when Laura Lee wanted it.

He set the mug down, went to the bed and brought back a pair of pillows along with a large quilt embroidered in pink-and-yellow flowers.

"With all the rain, I imagine the snow will be melted by morning," she said, holding her tea but not drinking it. "The train ought to be running again."

He set the pillows behind them, then spread the quilt near their feet. He didn't bother with his tea but left it where he'd set it down.

With the reward money she had coming in the morning, she could go wherever she wanted to. Buy herself a grand mansion if she had a mind to.

"Darlin'," he said, looking at the fire, watching the way red-and-orange flames danced and twisted into one. "Can you tell me why collecting that bounty was so important to you? I understand about how you felt he owed you…and I agree that he did, and I know how you wanted him safely behind bars, it needed to be done… but the money…why did you want it?"

He had to ask but fear of the answer made him feel colder than any bath or snapping hearth had the ability to warm. That tidy sum of money gave her the ability to find her place in the world without him. Was it what she wanted?

"Jesse," she whispered, turning toward him, her legs crossed, the flannel gown pulled taut across her knees. She ducked her head, stared down at her hands cupped about the mug. "I'm sorry I didn't tell you. How could I when you could have so easily made me stay. Only a word and I would have."

"I'd have used every word in the dictionary if you gave me the chance."

"Just one would have worked. But if I'd stayed, I'd have never known."

It felt like he couldn't breathe. Whatever she had been looking for she had discovered. In his favor or not, she knew.

"You needed to know if you loved me or my home, darlin'?" Nothing was to be gained by avoiding the dagger poised over his heart. "The ranch and me, we were all tangled up, isn't that right?"

"I never wanted to leave you. It's just…how else was I to know unless… I thought I needed to have my dream before I would know. And you were going to sell the ranch! It was my price to pay, not yours."

He took the mug from her fingers and set it beside his. Tea sloshed over the rim. He lifted her face, saw silent tears dripping down her face.

"Come here to me, darlin'." He opened his arms and she crawled into his lap. The towel draped about his hips held by a thread. He kissed her cheek, his heart in the gesture since he didn't know if he would ever do it again. "You have a right to find what's in your heart."

The worst of the storm was coming closer if the increasingly violent lightning flashes and pealing thunder were anything to judge by.

"Will you tell me what you found?"

She nodded, kissed his lips lightly. He felt them tremble. "I had a dream. But when I chased it, it was just gone. Like the pot of gold at the end of the rainbow. The thing I thought I loved beyond anything else vanished and there you were. I know you said you don't resent me. But after what I did, do you—" She turned her face toward the fire, blinking her eyes fast.

"Do I love you?" How could she not know how much? "Look at me, Laura Lee… What is it you see?"

She turned her face toward him, eyes closed and mouth trembling. He kissed her, kept at it until he felt her lips respond and give the kiss back.

When she at last looked at him, she smiled. "Well, I see it but I don't deserve it."

"That's just the thing about love, isn't it?" he said. "We don't deserve it, it's just a gift."

"Yes." With a sigh, she tipped her head back, exposing the delicate column of her neck. A lightning flash scoured the ceiling, thunder exploded a second behind it. "I love you, Jesse."

He pressed his lips to the spot on her neck where her pulse beat. "Love you, too." His words were garbled because he was nibbling a delicious path down her throat. "You taste so good."

"Yes, well…"

She curled her fingers in his hair, drew his mouth away from her neck. Couldn't say he minded since she settled her lips on his before they had time to cool from her throat.

Without letting loose of her mouth, he shifted her weight, lowered her down to the quilt, then lay half on top of her.

Looking down at her smile, he knew he was the luckiest man alive. He touched her, felt the shape of her ribs, stroked down the curve of waist and hips.

Cool air brushed his bottom as his towel gave

way in the back. In the shift onto the quilt, her gown had become pushed up past her hips.

The only thing separating his hard belly from her soft one was a thin rectangle of fabric and holy vows.

"This is as far as we go until you marry me," he said. With more willpower than he'd ever been called upon to exert, he lifted his hand from her thigh, stroked the curve of her smile instead. "So, darlin', will you marry me? Tomorrow morning?"

"I'll marry you, but not here. Let's go home to Forget-Me-Not."

"Day after tomorrow then."

"Not a day later."

He rolled off her, yanking her gown down past her knees. Then he knotted the towel around his hips.

"Sleep with me here by the fire," he said, pulling the quilt over his legs, then holding the edge open for her to join him.

"Since the dog's got the bed, I suppose I must." Her dramatic sigh lifted her breasts in a beguiling way, but he'd think more about that the day after tomorrow.

Pillow to pillow, they snuggled down, watching lightning split the dark beyond the window and holding each other tighter when thunder shook the building.

"I'm a happy man." Her smile was inches from him, so he kissed it. "I love you, darlin'."

"No more than I love you." The beautiful whisper rustled over his face.

"Funny thing about anticipation," he observed. "It feels good and bad at the same time."

"Day after tomorrow feels like it just got a hundred hours added to it." She kissed his nose, then turned on her side.

He drew her in, her hip tight to his belly. Swiping the hair away from her neck, he nibbled.

"That tickles. Go to sleep. It will make tomorrow come faster."

They lay in silence for a while, but he doubted she would be able to doze off any more than he could.

"Laura Lee Creed," he murmured in her ear. "I like it."

She nodded, closed her eyes with a dreamy smile on her face.

Would tomorrow really come faster if he was asleep? He reckoned he was about to find out.

Chapter Seventeen

Something tickled Jesse's nose. He swiped at it, then turned over. It had taken a very long time to fall asleep but once he had, blamed if he didn't need to get back to it.

The unidentified irritant tickled his ear. He heard a feminine giggle and cracked open one eye. Something red swayed in his still blurry vision.

His long johns?

He sat up, yanked the underwear down and his fiancée with it.

"Time to get up, slugabed. We don't want to miss the train." Finely shaped brows arched over the loveliest blue eyes he had ever seen.

Laura Lee was already dressed, he was a bit disappointed to find. While he would not touch her inappropriately, he didn't mind looking at her.

"You've got pretty toes, darlin'." That was one

thing he could see since they poked out pink and pretty from under her skirt. "You ticklish?"

He reached for her but she scurried out of his reach and scrambled to her feet.

It was a great relief to see her completely recovered from yesterday.

"The sun is shining and I have errands to run," she said. "Do you want to come along or stay here with Chisel?"

Glancing at the bed, Jesse saw the dog watching, his long pink tongue lolling. "If one of those stops is the sheriff's office, I'm going."

"Hurry then," she said, digging through her valise until she found her brush. She drew it through her long golden hair in quick, brisk strokes.

He looked forward to the time he could sit, take his time while watching her do it.

It didn't take long to dress. Boarding the train for home couldn't happen soon enough.

With her hair finished, she sat on the bed, leaned over and tugged on her boots. Glancing up, she smiled at him while she tied a pair of fancy bows.

His heart warmed over. It wasn't only the sun that was shining this morning.

Standing quickly, she smoothed her skirt.

Impossible, he thought. A miracle and nothing less, that the girl in the garden was going to be his wife. He felt like a living, breathing grin.

"I have a couple of stops to make after we visit the sheriff," she said.

"Spending some of your money? There's going to be plenty of it with all those rewards."

"Well, yes. Something like that."

Going up on her toes, she kissed him. He answered the call and things heated up…for a long time.

In the end, they came out of the room, flushed of face and eager to get home.

After leaving a bit of money on the bed, on account of all the fur Chisel was leaving behind, they walked hand in hand to the sheriff's office.

It didn't take more than ten minutes for Sheriff Hank to pay off the rewards.

Next, Laura Lee went to Flora's Feathered Bonnet Shop. She purchased a small hatbox, put all the reward money inside, then tied it up in a bow of yellow lace.

It was an odd way to carry a small fortune, in Jesse's opinion. He totted it under his arm, watching for shadows that shouldn't be or movements too sudden, even though it was unlikely that anyone would guess there was anything but a hat inside.

Moments later, he followed Laura Lee into the café across from the hotel.

Stepping inside, he was impressed at how clean everything was. Tables gleamed, the floor looked like it had just been swept and enticing scents drifted out of the kitchen. This restaurant with checkered curtains in the windows and pumpkins on the tables seemed out of place for Beaumont Spur.

A young woman, tall and slim of figure, swept out of the kitchen's swinging door carrying a tray with two cups of coffee balanced on it.

"Table beside the window, Miss Quinn?" she asked, giving Jesse a nod and a smile. "Breakfast?"

"That would be lovely, Juliette," Laura Lee said.

"Bacon, eggs and toast for you? And for the gentleman, let me guess." She flipped a thick black braid entwined with a blue ribbon that matched her eyes over her shoulder. "You look like a steak-and-potatoes man."

"You must have the sixth sense, ma'am. That's exactly what I'm craving."

"I do have a knack for reading my customers' appetites. Nothing more than that." With a quick wink, she set the coffee on the table, then spun about and went back through the swinging door.

He set the hatbox on the table.

There was only one other customer in the dining room. An older man who shot them a sullen glance before he turned his attention to the doorway the waitress had gone through.

Sitting down, Jesse reached across the table and took Laura Lee's hands in his, caressed her slender fingers. "Are you happy, darlin'?"

He knew she was. The same joy glowing in her eyes warmed his heart through.

"I'm half afraid to be this happy."

He smelled the steak as soon as it began to sizzle in the pan.

The woman—Juliette, Laura Lee had called her—came back out of the kitchen carrying a pair of babies, one on each slender hip.

They weren't twins. The baby boy looked a few months older than the baby girl.

She set them at the table with the old man, tying each baby to the chair back with a long, fat ribbon.

The baby boy began to cry. The baby girl sucked on her fist while the old man watched Juliette hurrying back to the kitchen. The scowl on his lined face gave him an impatient look.

"Don't expect me to keep them happy!" he called after her. "Just bring me my food, girl!"

Moments later, Juliette carried breakfast to Jesse and Laura Lee's table. "I hope you enjoy—"

"When are you going to learn to tend to family first!"

The outburst made both babies cry.

Juliette shrugged, rolled her eyes. "If you folks will give me a minute?"

"Father Lindor—" she spoke firmly but not unkindly to the man "—we've discussed why customers must come first. Without them, we will find ourselves living in the fields."

She patted the little girl's hair, then kissed the boy's cheek. "Grandpa didn't mean to frighten you, sweetlings. Sing them a song from your seafaring days, Father Lindor, while I fetch your breakfast."

Jesse ate his food, listening to Juliette humming in the kitchen. The woman must be as good-natured as she was patient.

A shrill whistle announced the arrival of the train.

"Let's go home and get married, darlin'." He stood up, reached for the hatbox.

"Leave it here, Jesse."

"What…why?" He reached for it again but she stilled his hand.

"I don't need it."

"You sure about that? You might want to—"

She cut off his protest by shaking her head. At the same time, she slipped an envelope between the box and the yellow bow.

"I don't need anything but you. Sell the ranch if you still want to." She touched his cheek, ran the backs of her fingers along the rough stubble he hadn't shaved off in days. "If we live in a tent and wander like nomads, I'll be happy. If all I ever have is you, it's blessing enough."

The train whistle blew again.

"Let's go home." He swept her out the door, well aware that that she had given him a great treasure and it was not in a hatbox.

A day and a half later

"Scoot over closer, darlin' wife." Jesse leaned sideways, kissed her cheek. "Say it just one more time."

Laura Lee didn't know how she could scoot closer given that she was already hip to hip with him on the wagon bench.

"I, Laura Lee Quinn, take you, Jesse Creed, to be my lawfully wedded husband."

"Still can't believe it happened." He shifted the reins to one hand, put his arm around her shoulder, then hugged her against him. "I never knew a bride could be as beautiful as you are...and will be. Not that I don't like the gown, but I'll like it better when it's tossed over the back of a chair."

She hadn't known she could be so pretty either. While the cloud-like gown made her feel like a princess from a fairy tale, it was the smile on Jesse's face as she walked down the aisle on Bingham's arm that made her feel a cherished beauty.

That noon, first thing after getting off the train,

they had gone to the boardinghouse to rest and plan a hasty wedding. While she knew she could live anywhere, as long as it was with Jesse, she had dearly missed the ranch house, the stream and the bridge over it, even the big barn and the paddock.

In their haste to get home, they hadn't expected much in the way of a wedding celebration. Speaking vows with this faithful, brave and handsome man…it was all she needed.

Of course, Auntie June thought otherwise.

As soon as Laura Lee and Jesse had told her their intentions to be married by sundown, the town went topsy-turvy. She'd been whisked off to the dress shop at the same time Jesse had been carried away to the tailor.

The women of Forget-Me-Not rallied about her. Joyful to be a part of the happy event, they went to work.

Some of them scrubbed the library until it glowed. Others came directly behind them to hang garlands of pine and lace. It wasn't the season for flowers, so the food tables set up in the corner of the room were decorated with straw, pumpkins and softly flickering candles. The mantel over the hearth was decorated in evergreens and berries. The library smelled like a forest, fresh and bountiful with promise.

This close to Thanksgiving, Laura Lee had so much to be grateful for.

"Tell me the other part," he said, "the vow you made on the train."

"I vow to keep you fed. Make potatoes and pie?"

"That…but no, the other one about keeping me warm on winter nights."

"As I recall, the many ways you thought of me doing it made the woman ahead of us on the train change seats. You ought to have whispered more quietly."

The moment the wagon crossed the ranch's property line, Chisel roused from the nap he had been taking in the back. He leaped over the side and sniffed at familiar places.

She could barely wait to do the same. Not sniff, of course, but clean the kitchen, sweep the floors…become reacquainted, make the place her own again.

But before that—her heart turned flips in anticipation of it—she would make the man her own.

He was hers already because of the vows and the love between them, but the bond that would seal them as man and wife… Well, all she could do was gaze up at the brilliant display of stars and imagine the ways it might happen.

Caught up in dwelling on images that she used

to shy from because they were forbidden, she was surprised to find that Jesse had pulled the wagon into the paddock.

Working together, they made a quick job of settling the animals. Walking back toward the house, Chisel raced ahead of them, yipping in pleasure at being home.

When Laura Lee crossed the bridge, she stopped to look at the precious four walls. With Jesse's arm about her shoulder and hers tugged tight around his trim, muscular middle, she knew all over again that this was where she was meant to be. Not the four walls, she didn't mean, but tucked under her husband's arm.

Breathing in a lungful of cold air, smelling smoke in the air, she watched the house. Through the window, she saw the warm glow of a banked fire. Someone must have come beforehand to prepare the love nest for them. Unless she missed her guess, the kitchen would also be stocked with food.

Jesse wrapped both arms about her, rested his chin on the top of her head. "We made a wish once, remember? We held hands and wished upon a star."

"And here we are."

He took her hand, twined his fingers through hers and lifted their joined hands toward thousands of dreams to wish upon.

Moving their hands west, east, then in a circle, he stopped, then extended his finger to an especially bright sparkler. "That one's Venus." The warmth of his breath tickled her ear. "I'm making my wish on that one."

"Oh…well, I have a very good feeling about Venus."

"A kiss then, to seal the wish." He turned her, tipped his head down for a kiss.

At the instant before his lips touched hers, she ducked out of his embrace. "Catch me if you can, husband."

Spinning about, she dashed toward the house, her chiffon wedding gown blowing a cloud about her knees. The hood of her cloak fell away from her face. Cold air rushed through her hair, tugging the pins loose. She shook her hair free.

Jesse's heavy footsteps pounded the earth a short distance behind her, so close that she heard his breathing, felt the heat of it nearly at her neck.

He caught her waist at the foot of the stairs, spun her about. Scooping her up, he carried her up and across the porch. When he opened the front door, warm air rushed out like a blanket folding about them.

Stepping over the threshold, he somehow managed to loosen the top half of her clothing. A few of the fantasies she dreamed of on the way home were coming true and they hadn't yet stepped fully into the house.

"Welcome home, Mrs. Creed," Jesse said, then clicked the door closed with his foot.

* * * * *

COMING SOON!

We really hope you enjoyed reading this book. If you're looking for more romance, be sure to head to the shops when new books are available on

Thursday
28th June

To see which titles are coming soon, please visit
millsandboon.co.uk

MILLS & BOON

MILLS & BOON

Coming next month

ONE WEEK TO WED
Laurie Benson

Charlotte's gaze dropped to Andrew's lips just as a giant boom reverberated through the hills. They both turned towards the house to see more colourful lights shoot into the sky and crackle apart.

'I'm thinking about kissing you.' He said it in such a matter-of-fact way, as if the idea would not set her body aflame—as if the idea of kissing this practical stranger would be a common occurrence.

Charlotte had only kissed one man in her life. She never thought she would want to kiss another—until now. Now she wanted to know what his lips felt like against hers. She wanted him to wrap her in his arms where she would feel desirable and cherished. And she wanted to know if his kiss could be enough to end the desire running through her body.

He placed his gloved finger under her chin and gently guided her face so she was looking at him. The scent of leather filled her nose. There was no amusement in his expression. No cavalier bravado. Just an intensity that made her believe if he didn't kiss her right then, they both would burn up like a piece of char cloth.

It was becoming hard to breath and if he did in fact kiss her there was a good chance she would lose consciousness from lack of air. But if he didn't kiss her…

She licked her lips to appease the need of feeling his lips on hers.

He swallowed hard. Almost hesitantly, he untied her bonnet and put it aside. Gently, he wrapped his fingers around the back of her neck, pulling her closer, and he lowered his head. She closed her eyes and his lips faintly brushed hers. They were soft, yet firm, and she wanted more.

Continue reading
ONE WEEK TO WED
Laurie Benson

Available next month
www.millsandboon.co.uk

Copyright © 2018 Laurie Benson

LET'S TALK

Romance

For exclusive extracts, competitions
and special offers, find us online:

- **f** facebook.com/millsandboon
- **◎** @millsandboonuk
- **𝕏** @millsandboon

Or get in touch on 0844 844 1351*

For all the latest titles coming soon, visit
millsandboon.co.uk/nextmonth

*Calls cost 7p per minute plus your phone company's price per minute access cha

Want even more
ROMANCE?

Join our bookclub today!

'Mills & Boon books, the perfect way to escape for an hour or so.'

Miss W. Dyer

'Excellent service, promptly delivered and very good subscription choices.'

Miss A. Pearson

'You get fantastic special offers and the chance to get books before they hit the shops'

Mrs V. Hall

Visit millsandbook.co.uk/Bookclub
and save on brand new books.

MILLS & BOON